Montana Son

By

Alek Leslie

This book is a work of fiction. Names, characters, places, and incidents either are products of the author's imagination or are used fictitiously. Any resemblance to actual events or locales or persons, living or dead, is entirely coincidental.

First Edition

Designed and edited by Theresa Leonard

Maps - State of Montana Map 1881 ©iStockphoto LP
Cover Art - ®Bigstock, ©iStockphoto LP, ©Shutterstock, Inc.
State of Montana Map 1866 – Mitchell's New General Atlas
(Philadelphia: S. Augustus Mitchell)

Printed in the United States of America

Published simultaneously in Canada by
Rowe House Publishers

Leslie, Alek
Montana Son : a novel / Alek Leslie

ISBN-13: 978-0-9938600-0-3
ISBN-10: 0-9938-6000-1

Montana Son

For my mother, my inspiration

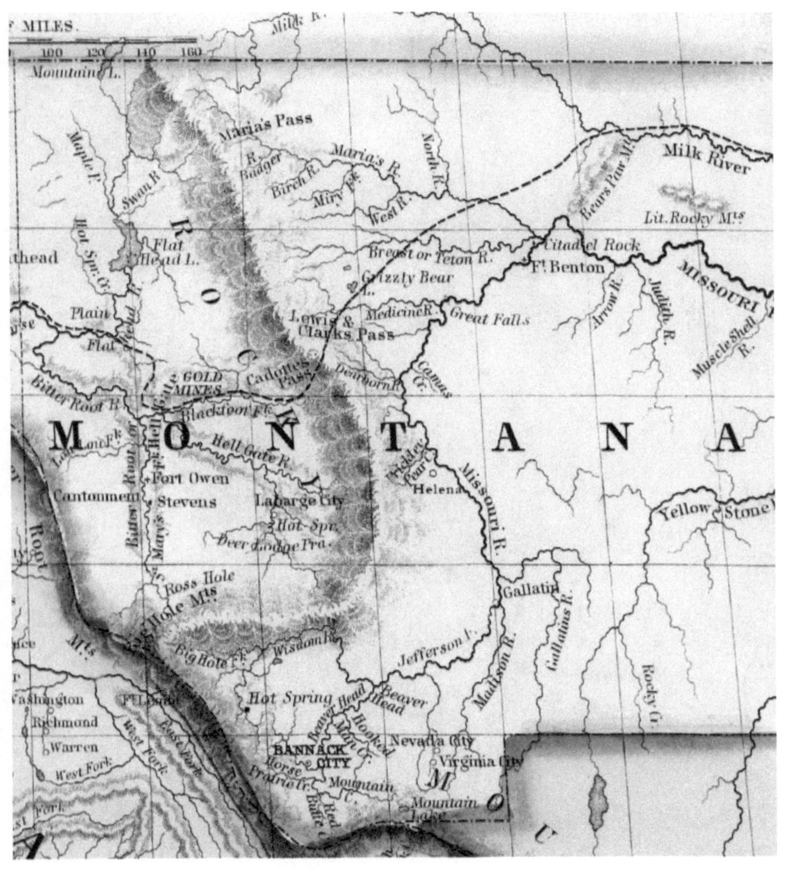

Source Citation: Mitchell's New General Atlas….
(Philadelphia: S. Augustus Mitchell, 1866), 44.

Part 1

A new town

Chapter 1

I was born under a Montana sky. Slept in a pine dresser drawer until I started clinging to my momma's panties. She said I got that fetish from my cousin, Tommy.

Wasn't the first born in this new territory, so no official announcements heralded my birth; but I did have a distinction of my very own.

However, this story doesn't begin with my birth. It begins with the birth of a new town upon the discovery of a precious metal called.........gold.

It's late afternoon; the sun's starting to cast longer shadows. Upon first glance, southwestern Montana is a mixture of barren rock formations and fertile lushness. But tucked into the foothills of the Tobacco Root Mountains, throngs of tents, brush wickiups, log cabins, and stone homes were springing up daily, winding around a narrow gulch with a vast promise of wealth.

Trees dapple the hilly green peaks that cascade towards Virginia City, the biggest of a cluster of mining camps stretching twelve miles along gold filled Alder Gulch. Most of the businesses and residences within the town could be found on Wallace Street. Plainly constructed buildings were made of hewn logs or planed wood, while the more 'fire proof' businesses boasted brick and stone construction. Even more impressive were the facades playing tribute to Greek, Gothic, and Renaissance influences.

Even though this mining town was just in infancy, it offered many one and two story establishments. The Donevan hotel was one of them. The white washed boarding house looked appealing to Sean and his father.

Frankly, anything with four walls and a bed would be appealing to the two weary travelers. They had been riding since sun-up everyday for the past few weeks, eager to stake a claim.

Sean walked into the hotel and was quickly greeted by Donevan Langtry. He was a short fellow, rather portly, with spectacles and a very cordial smile.

"Hello sir. How may I help you?"

"We're looking for two rooms," Sean said as his eyes roamed the quiet dining room, still pungent of smoked tobacco, and winding staircase that led to the sleeping quarters.

"I'm afraid I have just the one though it has two single beds."

Sean's weight shifted into the heels of his boots, creaking the floorboards, when he peered at his father sitting sleepy eyed on his horse. "That'll be fine."

He committed to a week's accommodation and signed the register.

Donevan studied the signature, pleased to see it was more than just a letter 'x'. "How many horses do you have, Mr. Thomas?"

"We have two," Sean replied.

"Fine, then. Bale of Hay Livery is three businesses to the left. Your room is just up the stairs, number four. We have a dining area with nightly entertainment," he said, pointing to it, "and of course, a fully stocked bar. You mining men?"

"Yes, we are."

"Well then, you'll feel right at home. Most of the men staying here are miners."

"Thank you, Donevan," Sean replied with a tired grin.

He walked out to his father. "It's gonna be cozy. We have one room."

"Doesn't bother me one bit," Robert spoke languidly.

Sean mumbled, "You're not the one who has to put up with the wretched snoring."

They tied the horses to a post, gathered their saddlebags and tools, and shuffled up the hotel stairs. Moving along the dim and musty hallway, they reached their sparse room where Sean didn't linger. The bed squeaked with the weight of his possessions as he recoiled from his bedraggled presence in the oval mirror above the pine bureau.

"I'll tend to the horses," he offered.

Strolling out of the hotel, he looked up and down the lengthy street, surveying it quite peaceful this time of day. His mind abruptly changed when a sixteen horse team came barreling along, pulling three wagons through the narrow road, summoning dust clouds to cling to the dry air.

He wiped his eyes, walked the horses to the livery and decided to stretch his lean legs a little further. Ambling along the cottonwood boardwalk, he passed several businesses before he came to the first saloon. Just beyond the drinking establishment, he could make out new construction. A horde of carpenters were busily working on framing walls or putting up false fronts, hammering in nails and sawing wood.

Entering the swinging doors of the Golden Nugget saloon, his boot spurs jingled to the solidly constructed softwood bar.

"What'll it be?" the bartender asked blankly while toweling a thick glass bottom.

"I'll take a beer and a shot of whisky," Sean replied.

His attention was quickly taken by two gentlemen discussing commerce. "The building and property are only worth seven hundred," one spoke to the other in hushed tones. "Just think, in a few weeks I bet it'd be double. It's an easy way to make money, Hal. We should do it."

His companion showed enthusiasm, nodding and raising his bushy black eyebrows.

"You new in town?" the bartender spoke curiously as he woke from a cataleptic trance induced by a trickle of thirsty patrons.

"Just arrived from Colorado," Sean replied with eyes focused on the broad mirror hanging above the necks of whisky bottles, and the man reflected in it with dire need of a sharp razor and hot bath.

"Have your own gold rush there?"

"Easy mining's been played out. It was time to look elsewhere. And judging by the slew of shops and new builds taking place, streams must be filled with prosperity."

"You got that right! I hear many pulling scads of up to one hundred and fifty a day out of Adler Gulch. Heck, I saw a nugget," he voiced with avaricious envy, "must have been worth six hundred: fine specimen. Reckon you'll have to purchase a claim, though. There are other prospects, as well," he said, nodding toward the men hunched over and murmuring between pints of ale.

The tall, red-headed bartender introduced himself, "Name's Ned Monaghan."

"Sean Thomas."

Ned, who couldn't be more than seventeen, said he would be out at the gulch if he didn't have to look after his father's saloon.

"He's sleeping off another one," he said, visibly perturbed.

"Ain't that the way it is sometimes. Say, if I were in need of female companionship, where would I be looking?"

"I'm afraid you got more chance of finding gold than any female kind in this town. But, between you and me, I hear some lovely working ladies should be heading this way in a month via Overland stagecoach."

"A month!" Sean exclaimed in disbelief.

Ned inched closer to him and whispered, "Well, there's a restaurant called Young American Eatery over at Merriweather Inn run by a Wilbur White. He has three pretty servers scantly clad in corset dresses. I know they'd give you more than just a fine meal, but you didn't hear it from me."

"Thank you, Ned, for advice on where I should feed my appetite."

Ned smiled devilishly.

Sean finished his beer, chased it down with the whisky, and set off for the hotel. On his way, he passed a Barber Shop in need of a customer. It was all the more reiterated by a little boy with a freckled smile donning a sign, screaming, "Shave and a haircut, two bits!" to an empty street.

While Sean sat in the chair, he heard more gold stories while Joe Flannery made smooth upward strokes with his straight razor.

"I hear one man pulled a sagebrush bush out the ground and just shook the gold from its roots," the stout, middle-aged man said matter-of-factly while the bristly whiskers were scraped restoring Sean's youthful face.

"You have a lot of crime in this town?"

"Not since a Vigilance Committee's been started. Heck, they hung a man this past March for disorderly conduct. You best be wise and leave that gun you have holstered in your room," Flannery advised.

"I don't go anywhere without my gun."

"Suit yourself. Keep a close eye on our juniper and cottonwood trees though; favourite hanging trees for our lawmen. Just might make you change your mind...."

Sean began to doze while Flannery blathered on about the vigilantes' feats, the odd word sinking into his weary head.

"Howitzer....shot....strangled....burned!"

Flannery snapped a towel, flashed a mirror, and kindly held out his hand for payment, thus ending Sean's slumber.

His walk continued westward until he noted the Merriweather Inn a few doors from the Barber Shop, and the Eatery Ned recommended. Curiosity got the better of him so he ambled in for a quick peak, his view quickly obstructed when Wilbur White appeared.

"May I help you?" the homely man drawled.

"Just checking out your dining establishment," Sean said, peering over Wilbur's bald, glistening head to see a sultry dark haired server giving a patron his meal. She was wrapped so tightly in deep red ruffles, her pale breasts heaved as she glanced up, smiling, winking. "And I see you have ample to taste."

"We'll have a lot more on the menu this evening," Wilbur replied with a subtle smirk exposing stained, wide gapped teeth. "I'm sure there'll be something here to gratify your hunger." He licked his lower lip, brimming with more confidence than a cock in a henhouse, that satisfaction comes guaranteed with every dish strolling out of his kitchen.

As Sean walked on, he smiled glancing at the array of shops the town offered considering Virginia City was formed just a year ago. This kind of phenomenal growth could only mean golden streams were nearby.

Returning to the hotel, he was pleasantly surprised to find the room empty. It would afford him some privacy to get changed. Going out tonight, he would do it in style. He was young, easy on the eyes, and in need of a lady's attention. Sleep was something he could do when he was much older or dead!

Robert came in with a towel around his neck while Sean was buttoning up his vest.

"Where you off to all dressed up like a peacock?"

"Supper," Sean answered while admiring his reflection in the mirror, combing fingers through dark hair. "Care to join me?"

"No, I'm pretty tired. Bring me back a sandwich or something."

"You're not gonna get it for a while."

Sean grabbed his jacket and glanced at his gun, left to hang in its holster over an iron nail in the wall.

"That's fine. I'll survive." Robert yawned with a slow stretch on the bed.

Sean gave him the once over. "You know, you're starting to show your age."

A spiteful glare burned back, followed by a heaved pillow, narrowly missing Sean's coiffed head.

"Get out of here!"

As Sean descended the stairs, music wafted from the sparsely decorated dining room. Curious, he moved that direction until Donevan approached him.

"Mr. Thomas, are you finding the accommodations to your liking?"

Sean thought, *the room is clean and the bed is softer and drier than a saddle and wet ground.* "Suits me just fine," he said, eyeing a tall, curly blonde woman crooning around munching miners.

"Does she sing here every night?"

"Colleen Tate and her cousin, Amanda Wilkes, who plays the piano, perform here twice a week. The singing is new to the hotel, on a trial basis, to see if it encourages more patrons or draws them away."

Donevan spun around, armed with cuspidor in hand, but was too slow to catch a black ribbon of tobacco that spat from a miner's puckered lips onto his clean wooden floor.

"Now, why would a pretty voice like that draw people away?" Sean asked.

"It's not always a question of the voice but of the choice of music," Donevan advised, wishing he could choose whose fleshy cheeks straddled his bar stools every night. "Would you like a table?"

"Well, I for one find the music refreshing," Sean said, avidly eyeing the melodies gushing from the voluptuous singer's mouth. "Yes, please do."

Donevan picked up on Sean's keenness for Colleen, seating him directly across from her.

Sean felt very privileged until he saw a lone man to his left with the same vantage point.

"Would you like anything to drink, Mr. Thomas?"

"A beer would be fine," he said, holding his gaze on the woman singing 'Then You'll Remember Me'.

Man on the left cleared his throat, bringing Sean promptly brought back to his solitariness at the table. His sharp eyes measured the man with scrutiny to discern cleanly-shaven, well-dressed in black broadcloth jacket and vest, keenly staring at singer, grin as plain as day.

Sean thought, *at least I'm hiding my pleasure.*

Colleen finished her enchanting aria and whispered a thank you to the diners. "My singing will resume shortly."

Turning to her cousin, who was busy leafing through sheet music, Colleen muttered a few words before walking to the grinning gentleman on Sean's left and eagerly clasping his hands. She beamed attentively, batting big brown eyes.

Sean turned away with much disgust, which didn't last long.

His interest shifted to the petite woman with curvy brown hair playing the piano. The tune was rather slow and melancholy, somewhat classical in nature, flowing curiously through his ears yet foreign to his mind.

He was intrigued by it, then by her: hands flowing so gracefully across the black and white keys, body moving with a lovely passion. It was so captivating a feeling was evoked inside of him, though it wasn't the feeling he wanted evoked that evening.

She was wholly absorbed in playing that piece and he was wholly absorbed in watching her. He thought, *where did this woman come from and how did she end up in a place like this.*

Most of the patrons were grumbling and chewing, oblivious to how well she played. Maybe they didn't care for the tune; maybe they missed the singing. They could be swinging from the rafters and this woman would never have noticed, and neither would Sean.

However, Donevan noticed the rising clatter amid scowling faces and irritably marched over to Colleen, still eye-locked with her male companion.

He whispered terse words.

She replied, holding up five slender fingers.

Donevan stomped to Sean and began muttering the specials for the day.

Sean was ready to tell everyone within earshot to shut up, but Donevan's snarling face deterred him.

When Amanda finished her solo, Colleen was soon by her side singing 'Home Sweet Home' which hushed the querulous crowd.

Sean curtly ordered the Irish stew and a whisky before resuming his enthrallment with the pretty performers.

As soon as Ethan Holden broke his enamoured fixation with Colleen, he observed the solitary man to his right holding a recognizable fascination with Amanda. "She's wonderfully talented, don't you think?" he asked bluntly.

Being caught by surprise, Sean replied, "She has a natural way with the piano."

Ethan stole another glimpse of Sean, observing that he was cleanly attired and freshly shaven. Not the usual sort in town. Scanning the room, most pan diggers shook dust and dirt from their jackets every time their forks dug into plates or their arms lifted fiery drinks.

Curiosity about this new face in the dining room took rampant hold. Extending his hand, he introduced himself, "Ethan…Ethan Holden."

Ethan was tall and lean with deep brown eyes, and a warm smile.

"Sean Thomas," he replied with a firm handshake.

"Say, ah, you mind if I join you, Sean? I hate eating alone," he said with hope that Sean was a banker because he was in need of a substantial loan.

"Be my guest, but I can promise you the view of me is not near as pretty as the view of her."

Ethan grabbed his glass and placed his eager self in Sean's view. "I work at Beaverhead Sawmill. It's about twenty miles southeast of Virginia City."

Sean registered no expression.

"I plan on opening a hardware store right here on Wallace Street. Supply the miners with their picks, shovels, pans," he informed with verve.

"Well, judging by the number of miners here, you should do very well."

It wasn't the answer Ethan was probing for but at least his supper companion was talking.

An awkward silence fell across the table.

"Hell, I'd probably come to your store," Sean said airily. "I'm always breaking my pick."

Ethan smiled limply. His supper companion was cleanly attired and polite, but still a miner; no loan tonight. He couldn't hide his barefaced disappointment. "Where've you come from?'

"Denver: just arrived with my father. We're rooming upstairs. And if these miners ever learned to chew with their mouths closed, you'd probably hear him snoring," he spoke heavy with sarcasm.

Ethan laughed, sensing Sean had an easy manner and a genuineness that he rarely saw in people. He changed the focus to the ladies.

"The blonde singer in the apple-green dress is Colleen. I've been courting her for, oh…about six months," he said with a contented grin. "The woman playing the piano is her cousin, Amanda, and she sadly doesn't have any suitors at this time."

Their attention was briefly taken by belligerent slurs with deafening demands for an Irish ballad.

"The ladies should be finished soon," Ethan said with protective eyes over the women.

As the hard liquor flowed, demagogues were coming out of the woodwork. Donevan was running off his feet to keep the dining room from turning into a boxing ring.

Sean and Ethan finished their meal and had one final round of drinks.

Colleen announced her last song after a noticeable glare at her cousin. "It is called 'Was My Brother in the Battle' by Stephen Foster."

"Donevan isn't going to like this too much," Ethan averred, fervently shaking his head.

"I find the piano accompaniment to Colleen's voice very complimentary."

"Oh, it's not that. Donevan would prefer it if we forgot there was a war going on. These people don't get along as it is. This song will only pick out the Northerners from the Southerners. We wouldn't want to have our own Virginia City brawl right here. Vigilance Committee would love that...hang more men from their rafters," he said scathingly.

Sean was very impressed with the entertainment. They could sing about how white the moon was and he'd still be interested. He felt very fortunate that this kind of amusement was a few steps from his room, and that this pretty parcel with curly locks was sitting without a suitor, in a town loaded with single men.

"Why don't I introduce you to the ladies?" Ethan offered. "But I have to warn you, I think Amanda is more interested in books than men."

Sean acknowledged his offer with a subtle smile but was incredibly pleased.

Colleen and Amanda finished the song unscathed and stood together, smiling. They lured a few claps, some polite nods, and a standing ovation from Ethan. Colleen rushed to him and they immediately held hands.

"That was wonderful, Colleen. Angels weep at your voice," he said warmly, knowing how much she adored a compliment.

"Why, thank you," she said in a sweet southern drawl.

"Colleen, this is Sean Thomas. He's a miner: just arrived from Colorado."

She subtly perused him. "Well aren't you just about the best dressed miner I've ever seen."

"Maybe I could introduce him to your cousin. What do you think?"

"Well, I think that'd be fine," she said tickled pink.

After Amanda gathered her sheet music she found Colleen and Ethan talking to a tall, unrecognizable man.

This was the first glimpse Sean had of her face and he was not disappointed. She had soft features except for full round lips, which were beautifully framed by a glowing, fair complexion. However, he couldn't help but notice that those lips weren't smiling. By that point, her cousin was calling and waving her over in a rather embarrassing manner.

Patrons kept glancing at Colleen, then Amanda, then Colleen, like they were watching a pendulum swing.

It irritated Amanda to no end when her cousin caused unwanted attention. She walked over, obviously annoyed.

"Amanda, wonderful performance this evening," Ethan praised, hoping her icy mood would melt.

"Thank you," she spoke quietly and in a much subtler accent than her cousin.

"This is Sean Thomas."

"Mr. Thomas," she said, extending her hand.

He took it and kissed it.

She couldn't quite find the words to respond. Her hand hadn't been kissed since she was back in Arkansas, surrounded by educated and wealthy bachelors promising undying love for, in what seemed like, a lifetime ago.

Normally, Sean wouldn't have made such a bold mark of affection, but she was a southern lady, no doubt, and it seemed the proper thing to do.

"It's a pleasure to meet your acquaintance," he said with softness in his hazel eyes.

His gaze lingered on her intensely deep eyes, shadowed by long curly lashes, and couldn't help but take in those full round lips again, a burst of ruby red against porcelain skin.

Becoming too conspicuous, Amanda announced abruptly that it was time to go.

"Quite right," Colleen said. "My brother's been waiting for a while now and we should be heading home. Would you gentlemen mind walking us to our carriage?" she asked, smiling sweetly, flashing brown eyes again.

Ethan said he wouldn't have it any other way, grasping her arm.

Sean and Amanda followed closely behind.

He broke the silence saying, "I thoroughly enjoyed your performance this evening. You played a song I've never heard before." His voice hinted admiration.

"That was part of a composition called 'Moonlight Sonata' by Ludwig van Beethoven," she said confidently while looking onward.

"It was very," he paused, "different...good, but different."

Sean thought, *what an asinine comment.* He didn't think it appropriate to say that it stirred him inside.

They stepped out of the stuffy hotel into an invigorating easterly breeze. The clear sky was a portrait of brilliant stars.

Tommy was lying in the carriage, eyes closed.

"Tommy, get up!" Colleen shrilled hastily. "It's time to go!"

Startled, her twelve year old brother bolted up.

"Evening, Mr. Holden," he spoke barely audibly.

"Evening, Tommy," Ethan replied. "Have a safe journey home." He then hugged Colleen.

Amanda warily peered into Sean's eyes. "Good night, Mr. Thomas."

"Miss Wilkes, it was a pleasure to meet you this evening and hear you play. I look forward to your next performance," he said with charming enthusiasm.

Tommy led the carriage away.

"Well, that Sean Thomas sure is a sight," Colleen declared. "I hope we get to see more of him and that very attractive smile."

Amanda thought about the polite man with intriguing eyes and thick dark hair. She had never met anyone like him in this town and wondered if he had a good mind, or was just like all of the other men in this town, dull-witted and driven by golden dreams. Nonetheless, she couldn't forget his eyes. It was like looking through to one's soul. She felt sensitivity and that was attractive to her.

As the carriage pulled away, Ethan offered to buy another round of drinks and Sean was very obliging. His thoughts flashed to the Eatery and the three sultry servers but were easily dismissed at the thought of Amanda Wilkes, who had captivated his attention this evening. He was determined to find out all about her through his new friend, Ethan.

Chapter 2

The sun was blurrily streaming through tall, dust soaked windows as Sean descended the narrow staircase to the bustling dining room. He found a small table by a tiny window.

Miners were busy slurping their coffee or crunching their bacon in a hasty fashion. The older men with long, mangy beards that brushed into runny eggs were already rubbing their backs, while the young men with fervent grins were shaking with anticipation that this might be their lucky day.

After Sean ordered breakfast, he peered out of the window, observing the formidable wall of mountains that would exist long after his bones turned to dust.

Coffee and a plate of bacon with scrambled eggs came quickly. He ate ravenously when his father appeared, clean shaven in a white shirt and suspendered dark brown trousers. Scraping his chair out, he swallowed severely at the sight of his son's breakfast.

Donevan instinctively rushed over with a cup of coffee. "Hope I'm not being too bold."

"No, that's fine, but hold the food today. I'm not hungry," Robert answered.

"Everything all right, Bob?" Sean asked between mouthfuls of food.

"My stomach's queasy. It'll be fine by mid-day. I purchased a claim and we're good to go. How's Virginia City at night?"

Sean couldn't hide his smile. "She's just fine!"

"Is that so? Let's hope you're just as lucky at finding gold." After sipping his coffee, he rubbed a cramping stomach. "I have to go searching for an outhouse. Meet you at the livery."

Sean tossed money on the table and took long strides out of the busy establishment, onto the busier road as a mass exodus of gold seekers moved west to Alder Gulch.

The horses were groomed, saddled and bridled by the time Robert arrived, looking no less relieved. They mounted and clucked to their horses.

Small bits of conversation could be heard among the clanging of tools as they journeyed with the sun on their backs.

"When gold was discovered last year, the creek was tangled with alders," one miner said.

"You know Jedediah Brown just pulled out two giant nuggets and his claim not more than thirty feet from mine," another boasted.

Alder creek was lined with miners from as far as the eye could see. Their backs were either arched as they drove their picks and shovels into bedrock, or over barrow loads of dirt that were wheeled to sluice boxes. Others were on their knees, dipping pans into sand and gravel, hoping the 'colours' of gleaming gold would shine back.

Sean and his father found their claim among the ramblings of the Rocky Mountains.

By mid-morning, it was already a hot and sweltering day when Robert plunged his shovel into the ground and skittered, grinding his knee against stones.

"Bob, you all right?" Sean asked with concern.

"Still feeling unwell," he grumbled, sitting down and letting the water run from his canteen in great gulps down a parched throat. "Stomach's unsettled. Think I'll head back to town." Trying to stand, he stumbled again.

Sean rushed to his aid. "I'll go with you. Just give me a minute," he said, collecting the tools. His offer to procure sodium bicarbonate at the drugstore did not garner any objection from Robert.

Returning quickly, he was pleasantly surprised to find Colleen and Amanda at the piano with Donevan perusing their sheet music, dourly shaking his head.

Taking the steps, two at a time, he soon creaked open the door to find his father already asleep, his snore still thunderously strong despite the paleness of his bronzed skin. Sean diagnosed the cause of his malady as a fast-paced journey to Virginia City that must have worn on him some, and believed that the cure could be found with ample sleep and medicine gently placed on the bedside table along with a glass of water within reach.

Figuring his doctoring was done, Sean searched out his copy of Dickens 'Great Expectations' and moved downstairs.

Amanda was still at the piano glancing at the worn keys while Colleen and Donevan scoured through sheet music.

"Colleen, please no songs about war, gospel, or classical nature. We want light, melodious…..I'd like to stay here and drink more of your liquor, music."

Sean nonchalantly sat at his usual table with full view of the women, while Donevan resolutely approached with a longing for no view of the women.

"Well, I guess we just stick to parlour songs," Colleen recommended. "I, for one, like getting away from the farm so let's give Donevan what he wants. Are we on the right musical sheet, Mandy?"

"Yes, you have my agreement. Let's see….a song that doesn't have cotton fields, battles, death, darkies, master or God….how about 'Come Where My Love Lies Dreaming'?" Mandy asked emphatically.

"Look's good…I mean sounds good," Colleen replied, turning to her gloomy cousin.

"Mr. Thomas, can I get you something?" Donevan asked with a look of profound frustration as deep as the creases on his aging face.

"I'd like a cup of coffee."

"Of course. Would you like to try my wife's apple cobbler? Just come fresh out of the oven," he enticed.

"Fine." Sean cracked the spine of his novel feeling confident this ploy would catch the bookish woman's attention.

Colleen leaned into her cousin. "Sean Thomas is here and he's…he's reading."

Mandy took a curious glimpse.

"Why don't you go over and talk to him," she urged.

Mandy shook her head, still nettled that she'd be playing parlour songs.

Leaning in closer, Colleen spoke discreetly, "You're nineteen years old: not a spring chicken anymore! Your womb's bound to be a barren wasteland if you don't do something about it!"

"Colleen, stop it!" she cried curtly.

"He's about the cutest miner I've ever seen. Don't lose this opportunity."

Mandy's eyes narrowed over furrowed brows.

Colleen thought she looked like a pouty child being asked to do morning chores. She decided to pull the wool from her disgruntled eyes with one more tactic.

"You know if you got acquainted with Sean Thomas even as a friend, you may never have to talk to old, smelly Lonny Hopper again. Why, right now he's drooling in his glass as he gazes at you."

Mandy glanced at the bar and there was the repugnant man, half-baked, gawking at her like she was a tasty treat. Repulsed, she pushed her bench out with a squeak, gave Colleen a cursory glance, and slowly walked over to Sean. Unsure of what she was going to say, she put on a contrived smile and started with, "Good afternoon, Mr. Thomas."

Sean casually peered up from his book. "Good afternoon, Miss Wilkes. Please call me Sean."

"I hope I'm not disturbing you, Sean," she said rather sweetly.

"Not at all. Please take a seat."

Glancing at crusty Hopper, she made a point to grind her chair across the pine planks and give Sean a noticeably big grin. She even batted her wavy eyelashes once or twice, knowing full well how to lay on the charm when it worked in her favour to do so.

Sean was conceitedly happy his plan had worked, believing he had her full attention. It was as plain as the nose on his face.

Even so, she layered it on thick like molasses.

"Please, call me Mandy."

Donevan appeared with coffee and the apple cobbler. "Would you like something?"

Her mind screamed 'I'd like you to get rid of creepy Hopper, who won't stop ogling me with his weeping, glassy eyes and slurping, droopy mouth' but her mouth kept utmost propriety with a silent tongue.

"I will try your apple cobbler and a cup of tea, if you please!" she said sharply, hoping she could eat with such a ghastly view.

"Very well!" Donevan replied, thumping away.

Her attention focused on Sean. "What may I ask are you reading?"

"Great Expectations by Charles Dickens."

"I have yet to read that novel. How are you finding it?"

"Just started it myself. Haven't had lots of time to devote to books, I'm afraid."

Amanda nodded, wondering why on a sunny afternoon a miner would be reading.

Picking up on her perplexed countenance, he said, "I should be mining but my father took ill. Rode back with him and decided to stay close by."

Her face softened. "I do find Dickens to be a masterful story teller. I've read several of his novels: Bleak House, David Copperfield, and of course, my personal favourite, A Christmas Carol. I firmly believe that inspiring tale will remain popular for generations to come."

Donevan arrived with her tea and cobbler. Before lifting her fork, she peered at the bar, relieved only to take in a pudgy backside and oily horseshoe hairline.

Halleluiah, she thought, *my appetite has returned.*

"Though, I dare say," she admitted wholeheartedly, "that my favourite author is Nathaniel Hawthorne."

"Ah…..Scarlett letter," Sean said hesitantly.

"Yes, that's one of my favourite books. I've read most of his novels."

"Are you enjoying your cobbler?" Sean asked.

"It's very good though not as good as mine," she spoke proudly. "Needs a touch more spice."

"Well, maybe I'll get to make that comparison one day," he smiled, revealing deep dimples in his tanned cheeks.

She couldn't help but smile back, wondering how soon that day would come.

Sean sensed his time with Mandy was over when Colleen's piercing sigh jolted the peculiar relic to teeter off his bar stool.

"What time do you perform tomorrow evening?" he inquired.

"We begin at eight-thirty."

After a calculated pause, he asked, "Would you mind having supper with me before it starts?"

She pondered his request having been brought up proper, which meant asking the lady's father for permission first. But those were rules made in a civilized, cultured part of the world. Living in the wilds of Montana, she decided to throw proper out of her thoughts.

Besides, she couldn't remember the last time she was in the company of such a well-mannered, educated man and hastened at the thought that this might be her last chance with one. She figured if it got dreadfully bad she could excuse herself early, saying final preparations had to be made.

"I accept your invitation," she replied quite composed. "Why don't we meet here at eight o'clock?"

"Eight o'clock it is," he answered, very pleased for making the bold move.

She began to rise, reaching for coin in her reticule.

"No, Mandy," he said with a hand on hers. "It's my pleasure."

"Thank you," she whispered with eyes unable to leave his beguiling smile. "You're very kind."

Colleen approached. "Shall we see you tomorrow, Mr. Thomas?"

"Absolutely and please call me Sean," he said with a subtle nod.

"Good day, Sean," she smiled sweetly.

Colleen took Mandy's arm and squeezed gently as they strolled out of the hotel. "You can name your first born after me."

She was very happy with her cousin's persistent attitude on this particular occasion.

****

Mandy lingered in bed, smiling and thinking about her acceptance to supper with the charmingly handsome Sean Thomas.

Glancing at her dresses hanging in the armoire, she won-dered if she could get away with the pretty blue gown in a town like this. The crinoline had been removed with adjustments to its length, but it was still a formal ball gown. Grinning, she envisioned getting out of the rickety carriage, dirt and dust swirling around her, then frowned, feeling the dress may be too much.

Oh, who cares, she thought. She felt pretty in that dress and it could be the last opportunity to wear it.

Wandering into the small kitchen, she found Mable whipping up a cake, reminding her it was a special day. Birthdays weren't really celebrated, though Mable would always bake a cake. She had been a slave, along with her brother, Jacob, and dearly departed mother, Naomi, from the time that Mandy was born.

"Good morning and happy birthday, Momma," Mandy chimed, kissing her cheek.

"Why, thank you," she responded happily.

Mable smiled at Mandy's warmth and affection toward her mother and wished she'd see more of it.

Ellen Margaret was shorter than her daughter but shared Mandy's fair complexion and fine facial features; however, her blue eyes no longer sparkled and she rarely smiled. When she did, it seemed delicate and weary.

Mable passed Mandy her breakfast.

"Might be cold. Made it a while ago."

"That's fine. Couldn't get out of bed," Mandy said dreamily. "So many thoughts running through my head." She smiled until motherly eyes were upon her. "Just thoughts of you, Momma, and what we should do for your birthday," she spoke quickly, maybe too quickly. "I thought we could go into town and get you a dress."

"What for, Mandy? Your father doesn't take me anywhere. Besides, we have a lot of work to do. There's weeding and planting…"

"Oh, Momma, that can wait one more day. I want to get you out of this small cabin. How about some new shoes? Your shoes are looking pretty worn? We'll go shopping and dine at that new restaurant, Rosie's," she coaxed.

Ellen Margaret glared at her daughter. "You promise you'll be up bright and early tomorrow and I'll go with you today."

A radiant smile flashed across Mandy's face at the prospects of the day.

Jacob arranged the horses and carriage for the ladies on this July morning. Light clouds were quilting the sky, bringing a comforting respite from the scorching sun.

Mandy's father, Henry Wilkes, was already in the town, constructing a two-storey establishment on one of his empty plots of land.

On the way to Virginia City, Ellen Margaret seemed very relaxed despite her daughter's speedy pace. The carriage's wheels were leaving a trail of dust that lingered in the warm air for several minutes.

"Mandy, though I'm enjoying my time away from our cabin, I do wish you'd slow down! I'm going to lose my hat!"

"Sorry, Momma." She tugged on the reins slowing the horses to a walk. "Guess I'm just anxious to get to town."

Ellen Margaret looked at her daughter critically.

"You've always been a little fast with the reins. Maybe if I got out with you more, you'd change your pace. Sometimes it's hard for your momma to get moving."

The long and arduous journey from Arkansas to Montana had aged her considerably. She experienced poor circulation and suffered from stiffness and pain in her extremities all the time.

Mandy hoped that the short trip away from the ranch would help to ease her suffering if only for the day.

Halting the carriage in front of Donevan's hotel, she kindly escorted her mother into the darkened lobby, the sun's brightness still hidden behind soft clouds.

Donevan was standing hunched over the counter, keys in hand and pen on registry book. "Why, Amanda, how delighted to see you so soon." He feigned a huge smile.

"I'd like to introduce you to my mother, Ellen Margaret."

Donevan shook her hand lightly. "I see where Amanda gets her fine looks."

"Thank you, Mr. Langtry," Ellen Margaret blushed.

"Donevan!" Kitty Langtry bellowed, walking with a heavy step towards him. "Please try my newest dessert!"

She thrust a spoonful at his closed mouth.

He reluctantly opened thin, pale lips. "Why it tastes a lot like your other desserts."

"I've broken up my leftover cobblers, mashed them with fresh cream and will serve it in our stemmed glasses!"

Donevan cringed. "I'm sure the miners would take delight in that, Kitty. Allow me to introduce you to Ellen Margaret, Amanda's mother."

"Why, it's a pleasure to meet you." Kitty outstretched a sweaty, puffy hand.

Ellen Margaret shook it and smiled prettily into the plump woman's pale blue eyes.

"Would you like to try a taste of my dessert?" she asked with vigour, scooping a spoonful of cobbler mash.

"No, that's very kind of you but we have plans to dine at Rosie's and wouldn't want to spoil our appetite," Mandy said with sweet politeness.

"Oh, well, I best get back to the kitchen," she said as disappointment settled across her flushed face. "Please do come again, Ellen Margaret."

Mandy and her mother said good bye to the Langtry's and continued a meandering pace along the main street town.

"Kitty Langtry seems quite wonderful," Ellen Margaret commented.

"She is for the most part though she gets a little cranky at night. I think it's because she doesn't have time to stuff those sweets into her wide girth and the sugar rush has worn off. Frankly, I'm surprised she has any cobbler left to make that new dessert with cream."

Crossing the street, they waved away a swarm of black flies fresh from a mound of reeking horse manure.

They entered Armstrong's boots and shoes, and walked out with a new pair of black lace-ups; and were even more fortunate to find a frilly top and skirt at a nearby Dress shop. Mandy proudly stated her mother would look wonderful at supper this evening.

There was plenty of time to talk. Wallace Street was so long her mother was winded by the time they entered the newest section. This part of town was bustling with carpenters, their wagons brimming with boxes and lumber.

Breathing in the scent of freshly cut pine, Mandy felt the softness of the sawdust and shavings under her shoes as she searched for her father's property. Rasping saws and pounding hammers filled her sensitive ears and assaulted her temples.

Ellen Margaret held small hands to her own ears to muffle the sounds; however, Mandy was too busy admiring the birth of this block to care about her sense of sound. She was amazed to see how quickly a building was erected with its false front. Even though her father didn't have a flair for architectural style, his buildings were well constructed and sturdy. He never had trouble selling or renting any of his properties while gold was being pulled out of the gulch.

Of the one hundred new buildings, most would be a part of the main street by the end of summer. Henry's property and skeletal framing were finally found, but he was nowhere to be seen, and his men had no clue to his whereabouts.

They turned from the busy site for a mercantile that Mandy wanted her mother to see. Ellen Margaret was happy to enter the store, catch her breath, and hear nothing but the creak of her footsteps on the wooden planked floor.

Mandy spotted her friend with glee behind the polished counter.

"Momma, this is Marie Champlain," she said.

"Bonjour, Madame Wilkes."

Marie shook Ellen Margaret's hand, nodding kindly.

"I've been hoping to see you, Mandy. I've something for you," she remarked in a Parisian accent. "William!" she called, "please bring the package to Miss Wilkes." Her amiable gaze returned to Ellen Margaret. "I must say you've trained your daughter well. She is a wonderful pianist."

Ellen Margaret was delighted to hear such a kind comment.

"Mandy, this piece by Chopin may prove to be quite difficult for you to learn."

After handing Marie the coin, she clutched the music sheets to her breast, remarking that she would do her best.

While they ambled along the cottonwood boardwalk, Ellen Margaret turned to her daughter with a curious face. "So that pretty woman is married to Mr. Pratt."

"Yes, Marie says he's quite kind," she said skeptically, "though I do find it hard to believe she would have a better life in this dirty frontier town than the place she left in France."

"Maybe she didn't leave for sake of the country."

Mandy shot a glance her mother's direction while an awkward silence filled in the air.

They weaved around wagons and steaming brown mounds to the shade of a covered boardwalk. Mandy peered through the window of the sparsely filled restaurant.

"It's a lot busier at night," she said, turning to her mother, who was already focused on someone sitting at a distant table with another woman, the gentleman's broad back to them.

Ellen Margaret could pick out the back of that head anywhere. Quite often, she lagged behind staring at his head of curly salt and pepper hair.

Mandy recognized the sea of grey her father was wearing. She always hated that ugly jacket. It was two sizes too big for her father, and while it made him appear smaller, his fingers, as fat as tender sausages, though as strong as iron rods, crept out from the wide sleeves.

Rosie approached and asked if they wanted a table.

Mandy's head shook crossly as she pulled her mother from the restaurant.

"Come on, Momma," she spoke solemnly. "I'll take you somewhere else."

"You'll take me home!" Ellen Margaret commanded.

As they rode back, Mandy mentioned she was going to the hotel earlier than usual but could change her plans.

"No, keep your prior arrangements," she forced a smile. "I'll be fine. Let's go home and have some of that cake!"

That night, Ellen Margaret was happy Mandy wasn't there. When she sat down with Henry in her new clothes, she doubted he'd notice. As usual, he said very little.

Finally getting the nerve, her voice trembled, "Mandy took me shopping in Virginia City today for my birthday."

He nodded with a brief glance her way before going back to his half-empty plate.

"We looked for you at the new building but you weren't there. You were dining with someone at Rosie's."

Henry stopped chewing but his eyes stayed firmly on the plate.

Taking a careful breath, her shaky voice implored, "I want you to stop seeing her."

"What you gonna do if I don't!" his voice snarled as fists rocked the table.

Ellen Margaret jumped at his actions.

"You don't have a dollar in your name!" Henry bellowed. "I work so hard for this family, give you everything you need, yet you're so ungrateful!" His eyes glared in disbelief. "I won't stop seeing her because she gives me what you don't. I won't leave you," he vowed in a threatening tone. "Need I remind you that my father walked out on me when I was seven!"

"I know, Henry," she cried.

"But I won't leave her either and you'll never tell me what to do in my own home!"

He picked up his plate, tossed it in the dry sink and stomped away. "Don't wait up for me."

Ellen Margaret stared at the wide door as it slammed shut, the forced breeze feeling like a slap to her face. She thought, *another night alone in this small cabin.*

Mable came out from her room just right of the kitchen and gazed somberly at Ellen Margaret. "Why don't you play me a song while I wash the dishes?"

She wearily looked up. "Think I'll just retire early. I'm very tired, Mable. Good night."

"Night, Mrs. Ellen," Mable said forlornly as she fingered a new chip in the abused china plate.

Ellen Margaret's face remained shrouded in sadness even after she closed her bedroom door tightly.

Chapter 3

At the hotel, Sean was calming his eagerness with a splash of whisky; and gauging his appearance amidst a row of dark suited men through the oblong mirror when Mandy arrived in a satin brilliance.

The dress, the colour of her sensitive blue eyes with a lace bodice and puffy sleeves, flowed from her tiny waist like the deepest ocean. She'd be the belle at any southern ball, but here, she was just an ornately dressed lady in a room brimming with covetous, women-deprived men. They stared at her from every space, dining room to bar, like she was the biggest nugget they'd ever found.

She didn't care for the attention, looking nervously around the busy room.

Sean responded immediately, making quick steps towards her, his height and broad shoulders blocking most of the gawkers from her sight.

"Mandy, you look lovely tonight."

Patrons resumed their talking. The pounding of glasses on tables and cutlery clanking against tin plates slowly returned.

Ethan stepped in. "Sean, Colleen and I are heading along Wallace Street to see a vacant piece of property. We just wanted to escort Mandy to you. Enjoy your supper."

A table was waiting for them. As they sat down, Mandy confessed she was a tad bit overdressed.

"You could be wearing an old tattered robe and all eyes would still be on you," he said with a reassuring smile.

She was flattered and instantly put at ease.

"Pardon my interruption," a young woman said, grinning widely. "Would you be interested in a bouquet of flowers to brighten your table?" Fran Tucker addressed Sean.

"Why sure," he replied, eyeing the basket with bunches of wild roses and violets. "How much do they cost?"

"For you and your lovely lady, twenty-five cents."

Donevan rushed over, out of breath. "I assume you've heard more gold has been found at the gulch!"

After boasting with much elation that his tables were filled to capacity, he frowned at Fran, whispering harshly, "I told you not to come in here selling those wildflowers!"

Fran appeared devastated.

"That's fine, Donevan," Sean said, handing Fran the coin. "I'm eager to have these flowers adorn my table."

Fran smiled and gently placed her best looking bouquet on the red-checkered cloth. "Thank you kindly mister and my family thanks you kindly."

She scurried away like a cat being chased by a straw broom, figuring she wasn't getting much more interest from miners, or the few businessmen scattered around the room planning their enterprises around this new found wealth. Maps were out, hands were shaken, and excitement charged a lightness in the dimly candlelit room.

Donevan recited his supper specials with inaudible speed while a table of five men shook their gold-filled pouches his direction.

About ready to bolt, he interjected, "Might I suggest the roasted beef and potatoes. The beef comes from the Wilkes ranch," he smiled appreciatively at Mandy before glaring insolently at Sean.

Sean was so impressed he completely ignored Donevan, until the man started panting down his neck.

"Well, that settles it," he nodded to Mandy. "I'll try the beef!"

"Thank you, Donevan," she replied politely.

"How far away is your ranch?" Sean inquired.

"We're about eight miles northwest of the gulch," she spoke with nervous alacrity. "When we arrived here last fall, Virginia City was just a long row of tents and wagons. Gold had just been discovered that May. My father found property in the valley with a creek and fertile pastures declaring it would be the Wilkes ranch. Momma and I were in shock. Not another soul around except for our wagon party. It got even quieter when Colleen and her family moved further west."

When the drinks arrived, Mandy took a dainty sip of sweet tea from the wide-mouthed rim.

Sean smiled at the refinement; however, it was the inflection in her voice that caused an insatiable curiosity of her roots. His new friend, Ethan, would not shed any information about her, despite the copious amounts of free flowing whisky that went from glass to mouth.

"Mandy, if I may be so bold, where have you come from?"

Her face showed a twinge of sadness. "I'm from Arkansas. We had a ranch east of Little Rock. Are you familiar with the area?"

"I've never been there but I know where it is."

She thought, *at least he knows some geography.*

Continuing, her voice remarked, "It was a wonderful place to grow up. We had schools, grand balls, culture, and music." Reminiscently, she looked away.

"And it has definitely influenced you," he said in earnest. "You're a wonderful performer."

Sean wondered about the move to Montana, but he'd been bold once, so he formulated another way of getting his answer. "Must have been something pretty important to move from Arkansas to Montana."

There were lots of reasons why, but she chose to speak of two of them. "I believe it was the impending war that put the idea in my father's head. He felt the war would be fought on his fields, and bring devastation to his land and the economy he relied on. He had also heard about opportunities in the west: the discovery of gold in Colorado and the chance for a fresh start in life."

She decided not to elaborate on the fresh start. "After he convinced my uncle and cousins to join us in 1861, plans to move to Colorado were in place. Little did we know how much sacrifice and work it would take to leave our home. That year, we sold most of our furniture, livestock, and slaves."

"It's not easy to leave your home," Sean said understandably.

Donevan returned, noisily rattling plates on the cloth-covered table.

Before thrusting her fork into action, she said, "We left our beloved ranch in the spring of 1862 as the civil war raged just beyond our county lines," she paused again with a sort of gloomy humour. "We were a sight: party of five wagons pulled by oxen, half a dozen hired hands, Father's thoroughbred horses, and fifty or so cattle trailing behind."

She watched him avidly sink teeth into one of those precious cows.

"Our wagons were loaded," her eyes expressing disbelief, "a cooking stove, tin plates and cups that clanked over every bump; barrels that creaked with the fullness of rice and flour, and ham and beans; that is, until their hollow remains were chopped up for firewood. Our tools repaired the wagons on more than one occasion. Seeds, saplings, and medicines, were crammed into every tiny crevice and stuffed with bedding. Rifles and ammunition were always in reach. We each had a job on that arduous trip northwest."

She stared into a dark corner while recollecting her thoughts. "The journey was the hardest thing I've ever done. We took turns walking a fair part of it. I felt it would go on forever."

Sean knowingly nodded, his mouth too preoccupied with chewing and savouring, and chewing and savouring, the beef that went down as smooth as butter, so unlike the beefed jerky and hard tack he was accustomed to grinding to a pulp in order to slide down his parched gullet.

"We made several stops along the thousand mile journey: broken wheels, swollen rivers, blocked trails, dreadful weather, and….utter exhaustion. The piano was removed and put back on the wagon more times than I could count," she smiled delicately.

"Momma refused to let that piano go. It was the last of her family's treasures. She said if the piano didn't make the journey, neither would she. It was the only time I ever saw her put up a fuss."

Mandy thought about how incredible that was considering what her mother had to put up with, and felt a pang of empathy which did not go unnoticed.

Eager to change the mood, she chirped, "There were happy times, though." She smiled and a small giggle escaped her mouth at the memory. "Tommy brought these tiny piglets and we had the most fun chasing after them when they tried to escape." Her smile faded into a frown. "Two of them survived the fire pit and our ravenous stomachs."

Sean watched Mandy with great intensity, admiring how she spoke so openly and sincerely.

"My cousin would sing to lighten up our tired and weary moods while my uncle played the fiddle, and some nights we had enough energy to dance around a roaring fire."

Mandy didn't tell Sean that she lost her temper at times, too. She silently recollected fitfully tossing her corsets out of the wagon, figuring they'd never be needed again. She also didn't divulge how she found them, lovingly coddled in her cousin, Tommy's arms, like a cherished blanket crusty with spittle.

Peering up from her glass, she was surprised to find Sean's focus no longer on his dinner plate.

"You mentioned your destination was Colorado?" he asked, stabbing at the few potatoes mottling his dull grey plate.

"Yes, originally it was Colorado. When we arrived in Denver three months later, we saw it was already densely populated."

"Believe it or not, by 1860, population of Denver was in the tens of thousands," Sean nodded affirmatively. "I guess that's why they call it a gold rush. Nothing forms a town quicker than a gold rush."

"With winter soon approaching, my father claimed one hundred and sixty acres of free property east of Denver provided he work it for five years. Momma wasn't well so I stayed with her and Colleen at the Rosewood hotel. Two sod cabins were built on this new land with the help of our hired hands. However, my father was never happy with the Colorado plains. He claimed it was too arid for farming and there wasn't enough fresh water for his cattle, so he often came into town at night to cheer himself up."

She glimpsed the food getting cold on her plate.

"One night he met a man named Orville Smith, who made considerable money buying and selling property in

Denver. Father was quite impressed. Mr. Smith was heading north where gold was just discovered in Bannack, with high hopes of achieving success there. Father couldn't contemplate moving so late in the year, though Mr. Smith's words lingered in his mind while his cattle fetched good prices at the local butcher shops."

"I can see why, Mandy. The beef was delicious!" Sean exclaimed with shameful hope that her uneaten half-slab might end up in his stomach.

"Hereford cattle are not as tough as Longhorn. I believe it's the best beef you'll ever taste," she boasted proudly.

"So how did you ever get to Montana?" Sean persisted while suppressing his voracious fork, pinning it against the checkered cloth.

"We had a difficult winter and lost seven of our cattle. Father's small herd was not going to be sufficient for demand and a cattle drive was out of the question while the war continued. Then, by spring, gold was discovered again in Montana territory. Father's mind was made up as soon as he heard of the second gold rush. With conviction," and she thought, *sheer determination*, "he said 'Montana is the place to go.' As one could imagine, Mother and I were none to pleased."

Her reticent mouth would not confess wishing she'd vanished in Denver with her mother and Colleen.

"Montana was another seven hundred miles north," she said grumpily. "However Father's decision was already made."

Distracted by thoughts of him and what she saw in town today, she hoped her discontent was not too transparent.

A smile adorned Sean's face, revealing deep dimples again. "I'm from Denver, Mandy. I know exactly what it was like. To think, we may have crossed paths, though I'm sure I would have remembered."

His words warmed her heart. "How long did you live there?"

"A few years," he replied. "I'm originally from Illinois. My mother worked as a schoolteacher. My father headed to California when I was very young with golden dreams. He is part adventure seeker, part gold seeker. When my mother took ill, he had to return home. We had some good years as a family before she passed away," he said, thinking back.

Mandy expressed her condolences.

"After my mother died, Father got anxious and thought maybe we could go gold seeking together. We went to Colorado but didn't have any luck. Figured, we'd give it one last shot in Montana."

His eyes lingered on her delicate, slender fingers slicing at beef, until she glanced up, her chewing abruptly halted.

After a hard swallow and burning cheeks, she was set to speak, when he interrupted, "News travelled about the gold in Alder Gulch and we felt the timing was right to come here. We hope to take advantage of that Homesteader's Act and get our own one hundred and sixty acres of land. We intend to settle here for good."

"Did you live in Springfield, Illinois?" she asked inquisitively as meat clung to her fork in mid-air.

"No, we lived north of Springfield, in Ottawa."

"I see," she said with disappointment. "I thought maybe you might have heard Abraham Lincoln speak publicly."

"I did, on a hot and dry August day amongst tens of thousands of my closest friends, I heard Lincoln speak," Sean said blithely.

Mandy's eyes lit up. "What do you remember about that speech?"

Set to say a speedy response, he changed his mind, believing she'd never get though her meal if he did.

Besides, he figured the experience was worth hearing about.

"Well, I remember most vividly how Lincoln said all men are created equal and that there is no moral right with one man's making a slave of another. Lincoln used the word 'hate' when he spoke of the injustice of slavery. He spoke passionately about the movement of slavery into Kansas and Nebraska, and the prospect that it would spread to every other part of the country, even the wilds of Montana. With the prospect of free land and the railroads being built across this vast land, I imagine he felt that danger more imminent. It was an excellent speech. Lincoln was engaging, humorous, and compassionate."

"We have two slaves who came with us from Arkansas," Mandy confessed. "If they remain personal property, would this territory eventually become a slave state, or would they have to be freed. I assume we will find out at the end of this war."

"I find it hard to believe that there is a war going on. We are so distant from it."

"I understand why it has come to this, but it's still a tragic loss of life," she said sadly, thinking of Sean and how he'd be on some battlefield, or even worse if he still resided in Illinois. For once, she was grateful to be in Montana, in the company of such a fine and handsome gentleman.

"I feel that a right which makes one man slave to another is no right at all," she said matter-of-factly. "Freedom to these people will be a wonderful thing. It's like a return to man's natural state: equality for all."

"I agree," he spoke with conviction. "It's a fight that has to occur. Slavery must end. Sometimes conflict is the only way to resolve man's problems. Conflict is everywhere. Whether it be over property, rights, politics, and whenever there is a clash, somebody loses. In Colorado, Indians are being pushed off their lands. They've retaliated by attacking settlements: Have gone as far as brutally killing a white family. It's frightening when you see the atrocities conflict has caused, yet we continue to fight. It seems to be the only way to make the changes we need to…..to survive."

Sean filled his lungs, carefully formulating his next words. "I've never been able to walk away from it, even though I know it always ends in somebody losing."

His confession made her curious. "Do you own a gun?"

"Only to protect myself," he answered unwaveringly.

"To defend yourself if you ever run into any conflict?"

"I respect laws, just as any other man should do, but where there are no laws, a gun can be the only thing stopping you from an early grave."

It was nearing eight-thirty.

"I apologize if our conversation got a little intense." His face softened with sincerity.

"Oh, I'm more interested in hearing a man talk about his moral and ethical trials than how much money he has, or how big his cow patch is," she declared genuinely.

She saw passion in this man tonight, although, she wished it wasn't sparked by the thought of conflict. "I thank you for supper and look forward to seeing you again."

Pausing, a brilliant thought entered her mind. "Would you like to picnic with me on Sunday after church. We could meet at the creek behind the ranch," she proposed, praying it didn't sound too forward.

Sean didn't hesitate, though he smiled subtly, "I would like that."

"I'll just go get some paper to draw directions."

"Mandy, I have a map. Why don't you add your details to it?" he offered, pulling it from his pocket.

She collected a pen and inkwell, and mapped out the creek and locations where he should search out property.

Colleen arrived and whisked her to the piano. Moments later, Donevan hustled over, ready to claim the dirty dishes.

"Not so fast!" Sean muttered, sliding Mandy's plate his direction.

Ethan arrived, hauling drinks from the bar. The tall, beaming fellow was thrilled to announce he'd chosen a spot to build his hardware store. He just had to search out a banker and settled on bouncing from table to table after shots of liquid confidence.

"I'll help you get to that point," Sean averred in a celebratory mood, while his teeth gnawed at the last of the roasted meat. He glanced at Mandy, who made him feel like the luckiest man in the world. Sharing the company of such a smart and desirable woman was truly delightful in many ways.

Chapter 4

Mandy sauntered into the kitchen, yawning and rubbing her eyes.

"Mornin' Miss Mandy," Mable chirped, flipping eggs.

"Breakfast smells good," she said with a stretch.

"I'll have it ready in a minute, child."

"Mable, will you teach me how to make your apple cobbler?"

She turned from the stove. "Why you wanna do dat? Get dem pretty fingers all floured up?"

Mandy tilted her head down with a small smile.

"What's his name?" she asked with a little snicker, thinking it'd be the only thing to get Mandy working in the kitchen.

"It's Sean. I promised him a piece of my apple cobbler and I'd like to give it to him today."

Mable's hand fell to her hip. "I knew it! You never shown any want to bake and come to tink of it, you never shown any want to cook eider!" she grumbled. "You let me know when he wants your beef stew and maybe I get out of da kitchen one day!"

While scraping bacon onto an empty plate, Mable felt sullen eyes on her stiff shoulders.

"Well, child, best get movin' if you want dat cobbler today. Roll up your sleeves, get da flour and grab dat jar of apples!" she pointed.

Mable continued to bark out ingredients as Mandy rushed to put them on the table.

The door opened suddenly and her father ambled in. Turning to Mandy with an all too familiar austere glare, he barked, "Go get clothes on! The day's half over!"

Reaching for a cup from the corner cupboard, he passed it to Mable, who stayed quiet, as he rubbed a throbbing forehead. It was all too apparent he'd had a late night, moving as slow as a snail.

Mandy scooted off before the words left her father's bellowing mouth and re-entered cautiously after the door clicked closed.

"Let's get cracking, Mable," she said eagerly.

"Eat your breakfast quickly. I'll start mixin' da apples with da spices."

Ellen Margaret entered the room. "Mandy, we've got to get to church. Hurry up and finish your breakfast!"

She gave Mable a desperate, pleading look.

"Next time, Miss Mandy, you do it all youssef; so you'd best be watchin' what I'm doing."

"Thank you, Mable," she squealed.

During Sunday service, Mandy was distracted by thoughts of Sean. Pastor Kennedy's parables became mumbled utterance as she contemplated which books would be brought to the creek, and what she would wear.

When his voice amplified with a slap to his Bible stand, she jolted on the uncomfortable wooden pew.

Her prayer for a quick morning in the stifling church would not be answered. Instead, a call to worship, five hymns, a lengthy scripture, and benediction, would make her feel bound in the building for an eternity. She had to stop tapping a nervous foot; otherwise, her mother would catch wind of the reprehensible meeting.

"Amen," Pastor Kennedy announced.

Mandy sighed in relief.

Her father didn't attend church since arriving in Montana territory. There was too much to do on the ranch and in the town. Before that, it was building Montana's biggest barn to house his cattle and prized possessions: his thoroughbred horses.

When church was letting out, Mandy took her mother's arm and quickened her step past the venerable man of the cloth because a stop with him would surely have lasted several minutes.

She also blocked out the sweet calls from her dear friend, Judy, whom she had been remorsefully neglecting the past few days.

With sunlight on her face, just inches from the doorway, she got cornered by Ethel Kennedy; and her mother held her firm.

"Amanda, Ellen Margaret, how nice to see you ladies this morning?"

Mandy gave a brief nod; however, her mother was more than happy to talk.

"Well, Ethel, we must have you over for tea soon. We get awfully lonely on the ranch, don't we Mandy?"

She wanted to confess 'except for today! I'm meeting a handsome, kind man if I ever get out of this church, Momma!'

"Would you like to come by for a visit tomorrow afternoon?"

Set to explode, Mandy started ushering her mother towards the door.

"I'm quilting with some ladies from the church tomorrow afternoon. Perhaps, later this week," Ethel offered.

Ellen Margaret had just enough time to nod before she was on the front steps. "Let go of me! You're being very rude!" she pointed out.

"I'm sorry, Momma. I have to go to the outhouse and would rather go to ours, so could we go home now before I have an accident?"

"Fine, but you are acting strangely, though," she managed to say before being hoisted into the carriage gently, but quickly by Mandy's support.

The carriage moved along at a calamitous pace.

"Mandy, slow down!" her mother fretted. "You're going to kill us and on the Lord's Day too! I think you should have used the outhouse at the church."

"It was occupied. It's always occupied by the elder Johnson brother. That man's internals run like clockwork all right. Church clockwork! It's uncanny how he bursts down the aisle like his pants are on fire just before the Pastor's final words. You remember how I waited that one time and I'll never do that again! I just about had to boil my clothes…"

"That's enough, Mandy! I had to put up with the fetid….I had to put up with it too!"

Mandy slowed the horses. "I'll be fine. I just feel a sense of urgency. Can't wait to go to the creek and eat my food in peace, spend the afternoon reading, and basking in nature's glory," she smiled.

At the ranch, Mandy rushed to the log home, forgetting to help her mother from the carriage seat.

"Mable!" she called, before opening the door to find the basket perched on the kitchen table.

Mable was already chopping vegetables for supper.

"Thank you so much," Mandy said with a hurried hug.

"Packed enuf in dat basket to feed a small army. Don't know how much your friend eats."

Mandy thought, *neither do I, but I'm going to find out all about his appetite and hopefully much more.*

"Well, I must change and be on my way. Don't want to be late!" she squealed, showing Mable her gratitude with another appreciative squeeze.

After sliding into a light pink muslin dress, she snatched a couple of books and was ready to grab the basket when she turned, the folds of her dressing twirling around slender legs. "Does this dress make me look fat?"

Mable plunked her fists onto wide hips. "You have a twenty inch waist! You best be eatin' haf of what's in dat basket or you fade away to a shadow!"

Mandy beamed, walking out of the rustic abode and into her mother, who stopped her.

"I thought you had to use the outhouse?" Ellen Margaret asked, perplexed, with eyes on the new dress.

"I'm going there on my way to the creek. It's a more efficient use of my time," she replied, hurrying past her mother's heated glare.

Mandy hopped away until out of view.

The meandering creek that flowed from Ruby River could be heard; however, she was too busy pondering whether Sean would find the spot.

Soon, she was surrounded by Ponderosa pines, cottonwoods, and willows, where the sun found it difficult to peak through. Dotted along her path were blue and yellow violets that waved in the slight breeze. When she laid the blanket down, water could be seen glistening through the trees. Normally enamoured by the place and its peacefulness, she was too preoccupied with peaking inside the basket, very pleased to see it full of delicacies.

Sean came into view riding at a loping pace. At the last second, Mandy nervously decided to stand and look as proper as she should, smoothing her dress, and feeling for hairpins that swept the tresses from slim shoulders.

He walked towards her, making smooth strides while winding his way around a few trees with leaves that fluttered in the gentle wind.

In daylight, he was even more handsome, showing off an irresistible smile. She hoped her attraction to him wasn't obvious.

"Have any difficulty finding the spot?" she asked warmly.

"No. I was just taking it all in," he replied, squinting at the creek briefly before taking her in: upswept hair and pretty round face with sun-kissed cheeks.

Too keenly aware of his long gaze, she nervously glanced away.

Hoping to break her trepidation, he asked, "Could we take a closer look…at the creek?"

She smiled with a soft nod.

They ambled to the clear waters.

"Your father ever fish here?" he questioned, watching the waters ripple downstream.

"No. Neither my father nor I have ever fished here. Father doesn't have time for what he calls hobbies, though I would learn if someone would teach me. I'd learn just about anything. It feeds my soul," she spoke wholeheartedly.

"I love to fish. It feeds my stomach," he grinned. "I think fishing is more of a necessity, especially if you're hungry and there's no food. So, when you're ready, I'll bring my rods and teach you how to fish."

"I'd like that," she answered, returning to the blanket.

"Well, you might not like the worm part."

"How bad could it be?"

He grinned genially. "Well, why don't we find out next week?"

"Maybe, you should try my picnic food first. You may not want to come back."

"I highly doubt that, but only one way to find out."

She removed the towel from the basket to reveal it teamed high with sandwiches, devilled eggs, cheese, peas, cobbler, and sweet tea.

"Are you expecting anyone else?" He shouted, "Who ever it is, you can come out from behind the trees now!"

Her cheeks went a shade of scarlet. "I just didn't know how hungry you'd be."

"Well, let's find out."

They ate quietly amid the melodious sounds of meadowlarks and blackbirds in the gentle swaying trees.

"It's a very peaceful place," she admitted. "I come here every afternoon, sometimes with food," her eyes peered at the basket, "and sometimes just to read. I've brought a couple of books."

Sean perused the books. "Let's see…they all look fine except for Shakespeare. Never could get into his works. Like a good story, but written in a…simpler tone."

"I don't always agree with Shakespeare's choice of words; however, it's the way the words are brought together. The sounds, the poetry, the rhythm, all make a kind of music in my mind."

She thought of a quote that was appropriate and recited it.

> "I know a bank where the wild thyme blows,
>   Where oxlips and the nodding violet grows,
>   Quite over-canopied with luscious woodbine,
>   With sweet musk-roses and with eglantine…."

While she read, a wisp of hair had fallen and delicately danced on her cheek.

Being in the company of such beauty, in a land scarce of the female kind, Sean saw her as a rare and vibrant flower in the densely verdant forest.

"Mandy, I'll listen to 'Romeo and Juliet' anytime as long as you read it."

He didn't want to stop hearing the intelligent passion in her voice. He was in awe of her, the food, the place.

"Actually," she corrected, "this is called 'A Midsummer Night's Dream'. I do have 'Romeo and Juliet' here somewhere though. Whenever I think of that story, it reminds me of the circus, strangely enough."

Sean smiled peculiarly.

"These two colossal elephants named 'Romeo and Juliet' came parading along, pounding Markham Street. They made such ghastly noises when they raised their trunks," she paused, "I miss the excitement of Little Rock. The intensity of its gas lights, procuring silk parlour slippers, and the taste of sweet potatoes, mashed, candied. Do you miss anything about your town?"

Sean took reluctant eyes from the basket.

"Oranges, I guess. When my father found gold in California, he procured a dozen oranges. Thought he was suffering from a touch of scurvy. He came home with a hankering; sent me off searching all of Ottawa for Florida oranges. My mother made this orange pudding and when she grated the rind, the house held the sweet fragrance for days. I never forgot that," he said, putting blatant eyes on the basket.

Mandy tipped it his direction.

"Why don't you read some more Shakespeare?" he urged, reaching for another sandwich.

"Why don't we try another of my favourite authors, Emerson?"
Sean nodded with a rapacious bite.

<blockquote>
"In this refulgent summer,
It has been a luxury to draw the breath of life.
The grass grows, the buds burst,
The meadow is spotted with fire
And gold in the tint of flower.
The air is full of birds,
And sweet with the breath of the pine……"
</blockquote>

Peering up after a lengthy passage, she found him eyeing the basket again, thinking that he was either starving to death, or had an insatiable appetite.

"Are you ready for some dessert?" she suggested. "Thought you might like to try my apple cobbler."

She offered a piece and waited for his reaction.

He took his time with focused bites until the crumbs were brushed away, his hand now on a jar of sweet tea.

"Well, what do you think?" she asked, exasperated.

"I think that…that I may need another piece before I make my final decision," he spoke with humour.

"Well, you aren't going to get another piece until you tell me whose is better, Mr. Thomas," she spoke sourly.

He laughed in surprise. "Yours is truly the best apple cobbler I've ever tasted, and I'd really like to taste more."

"Well, how about a race to….to that rock over there. Winner gets the last piece."

"You mean…run to that rock and whoever wins gets the last piece."

He showed incredulity in her challenge. "I think I was pretty clear about that but if you're not interested, I'll eat the last piece."

"You'll want a head start," he urged.

She gave him a sharp look while standing and smoothing her dress. "Ready….go!"

The last time Mandy ran was as a small child and the clothing wasn't so weighted. She was grateful for the lighthearted youthfulness in her step.

Sean coasted to the rock, thinking there wasn't any way she was going far in her full dress. He turned to find her at the halfway mark.

Standing on an overgrown stone, she uttered, "I meant this rock."

Swaying confidently, she laughed until balance was lost.

He rushed to her. "Are you hurt?"

Grinning, she squinted up, "I'm just fine. Better get your cobbler before I get to it first."

His steady hand helped her feet find solid ground.

They returned to a blanket covered with chickadees pecking at crumbs.

He didn't shoo them away.

"Well hello little ones. You're hungry too."

Mandy found Sean to be so different from other men. He appeared so gentle, so willing to show his affection, and so at peace with himself.

Her eyes lingered on his outstretched palm and the tiny bird precariously perched on it, and she wondered for a laconic moment whether that hand could ever do any harm.

Thinking of her father, she spoke reluctantly, "It's time for me to go."

They packed up the dishes and folded the blanket.

"Would you like me to escort you home?"

"No, thank you. Some other time."

"I hope to see you at the hotel in a few nights."

"I look forward to it."

"Thank you, Mandy."

She meandered home thinking it had been a wonderful day. Her step was light and her future seemed bright.

Sean watched as she moved towards the small home and massive barn.

"Let's go, horse," he said, reining his gelding away.

Chapter 5

Mandy was at the piano keeping time with her cousin's soprano voice when memories of that Sunday by the creek with the man, who was probably watching her right now, inspired her to play her best. It was also the thought of him that could lead her to great distraction, so her eyes stayed focused on the black and white keys.

Once the last note was sung she glanced over to find he wasn't alone. Walking to him, she smiled softly.

"Mandy, this is my father, Robert Thomas."

"Mr. Thomas, it's a pleasure to meet your acquaintance."

He took her extended hand and gave it a gentle squeeze. "It's mighty nice to meet you as well."

Robert was as tall as his son. He had a thick head of salt and pepper hair, eyes of hazel green, and that familiar smile, displaying two deep dimples.

"Do you have time to stay for a while?" Sean asked.

She glanced at her younger cousin being wheedled into trying a beer.

"Ah….now that Tommy is allowed in the hotel, he doesn't want to rush home," she replied hesitantly. "Can only stay a few minutes, though; don't want to arrive home late."

"Why don't I get us a couple of drinks," Sean offered. "Mandy, what would you like?"

"Sweet tea, please."

"How long has your family been in the cattle business?" Robert asked.

"For as long as I can remember. East of Little Rock, our ranch supplied the Kings of cotton with the best quality beef. It was a prosperous time and Father did well. I imagine that's all changed now."

Robert smiled grimly, knowing much more had changed. His thoughts turned to his son, free from the horrors of war.

"How are you finding your search for gold?"

"Well, nothing so far," he said disappointedly. "We've remained in the same spot. After a week or two, we'll move further up the gulch."

"I hear it's back breaking work," she spoke with empathy.

"It's not easy, especially at my age. This will be my last try at the rush. I will stop after our next big find," he said, looking forward to that day.

"I hear you mined in California?"

"Yes and it played out fine. I made enough to pay for a small house. Sadly, I missed out on seeing the children grow for a number of years. Mining's a busy job. I did it….do it, six days a week. It can be arduous and rather dull."

Mandy nodded as cheering broke out at the bar, her quick glance unable to discern a scrawny light vested boy amongst a nebulous swarm of dark jackets topped with bowler hats.

Robert followed her eyes and found Sean's lips moving a mile a minute. "He can be quite talkative when he wants to be."

"Mr. Thomas?"

"Please, call me Robert."

"Robert, you mentioned children. Forgive me but I thought Sean was an only child," she naively presumed.

"No, Sean had a sister. She was two years older than him. Died at sixteen from tuberculosis," he said sadly. "They were very close, Mandy, very close. He doesn't talk much about her. Everybody handles loss differently. How one handles grief is an entirely personal thing."

Sean appeared and saw her sad face. "Miss me that much?"

Her cheeks went rosy as she thanked him for the tea.

"I was just talking to a Jeffrey Coates," Sean said. "Seems he's from Denver, too. Know him, Bob?"

"Can't say that I do, though miners are strange people," Robert informed. "They either keep to themselves or won't shut up. I prefer to keep to myself."

He picked up on Mandy's confused face.

"Sean prefers to call me Bob. It's more professional when you're working around a bunch of other men."

"I still call you father. Heck, I'll call you father now. Father, would you mind getting us a few more drinks?"

Mandy cut in, "Gentlemen, I really must be going." She stood and shook Robert's hand again. "It was nice to meet you, Robert or Bob."

"The pleasure was all mine," he smiled kindly.

"Sean, would you get Tommy for me. I'll go search out Colleen."

All five reunited at the lanky front doors of the hotel.

"I'll see you in a couple days," Mandy spoke with enthusiasm.

"We'll have to plan out our fishing expedition," he replied with whimsy.

Tommy piped in, "You goin' fishin'? I love fishin'."

Colleen chirped in, "That's good, Tommy. We're happy you love fishin'." Then, she sniffed blatantly, "What's that smell on your breath? Is that….beer?"

Her mouth rambled on in the ear her fingers were pinching to the porch steps.

As Mandy peered at Sean, her eyes twinkled; and he responded with his charming smile.

She named that smile 'make me feel so warm and special inside' smile.

"I'll see you soon," she said blithely. "Good evening, Sean."

"Night, Mandy," he replied, watching her depart the hotel. Slowly, he ambled back to his father, who had a sly smile across olive toned skin.

"She's one fine looking lady. I see when it comes to women, our tastes are quite similar," Robert pointed out.

"I guess the apple doesn't fall far from the tree. Feel like heading down to the gambling hall? Try your luck at cards," Sean enticed.

"If it's anything like my luck at Alder Gulch, it'd be best I stay right here. Besides, we don't need any trouble in this town," he said sharply.

"Won't bring my gun! Just money and good luck."

"As long as we keep our bets low. You still want money to treat that lady to a good time."

"I plan on making money tonight so I can treat that lady to many good times," Sean grinned devilishly.

****

Sunday morning arrived. Sean peered out the small window of his room to see a cloudless sky. "Gonna be a warm one today."

Robert was just rousing from his bed. "Why don't you attend church with the lovely lady?"

"Can't," he mumbled, smoothing the folds in his jacket. "Got to search out worms. See you later on with supper."

Sean stole another glance at his reflection. "Damn, I'm a fine looking man," he intoned with fingers running though wavy hair.

"I'm sure the worms will find you irresistible."

Glaring at his father, he said, "Remember who's catching supper."

"Only if you can keep your attention on the fish, Romeo," Robert replied, shaking his head.

Sean walked to a mercantile, eager to just buy the worms rather than having to go digging or turning over rocks.

"Morning, Sir. What can I do you for?" Mr. Pratt, the stout, balding store clerk asked.

"I'm looking for worms," Sean answered while perusing the notions of the store.

"Have you tried searching at Boothill cemetery?" he asked with steely eyebrows raised over round spectacles.

"No, I thought I'd come here first."

"Well, we don't have worms, however," he thought aloud, scratching his head, "maybe I can convince my son, Willie, to go searching for some for say, a dollar."

"A dollar for worms?" Sean asked incredulously.

"Take it or leave it."

He didn't waste any time deciding. "I'll take it. Be back in an hour."

"That's just fine, sir. Willie, get your butt over here! This job requires your immediate attention!"

An eight year old boy with blonde, curly locks appeared from the back of the store.

"I've got an opportunity for you to make ten cents, son."

Sean headed towards the door and spotted some fancy chocolates in a glass display. "Could you pack up a dozen of these too?"

"Sure thing; see you, soon," Mr. Pratt smiled, thinking he just satisfied another customer.

On his way to the hotel, Sean bumped into Ethan.

"I was just coming to find you," Ethan spoke eagerly. "Thought you might like to see the property I purchased yesterday."

Sean peered at his pocket watch. "Sure, why not."

"It's just this way." He turned and they headed east into the bright yellow sun.

"I take it you were able to get the financing?"

"Yep, it's official. We have a bank in town and I believe I was its first customer." Ethan pointed, "There's the bank on your right."

Sean's glance at the impressive stone building was short-lived when he was forced to hop the boardwalk to get clear of a two-wagon train careening his way.

The town was it's busiest on Sundays. Wagons and carriages were creaking steadily along the narrow street in both directions, causing swells of brown clouds. Despite the gritty haze that stung at eyes and coated throats, storefronts were replete with patrons trudging along in their Sunday best.

They passed the Eatery and slowed to watch one of its tawdry servers beating carpet against a hitching post, her Sunday best scantily clad to blossoming bosoms.

Thirty yards past the Golden Nugget saloon, they entered the newly constructed part of town and didn't stop until they reached the first empty lot.

"We start building tomorrow," Ethan said with much excitement.

"I wish you much success."

"Say, you have time for breakfast?"

"If we make it quick. I'm picnicking with Mandy."

While they headed west, Ethan gave Sean a congratulatory smile. "So she's taken her head out of her books, has she?"

"For the most part, though I say she can read Shakespeare to me anytime," he said with pleasure.

"Shakespeare evokes boredom in me," Ethan remarked with a look of distaste.

Sean stopped to eye his friend. "Well, it arises passion in Mandy and I'm more than willing to encourage that feeling!"

"Well, well, Mr. Thomas, it appears you have a way with the lady," he grinned sheepishly while patting Sean's back.

With a cocky grin, Sean thought, *not yet but I plan to.*

Breakfast went longer than planned. Sean was burning the breeze to make it to Mandy in time, nearly loosing his balance and the fishing rods.

When he arrived, the blanket and basket were atop the forested ground, but Mandy was nowhere to be found.

He moved along the creek's bank, weaving around stately pines until her small frame came into view.

"I apologize for my tardiness," he said while she added stems of white violets tinged pink to a handful of wildflowers.

Peering up, she smiled brightly. "That's fine. I though I'd add some fragrant colour to our picnic."

"I had breakfast with Ethan. He's now the proprietor of Holden Hardware."

"That's wonderful!"

"Have you spoken to Colleen lately?"

"Two days ago. Why?" she asked curiously.

"No reason," he replied vaguely. "Oh, I brought you something."

He passed her a brown bag.

Mandy keenly peeked inside and lifted the flap of the box. "Oh!" she jumped.

Sean eyed the rejected package crumpled by her feet.

"Sorry! Try this."

She proceeded with caution and was pleasantly surprised. "Much better. Chocolates are my favourite indulgence."

They picked apart the picnic basket.

"Sean, what is the most important quality a person should possess?"

He didn't hesitate. "To be truthful. I hate liars. What's your opinion?"

"Honesty," she replied.

"It's the same thing," he answered quickly.

"Yes and no."

"What do you mean?" he asked with curious eyes.

She pondered an appropriate memory. "Back in Little Rock, we had a leap-year ball. I was escorted by a man named Andrew Jackson. After our first dance, he asked if he was the worst dancer I'd ever been with."

She smiled, thinking back. "I said, 'Andrew you are full of exuberance and youthfulness that I have never experienced before.' He had me moving and twirling so much, I nearly spun out the door. Truth would have been embarrassing to him. Might have made him feel bad. The next week, Andrew was more relaxed and controlled. Seems he found his step."

Rolling a pea between two fingers, her eyes implored, "I have a question?"

He nodded, his mouth full of food.

"When is Ethan proposing to Colleen? Speak the truth after you've completely chewed all of that food."

His laughter filled the air, while her face remained unflinchingly scrupulous beneath the wide brimmed straw hat.

Fighting every urge to kiss it and take her slender hands in his, he swallowed tensely, "Soon, Mandy. We should go fishing."

They took the mossy path that turned into a bed of dried needles when nearing the creek's edge, carting the rods and plump squirmy bait.

"Let me get a worm on your hook," he offered. "I'm going to drop it in the water and then I'll give it to you, so watch carefully."

Strong and brawny arms enveloped her as he closed the pole in her slender hands and slowly raised the line.

She enjoyed feeling his closeness so much she thought she liked fishing until he abruptly let her go, and walked away.

"How will I know when I have something?" she asked with a hint of desperation.

"Oh, you'll know."

Minutes went by and there was an easy silence.

Mandy watched as the tranquil, clear waters crested against sharp rocks.

Peering up, she asked, "How long does this fish catching take?"

Sean lifted his rod and pulled a shimmering fish from the water, making it look easy.

"What kind is that, Sean?"

"This is brown trout," he replied, unhooking the fish.

She watched as it wriggled and gasped for air.

"Trout has good flavour. Cooks up nice…."

As Sean spoke about fish, Mandy paid all of her attention to his lean and long body. His sleeves were rolled up revealing strong bronzed arms that, moments before, held her so tightly. He had such grace as he held out his line, smiling and chattering.

She thought, *my how he really enjoys ranting about fish.*

Her enthrallment with Sean's moving lips caused her to disregard when the line pulled, followed by the rod, into the water.

Sean reacted quickly, tossing off shoes and socks, and darting into the creek.

"I'm sorry," she cried as he waddled out, pants soaking wet.

"Why don't we try this again," he said encouragingly.

"I like it better when you put your arms around me. Makes me feel more confident," she suggested.

"Fine, but you're going to get damp," and, he thought, *I might not be able to keep my hands off of you, either.*

Sean ensconced himself around her again. Being considerably taller, he had to bend at the knees. Her scent of rose water was subtle as his cheek grazed a few curly strands that escaped hairpins loosened by the warm summer's breeze. Straining his neck, he delighted in the softness of her.

She didn't object. Angling her chin, warmth from his breath tingled her ivory skin. When the line went tight, he clasped her hands and lifted the flailing trout. Once they caught three good sized fish, she started for home.

Turning, she said, "I've got a name for our picnic spot."

He froze and waited, the fish tied together in his hand.

"Willowtree Creek," she spoke lightly as her eyes roamed the picturesque spot. "You'd better get those home," she pointed. "They're starting to smell."

He eyed the fish, ready to toss them back in the waters and kiss the lips he hungered for. "I look forward to seeing you on Tuesday," he said with deep resignation.

"Enjoy your fish supper," she smiled, walking away.

When Mandy reached home, her father was there.

"You been out at the creek a while," he stated.

"Yes, Father. Just lost track of time," she said warily.

A tense pause ensued.

"Go inside," he said gruffly. "See if your mother needs help." His stare stayed firm on his dusty boot.

Her father appeared deep in thought, so Mandy wasted no time heading to the cabin. When she entered, supper was prepared, the table already set.

Ellen Margaret eyed her daughter critically. "Best come back from the creek earlier, Mandy, or your father will come and get you. Go quickly and wash up."

Mandy handed Mable the basket with a mischievous smile.

Minutes later, she was seated at the hand hewn table across from her mother.

Henry sauntered in and splashed his hands in water warming on the stove.

Ellen Margaret softly shook her head, dreading when he cleaned his filthy hands in soon to be dish water.

The sounds of cutlery tapping china plates were already filling the kitchen, but were coming from Mable and her brother, Jacob's bedroom.

As usual, Henry ate quickly and rarely spoke during supper, though tonight he would say what was lingering in his mind.

"Talk from Texas is that Nelson Story is organizing a cattle drive. Gonna bring herds of longhorn cattle into Montana."

He shoveled mashed potatoes into his mouth.

"Why don't you write him a letter?" Ellen Margaret suggested softly. "Maybe you can work with him?"

Cutlery clanked the table, followed by angry fists.

"Dammit, Ellen Margaret!" Henry spat out. "When I want your opinion, I'll ask for it! Don't have time for a cattle drive! Nelson Story can drive that cattle to hell and back for all I care!"

Swinging his chair out, he leered at her, his face blazing red. The floorboards shook with his heavy footsteps and the mud slats crumbled when the door slammed shut.

"Momma, why do you let him talk to you like that?" Mandy snapped.

Sometimes you have to choose your battles and now's not the time," she replied somberly. Ellen Margaret's thoughts were on the woman Henry was probably off to see. She wondered if this woman was spoken to in the same heart wrenching tone.

Chapter 6

The following week, the dining room of the Donevan Hotel was bustling with hungry patrons. In order to provide prompt service and fast meals, Donevan hired another cook and server.

Sean was seated at his usual table but growing restless as Mandy performed her last song with Colleen. It had been another fruitless day at Alder Gulch, and even though the sight of her was lifting his spirits, he couldn't wait to have her full attention.

Colleen noticed how impatient he seemed, so she offered to collect the sheet music. Moving towards him, Mandy had a brilliant smile across her face until she spotted her father watching from the bar. In the blink of an eye, her face became very sober as she sauntered past Sean.

His confused eyes followed her to a stocky, firm-looking man.

When Colleen walked by, she discreetly shook her head as if in warning for Sean to stay seated. He assumed that the man was Mandy's father but couldn't comprehend the empty look on her face or the fact that she didn't make any introductions.

Mandy solemnly exited the hotel without any glance his way.

Sean sat bewildered, then disgruntled. He'd have to contend himself with sifting through dirt for days before she was even in the same room again.

Moving to the staircase, he passed Donevan.

"Say Donevan, who was that gentleman with Mandy?"

Donevan appeared puzzled. "Why that was Henry Wilkes, Amanda's father."

Sean nodded with little enthusiasm.

"Henry Wilkes owns this property and several others in Virginia City."

As Sean climbed the stairs, he couldn't help but think about how Henry Wilkes eyed his daughter with such apathy.

****

Dark clouds were rolling in as Sean and Robert were riding out to their claim.

Suddenly, Robert stopped.

Sean followed his father's glare to a man hanging from a juniper tree, arms pinioned to his torso. The branch creaked while a note fastened to his chest flapped whitely in the breeze against dark, somber clothes.

"What's it say, Bob?" Sean asked.

"Does it matter?" He shot hard eyes at his son. "What matters is you realize there's law here, and this is how they handle lawbreakers! Let's go! We've got gold to find!"

They worked a steady pace all morning, digging and sifting through dirt and small rock.

At noon, Sean handed his father a dinner pail.

"Maybe we invest in a rocker," Robert suggested as thunderheads smothered the blue sky. "It'll make us move quicker."

Thirty minutes later, the heavens opened. By the time they reached the hotel, their clothes were soaked through.

To Sean's pleasant surprise, Mandy was at the piano with a young girl in an indigo gingham dress.

He began to head over when his father halted him. "You may want to change son," he said as water pooled onto the pine planked floorboards.

Sean dashed up the spiral stairs to get into dry clothes.

"Do you know how to play the piano?" Mandy asked.

"No, Miss," the little girl replied.

"How about some lessons, then?"

Pigtails bobbed up and down as her head nodded frantically. "Yes, Miss!"

At that moment the girl realized Mandy had a caring heart.

"Have your mother come speak to me when she's available."

As the little girl squeezed passed Sean descending the staircase, a somber tune permeated the hotel. It ended abruptly when he approached her.

"I'm sorry about last night," she spoke lightly. "That was very rude of me."

Sean sighed as he sat on the bench while her gloomy eyes stayed on slender fingers.

"Why don't you play that song, Moonlight…"

"Sonata. Why don't we perform it together?"

"I'm afraid I wouldn't know what to do," he replied.

Gently, she placed his fingers over the keys and introduced his eyes to the notes.

"The left hand is generally the easiest."

He thought his attempt was pretty horrible but it did cheer her up.

Gazing at him, her eyes sparkled.

Sean couldn't hold back his desire for her any longer.

Leaning in slowly, their tender lips met and lingered until a glass clacked against the bar's counter.

He held her closely, her cheek innately resting against the warmth of his chest.

They sat lost in time until the atmosphere began to change. Grumbling miners were filling the room looking like drowned rats.

"Sean, can we talk about what happened last night?"

"Why don't we get a table?"

He took Mandy's hand to a corner of the room.

Donevan quickly followed with a pretty woman clad in a cotton calico dress and clean white frilly apron.

"I'd like you to meet Theresa. She'll be helping me wait on tables while we're so busy. Theresa, this is Sean Thomas and Amanda Wilkes."

Sean and Mandy nodded to the woman with the bright blue eyes and sweet smile.

"Amanda plays the piano while her cousin sings three nights of every week."

"I heard you playing with Mr. Thomas. It sounded lovely," she said, and thought that the kiss was even lovelier.

"See, you weren't so bad," Mandy grinned with mirth.

Sean chuckled. "That's a matter of opinion."

"Well, Theresa, just take the drink orders to Hal and bring any food orders to Kitty in the kitchen," Donevan advised.

"What would you two like this afternoon?"

Sean smiled. "We'll have two teas and two apple cobblers, please."

When Theresa was out of earshot, Mandy spoke about last night. "My father showed up unannounced and I was taken by compete surprise. To be quite honest, he's never shown an interest in hearing me play," she said with a disheartened face.

Sean was set to embolden her when she spoke again.

"My father's a very busy man. I do not see much of him. We do not…..we are not particularly close."

She stiffened while considering confiding in Sean about her father's lack of affection and atrocious temper. But, in the end, she shook away the thought, the feelings of betrayal and vulnerability winning over.

Sean clasped her hands and noticed they were cold and trembling.

"I've never really spoken to anybody about my father," she said in earnest.

With great efficiency, Theresa arrived with their teas and cobblers. Mandy instantly pulled her hands away.

Hesitantly, Theresa asked with concern, "Can I be of any further assistance?"

"No, thank you," Sean replied with eyes remaining on Mandy in a soothing way.

Theresa briskly walked away.

"You must understand that I'm very grateful to my father," Mandy began. "I've had an easy life, been afforded the opportunity to be educated, to learn to play the piano, and……to enjoy life. I've not told him about you, yet," she confessed with great disappointment in herself.

"Why?" Sean asked with concern.

"I don't know. I just don't want to take a chance that I might lose you."

Smiling confidently, he remained deeply baffled. "Mandy, your father will never scare me away," he said, squeezing her hand. "The only one who can drive me away is you."

She breathed a heavy sigh of relief.

"I'll wait 'till you're ready. However long it takes," he vowed.

Mandy was happy that she confided in him. It was a big step for her.

****

On an early summer morning, Robert Thomas stepped onto a sun-soaked street while Henry Wilkes slipped into the cool shade of the hotel's porch.

The tall doors swung open and Donevan peered up from his occupancy registry.

"Morning, Henry," he said, offering a brown envelope. "Morgan Terrence is just finishing his breakfast. Let me take you to him."

As they passed the winding steps, Henry paused.

"Most impressive," he observed while his wide hand brushed against the smoothly sanded risers. "Oak?"

"Yes," Donevan answered hastily.

"Suppose I could just take them considering I own this land," he boasted, his eyes gleaming with envy.

"Well, Henry," Donevan spoke anxiously, "I could make contact with the carpenter out East and he could replicate them custom to your specifications."

"Relax, Donevan!" his voice bellowed to the nervous renter wound tighter than a string. "I'm not gonna take your golden staircase, at least as long as these envelopes fill my palm."

They moved into the dim dining room.

Morgan was eyeing his empty plate when Theresa approached.

"Can I get you anything else, Mr. Terrence?" she asked sweetly.

"Well, Miss Theresa, I would love another plate of this bacon. It's absolutely delicious!" he smiled handsomely.

Theresa blushed a deep shade of scarlet at the charming, dark-haired man with intelligent blue eyes. "I'll get some more for you right away."

"Morgan Terrence!" Donevan announced. "May I introduce Henry Wilkes!"

Morgan shook Henry's hand. "Please, take a seat."

"How are you finding Virginia City?"

"To think it barely existed a year ago!" Morgan said implausibly. "These gold towns grow like weeds."

Henry thought, *they sure do and I've garnered profits.*

Theresa promptly returned with the fried pork.

"Thank you, kindly."

"I see you like your bacon," Henry commented.

"I do. This is the finest I've ever tasted."

"That's because it's home-cured and hickory smoked at my brother-in-law's farm just northwest of here," Henry divulged.

"Do say!"

"Have you seen the new construction alon Wallace Street?"

"I have and have also seen your new building. It's a fine sturdy construction. Will make an excellent establishment," Morgan praised as he crunched on the crispy animal fat. "I've thought about helping develop your other properties with much interest. How much were you thinking to borrow?"

"I don't have current estimates but it wouldn't take long to figure that out," Henry assured, his stout frame relaxing into the ladder back chair.

"Mr. Wilkes…"

"Henry."

"Henry, why did you purchase so much land?" Morgan asked with much intensity.

"I've always found that it's the land that gains in value. The more land, the wealthier the man," he said most sensibly. "You'll hear people in town speak of doubling their land values in a few months. I've just about tripled mine. Thought you might like a part of this fortune too."

"Land is only worth something if somebody wants it," Morgan pointed out matter-of-factly as a trickle of grease ran down his freshly-shaven chin. "Gold has already been discovered in the Prickly Pear Valley and I dare say people are already moving north. Henry, what happens when Alder Creek runs empty of gold? Is there enough in this town for it to remain viable?"

"There's still plenty of gold in Alder Creek," Henry stated with a convincing nod. "Hydraulic mining hasn't even begun yet."

"I've spoken to your men and they speak very highly of you. They say you work just as hard, if not harder than they do, and you pay them fair wages. I'm very much interested in partnering with you. Could we discuss this over supper, tonight?"

"I'm having supper with my family but perhaps tomorrow night."

"A family man?"

"A man who has to keep an eye on his family," he replied dryly.

"You have sons, Henry?" Morgan asked.

"I had a son. He died two days after his birth."

"I'm sorry….God works in mysterious ways."

Henry nodded grimly, though he felt God had nothing to do with it. The baby was just born too early. His complicated birth nearly took the life of Ellen Margaret and robbed her of the chance to have any more children.

"I don't tend to dine here," Henry scoffed as if the place wasn't up to snuff. "My time is spent at the Occidental Billiard Hall just east of the hotel. We can dine across from it at a place called Merriweather Inn. You like beef, Mr. Terrence?"

"Morgan. Call me, Morgan. Yes, I like beef very much. Even more than bacon."

"Well then, you'll like my Hereford beef served here and at the Merriweather Inn."

"How does a cattle man get caught up in land deals and construction?"

"The bloody war has stalled my plans of heading a cattle drive," Henry revealed. "A man must wear several hats to feed his family. Investing in this town has more than fed my family. It will fund my future cattle drives."

"How many acres do you have?" Morgan asked.

"I'm just shy of five hundred acres of prime grazing fields. Got my claim, convinced two hired ranch hands, who decided to stay in Virginia City, to make claims. I pay them higher wages in return for that land. In four short years, all of that land will be mine," he said with surety.

Morgan was very impressed with Henry Wilkes. He saw dollar signs in the hard working man and nothing more.

"You a gambling man, Henry?"

"That's how I got my Hereford cows and considerable prime property east of Little Rock."

"Then remind me not to play against you."

"If you insist."

They shook hands again.

"Word of friendly advice," Henry said. "Do your shopping at Pratt's. Avoid Allen's Mercantile. You will pay more for food supplies at Pratt's, however there's no plaster in their flour or pebbles in their coffee."

"Good to know. Bring me the financial numbers tomorrow," Morgan smiled subtly.

****

Days passed. Robert paid for another month's accommodation even though he felt it best to go north to 'Last Chance Gulch' where gold was just discovered. It was the sight of his lovestruck son that forced Robert to bury any dubious thoughts about his claim at Alder Creek.

They splurged on a rocker, which made looking for gold easier. The rocker was a bucket that moved like a cradle. Sean and Robert took turns mounding dirt into the upper end, then pouring water over it, and rocking it back and forth.

Sean's attitude remained resolutely hopeful. "Bob, I think our luck's going to change."

It was a humid day, but every now and then a soothing breeze would cool their bodies enough for the clothing to loosen its grip from their sweaty skin. Sean would sip water from his canteen and gaze at the mountains, untouched and majestic in size. It was such a stark contrast from the view along the gulch, littered with gold diggers and their equipment.

After mining had been through a place, it was forever changed. Soil would be eroded to bare rock and most of the nearby trees would be gone. Stream water was re-routed for sluices where dirt would be shoveled into wooden troughs before muddy water washed through, leaving gold behind in cleats.

"I was thinking about bringing Mandy out here for a little while tomorrow," Sean said. "She's interested in seeing the process."

Robert couldn't hide his discontented face. He wanted them to continue a strong pace along this claim of the gulch. If it were to be an empty part of the stream, they were less likely to get another chance the longer they waited.

Sean could see that his father was none too impressed with the idea, so he thought about bringing her out on Sunday. That was Sean and Robert's day off. It had always been that way when his mother was alive. It was the Lord's Day; a day of rest; a day of family.

Even though his wife had been gone five years, Robert kept that day of rest. He found a Methodist church in Virginia City to attend; however, Sean had turned away from religion after the deaths of both his sister and mother. They were such wonderful people and he couldn't understand why the Lord would want to take them, one so soon after the other. It devastated him, and he wallowed in grief, knowing despair was a lonely place. It didn't allow comfort, peace, or hope to enter.

Mandy changed all of that for him. She had beauty and talent: two qualities any man could fall in love with. But that wasn't what lured him in. When she played that first song so passionately, it stirred within him a feeling of sadness and a longing for something more. He was allured by her, and by how she felt everything and expressed it so openly, so bravely. She was so full of hope and promise that he started living through her rosy view of life. Whether it be scooping up wildflowers at Willowtree Creek, talking to a chickadee in the palm of her hand, or playing the piano, she lived in the moment. Sean lived in her moments and never wanted them to end.

Robert brought him back from his tender thoughts. "It's time to eat. Grab the dinner-pails."

As he did as asked, he decided he would bring her here. He would see her as much as possible.

****

That night, Sean and Ethan were sitting amongst scores of Irish migrants, wholly discernable, when they joined Colleen in belting out 'Tis The Last Rose of Summer' to the darkest corners of the room.

"Sean, its official," Ethan beamed, "Colleen and I are engaged!"

"Well, congratulations," he exclaimed, raising his glass.

"We wish to celebrate by having you and Mandy to my house Sunday evening for supper."

"Why, thank you, Ethan."

"We can also celebrate Mandy's birthday. She'll be one year older than she is now."

"And how old would one year older than she is now be?" Sean asked, quite amused.

"If I told you, Colleen would hang me out to dry. Southern women can be quite particular about certain things."

"Well how about showing some backbone! Besides, who am I gonna tell?"

Ethan revealed a crooked grin. "Nineteen, but if you ever tell, I reckon I won't see Colleen's lightness for several years."

"Ethan, you buy me a few more drinks and I won't even remember this conversation."

Sean lifted his empty glass.

"Say, how 'bout after tonight's performance we all go to the dance hall? It's just down the street," Ethan suggested while catching Theresa's eye, lifting two fingers.

"That's fine by me, though I haven't danced in ages."

"Well, there's no time like the present time."

Colleen called out in a boisterous voice, "That song was for you, Danny O'Connell, so I take kindly that you and everyone else stay silent for the next one. This song has been written by my dear cousin and it's our first time performing it together."

Once the patrons' voices turned to mumbles and low grumbles, the sounds of cutlery clanking tin plates and glasses knocking tables waned, so Mandy began tapping the keys. Colleen's soprano voice flowed through the smoky room.

"Take me to the river, to the place I know,
Hold me close forever, never let me go.
Where the waving violets grow,
Where time seems to move so slow,
Take me to the river, to the place I know,
Hold me now forever, never let me go."

"Where the sun streams bright its glow,
Where the crystal waters flow,
Take me to the river, to the place I know,
Hold me close forever, never let me go.
Where the wistful willows bend,
Where winding paths cease to end,
Take me to the river, to the place I know,
Hold me now forever, never let me go."

Mandy smiled as her cousin sang her poem so beauty-fully and secretly hoped that miners weren't ready to toss food at her.

After the song was finished, she turned, searching for the approval of one person in the crowd and would not be disappointed when he appeared and took her in his arms, regardless of her shyness towards public affection.

Sean whispered, "I'll gladly hold you in my arms forever."

With tears welling in her eyes, she softly replied, "If I knew my poetry would have this affect, I'd have read more sooner, thank you."

Ethan commented too loudly, "Hey now….they look more in love than we do."

Mandy hurriedly pulled away from Sean with a look of embarrassment in her rosy cheeks.

Colleen smacked Ethan. "Sometimes your mouth is bigger than your brain."

He recovered quickly, "Sean will be coming to supper, Sunday evening."

"That's wonderful!" Colleen cried with delight.

Mandy couldn't hide her happiness.

Ethan, the bearer of embarrassing and good news decided to try his luck once more. "Say, why don't we go to the dance hall for a spell? I hear it's a fine place to be."

"What do we do with Tommy?" Colleen asked.

"We'll take him with us. I'm sure there'll be lots of pretty girls for him to look at."

Sean waited for Mandy's response.

Hesitantly, she said, "Why not."

"What are we waiting for?" Ethan spoke eagerly. "Let's get out of here!"

Grabbing Tommy on the way out, they piled into the carriage and moved through the darkness into a warm easterly breeze.

Mandy tossed a shawl over her head.

"You cold, Mandy?" Sean asked, sliding his arm around her.

"I just don't want my hair to get dirty and tangled," she replied, thinking she didn't want her father to see her riding past the Occidental Billiard Hall.

When they opened the tall French doors, the dance hall was replete with enthusiastic and exuberant couples spinning around the room. Narrow wall sconces emitted a fair light that stretched erratic shadows along the paper lined walls.

Colleen clawed Ethan and yanked him to the sawdust covered floor. Mandy saw Tommy's wide-mouthed face with eyes that seemed fixated on the moves of the dance.

"This is called 'Triplet Galop'," Mandy informed.

Sean caught him drooling and knew that the dance wasn't what was catching the boy's attention. The woman wildly being spun around the room was wearing a sequined dress, her black bodice cut so low over large white breasts, nothing was left to a man's imagination. One swift flap of her arms and they would be jiggling out of her corset.

"You could dance with her if you like. Probably cost you twenty-five cents," Sean swallowed with eyes following the woman's hopping body. "You could probably dance with most of the women in this room provided you had money."

As the song ended, Mandy followed Sean and Tommy's fixation to a harlot with more skin showing than she did when she bathed.

In horror, she asked, "Are you going to stare at that painted lady all night long or are we going to dance?"

"Sorry, Mandy," Sean replied as his hand gently clasped hers while the other madly dug loose change from his pocket.

"Don't spend it all on one dance," he whispered to Tommy as the tune changed to 'Charming Waltz'.

Smiling at the gleaming coin, Tommy moved voraciously toward the black corset dress.

"It's been a while, so I hope I won't be the most terrible dancer you've ever had," Sean spoke with a nervous grin.

She smiled back and thought, *if you are, you'll never know*.

He was not the most terrible dancer, so Mandy was elated to be led through a stream of waltzes and schottisches, until the fiddler changed his tune to 'Jenny Lind Polka'.

Moving to an empty pocket of the dance hall, she asked, "Where's Tommy?"

Sean pointed to him, dancing with his head resting on the bobbing chest of the black sequined woman.

"How would he get the money for that?"

"Now, Mandy, what would make you think she's a hired lady?" he asked quite innocently.

"Well, let me see. Maybe, it's the fishnet stockings, or the knee length dress, or the way she's heaving her bosoms into my short cousin's face. Their making fools of themselves! What's worse, he might suffocate if he gets any closer to those...."

A commotion erupted on the dance floor.

Ethan bumped into what he would later call 'the brick wall'. He was a sturdy, stocky hulk; and, for what he lacked in height, he made up for in sheer muscle. The brute roared in a thick Irish brogue that he didn't care for Ethan's clumsiness. Ethan apologized, but was abruptly pushed off his feet.

Sean was just about to stomp his direction, the look of anger written all over his face, when Colleen grabbed Ethan and rushed toward the door.

The fiddler started up again, tapping his toe, wielding his bow, zig zagging to and fro. The crowds swallowed the Irish brute, and Mandy turned to see Sean's anger fading.

She cautiously took his hand and called for Tommy to exit the hall.

"You know I could have taken him," Ethan calmly said with shaking hands.

"I know, darling," Colleen replied smoothly. "For what you lacked in strength, he lacked in height, and it just wouldn't have been a fair fight."

"Did you end up spending all of your money, Tommy?" Sean whispered.

"She was worth every penny I had!" he exclaimed.

Mandy eyed Sean, who shrugged his shoulders.

He thought it a good time to ask her out to Alder Gulch on Sunday.

She looked to Colleen, who replied that she was coming into town to get supplies for their supper.

"Would you like me to borrow a carriage?" Sean asked.

"I can ride a horse," she replied staunchly. "Grew up on a ranch!"

"Well then, you can use my father's horse. He doesn't tend to go far on Sundays."

Mandy lightly kissed Sean's cheek before climbing into the carriage beside Colleen.

"We'll see you Sunday, Sean," Colleen drawled. "Best of luck to you at the gulch."

Chapter 7

A casual, warm breeze greeted Mandy and Ellen Margaret as they walked to the porch steps of the church, Sunday morning. Ellen Margaret praised God for such a pleasant day to visit the Tate farm.

"Mother, let me take the reins so you're not too tired for the ride back on your own."

"Hold your horses. Are you going to take it easy?"

"I promise I'll guide the horses at a walking pace this bright summer's day."

As they rode north, Ellen Margaret took in the beauty of the tall buttercups and pink primroses dotting the lofty, green pastures. All Mandy took in were thoughts of Sean, her dreamy smile as plain as day.

As they neared the farm, Ellen Margaret noticed her daughter's happy disposition but dismissed it as two close cousins spending Mandy's special day together.

When they arrived, Colleen appeared and asked her aunt to stay for lunch. Mandy's head shook profusely until her mother glanced her way.

"Well if it's not too much of an inconvenience, I'd love to," she stuttered, staring coolly at her daughter.

"I have fresh-baked sourdough bread with creamy butter, thick slices of ham, sweet tea, and, of course," Colleen boasted, "crunchy cucumber and carrots from our bountiful garden. I also made an apple pie."

"Sounds wonderful! Maybe you could teach Mandy to make an apple pie?"

"Not on my birthday, Momma," Mandy piped in.

"And not until Mable is put out to pasture," Colleen retorted.

It was a full hour before Ellen Margaret finished her meal, was given a quick kiss goodbye, and scooted away from the Tate home.

Sean was leaning against the hitching post when Colleen arrived into town at considerable speed. Mandy had a look of sickness when the carriage lurched to a halt. The dust drawn up and clogging her lungs didn't make circumstances any better.

"Colleen, I didn't know anybody could go any faster in a horse and buggy. I lost my hat and just about lost my meal," she choked.

"Well, we don't want to keep a grown man waiting now, do we," Colleen declared, gently pushing her cousin out of the carriage.

"If you hadn't been so cordial to my mother, we wouldn't have had to rush."

"Your mother deserves every bit of kindness she can get and you ought to know that!"

Mandy shook the dust from her dress and felt for the damage to her hair when Sean ambled over.

"Afternoon Mandy…Colleen."

Still combing her fingers through tresses and swallowing to curtail the swells of nausea, Mandy just nodded. Her attention was briefly taken by the barrage of people lining the boardwalk and steady movement of wagon trains and carriages travelling east and west along Wallace Street.

"We best be going if you're still interested in seeing Alder Gulch," Sean said.

Mandy hoped her gurgling stomach could handle the ride out to the gold stream as she climbed Robert's gelding. She felt Sean must have read her mind, or seen the green in her face, for he guided the horses at a walking pace, despite their late start in the day. Her uneasy constitution had settled by the time they entered the foothills of the mountains.

Strong hands wrapped around her small waist, gently bringing her to the ground. He smelled so clean and looked so good, it disappointed her when his hands fell away.

"It's so quiet here," she said, shielding her eyes from the scalding sun to scan the creek which winded from Daylight Gulch.

"That's why it's so busy in town. Would you like me to show you how we search for gold? I doubt you'd want to try it. Might get your hands dirty."

She'd been picked on enough, stiffly replying, "I don't mind getting my hands dirty! I just haven't had lots of opportunity. Show me what to do and I'll be more than happy to do it!"

"Would you like to try digging or moving the rocker?" Sean asked in a serious tone.

"I'll move the rocker. I'm not near as strong as you are," she replied sweetly.

After dirt was shoveled into the upper end of the rocker, Sean poured water over it.

"Now, Mandy, you rock it back and forth."

He watched her move the wooden contraption as finer material washed through a hole in the bottom.

"You can stop now. If there's any gold, it will be in the ridges. Gold is heavier and sinks to the bottom while the sand and stones wash through the hole.

"No gold, Sean," her head shook sluggishly.

"Well, let's try it again."

"Wait! There's something in the corner."

"What do we have here," he said, pulling a necklace out. "I think this belongs around your neck. It's not my gold, but maybe one day it will be. Happy birthday."

"How did you know? Who told you?" she asked as he placed the chain with small heart locket around her neck.

"It's going to take some kind of persuasion to get me to talk."

She laughed. "I thought we were supposed to be looking for gold."

"It's my day off. That's not what I'm searching for today."

Standing on the tips of her laced boots, Mandy's head arched, bringing tender lips to his. After slowly pulling away, her eyes taunted, "You want another one. Just reveal who it was?"

"Ethan," Sean divulged quickly before firmly planting his lips where he felt they should stay a little while longer.

Still in his strong and caressing arms, she asked, "How often do you do this process?"

"As often as you'll let me," he replied, trying to kiss her again.

"I mean gold digging."

"Oh, I imagine around say…two hundred buckets of gravel per day."

She was flabbergasted.

"Yep, Mandy. Roll up your sleeves. We've got a lot of work to do before supper," he said with humour.

She regretted when he pulled away and started scooping up dirt. Mustering up all of her strength, she rocked the rocker for several minutes!

"Well, I think that's enough for today. You're a good student."

She stood and rubbed her back, knowing she'd never be a miner. It would snap her spine like a twig.

"So, Mandy, tell me where you think we'll find gold?"

She walked along the creek's bank a few yards before stopping, mostly because she was tired, and her stomach growled. Turning, she pointed with confidence, "Here! You will find gold here!"

Sean directed the horses toward Donevan's hotel where Colleen was awaiting their arrival.

"Why, Mandy, you've got some sun."

She touched her hot, crimson cheeks.

"Sean, you worked my cousin too hard!" Colleen exclaimed. "I think it's a good thing, though. Mandy should get her hands dirty every now and then. We just don't want anything to happen to those fingers now, do we?"

"No, Colleen. Thank you for your concern and you do realize that if my hat hadn't blown away in your mad dash, I would still be quite pale, and besides, I get my hands dirty plenty of times!" she snarled.

Colleen interrupted, "What's that around your neck?"

"It's a necklace from Sean for my birthday."

"Very impressive," she said, grinning to Sean sheepishly. "However did you find out?"

"I have my ways," he replied, marching his father's horse back to the livery, thinking it a good time to exit the conversation.

As Colleen and Mandy proceeded to Ethan's house, Mandy thought it a good idea to fill her cousin in as to how many times she got her hands dirty the past week.

Colleen couldn't wait to get away from her cousin's busy mouth. It was still moving faster than a prairie wind when she rushed to the kitchen and slammed the door.

Mandy composed herself, climbed the porch steps and joined Sean on the porch swing.

They rocked in peaceful silence while the leaves of a nearby aspen trembled as bright meadowlarks sang a buoyant melody. The sudden banging of pots sent the birds fluttering away, and Colleen's ranting orders put an end to the tranquil quietness, effectively muting Ethan's pleas for politeness.

"Do you think we'll eat tonight?" Sean mused.

"Maybe we should escape to Rosie's. I'm about ready to chew off my fingers," Mandy remarked. "You think they could offer us a drink?"

"I brought a bottle of whisky and have a canteen of water if you're interested," he offered, walking to his horse.

"Oh, water would be lovely and bring over the whisky, as well."

She figured the alcohol might settle her ravenous hunger pains and ease her impatient attitude, which was about ready to boil over.

"Have you ever had whisky?" Sean asked curiously.

"I've had a sip every now and then," she said truthfully, knowing that it really was just a sip, and it was probably just once.

He popped the cork and handed it to her apprehensively.

The whisky blazed down her throat, and she coughed. After catching her breath, she croaked, "I don't remember it burning this much."

She didn't know if it was the liquor or the sunburn, but she was feeling heat; and that heat went from the top of her head down to the tip of her toes and everywhere in between.

Sean took a casual swig.

Her hand reached for another taste.

He hesitated, but her look of need was pathetically dire.

Taking a smaller sip, she didn't feel hungry anymore; didn't feel her sore back anymore, either. She just felt incredibly hot and stood to feel the air move, fanning herself with her hands.

"You feeling poorly?" he asked with concern.

"I'm just warm. Give me another drink."

"I don't think that's such a good idea."

"Don't think, Sean! Just give me another drink!"

His mouth opened in surprise when she snatched the bottle.

By the time supper was ready, she was intoxicated.

Sean seated Mandy across from her cousin. The food was already plated, and Mandy glared at it, knowing it was stew but thinking it had a funny smell. Lifting a pinkish-brown chunk from the plate with her fork, she inquisitively sniffed it. Biting her bottom lip, she asked rather rudely, "Colleen, what is this?"

"It's lamb stew. I thought we could have it instead of beef," she replied coolly. "Paid a pretty penny for it, too!"

"Is it supposed to bleed this much when I stab it!" she exclaimed with a confused look.

Colleen felt like saying *the only thing that's going to bleed is you, if you keep talking like this.*

She was unimpressed with her cousin's attitude. If looks were forks, Mandy'd be tined to death.

"Well, Ethan, is the meat undercooked?" Colleen glared his way.

He knew never to upset her because she had a temper.

"No sweetheart, the meat is perfectly cooked," he replied most assuredly, but even if it wasn't, he'd swallow every uncooked piece 'till the bottom of the pot.

Ethan poured everyone a glass of sweet wine.

Meanwhile, Mandy loudly scraped all of the lamb to the side of the plate.

"I don't think I want to eat any baby bah bah tonight," she cringed spitefully. "But the potatoes and carrots look scrumptious. Besides, what's wrong with Wilkes beef? You support my family when you eat my cows. Come to think of it, did these potatoes come from your garden, Colleen? If they did, I'm not eathing them either," she jeered and impressively downed the entire glass of wine in one swallow. "Now the wine I'll take more of. It's so sweet and feels so smooth going down."

Sean was speechless.

Colleen was horrified.

Ethan was amused.

Mandy couldn't stop laughing and fanning herself.

"Stop it!" Colleen begged.

"Only if I'm given something to do! Ethan, give me another dwink," Mandy cajoled, leaning in, smiling seductively while flapping long and wavy eyelashes over dazzling blue eyes.

He was more than happy to oblige until Colleen seized his arm.

"You pour her another glass and we'll marry when hell freezes over!"

"Mandy, honey, you've had enough to drink," Colleen drawled in a patronizing tone. "You're talking with a lisp."

"I'm not talking with a lithsp!" she spat out. "And if we're going to be honest with each other, you talk too loudly and sometimes you sing out of tune….."

She drawled out the word 'tune' a little too long.

Sean grasped her hand. "Why don't we go out for some air? You look a little flushed."

It was too late. Colleen stood up, pointing with the blade of her knife. "You need to shut those loose lips before you say something you're going to regret!"

"Like what, Colleen? Like I was berothed," her words slurred and jumbled, "betrothed before I ended up in this Godforsaken land!"

Colleen, for once, was at a loss for words.

"Well!" Mandy tossed back unruly wisps of hair scratching her burnt cheeks. "Considering I'm not getting any more wine, it'd be wise to get some air, besides this room is spinning!" she shouted while leering at her cousin.

Sean took Mandy's arm as her feet teetered over what felt like uneven floor planks. She was swaying and sweating, feeling much like a summer heat wave.

"I think I've had too much to drink and alas am going to be sick." Taking a few more steps, she nearly plunged off the porch, crying, "Now!"

Sean knelt on his haunches and patted her back but turned away. "That's it, Mandy."

When she rose, swallowing severely, she said she'd never done that before and would never do it again.

"What, be sick?"

"No, I think I'll do that again. I'll never drink again," her voice spoke deeply.

Smiling, he believed she was a fast learner. As his hand pushed the hair from an unhappy red face, he considered kissing her burgundy lips.

"Do you want to kiss me, Sean? Because I think that's….that's gross. I'm gross right now. Why did you let me drink so much?"

She looked like she might wail, but instead, knelt quickly to the ground again.

"I figured, since you're twenty, you know what you're doing."

Mandy turned to Sean in utter shock, wiping moist lips. "How do you know my age?"

Sean was at a loss for words but was soon distracted when Colleen slammed the door.

Ethan charged after her. "Please, Colleen!"

She leered at him, raising one finger. "Make it up to me tomorrow alone at Rosie's!"

Lunging at Mandy, Colleen used a strong hand to hoist her up. "Get in the carriage now!"

"How could you tell him my age, my confiding cousin?" Mandy whined pitifully.

"I never told him your age! Ethan….oh Ethan, hell will freeze over before you hear loving words rolling off of this tongue and anything else!"

Sean helped Mandy's unsteady body into the carriage.

"Colleen, let me take you home!" Ethan begged.

Raising one finger, her brows furrowed into fiery eyes. She didn't need to speak. Ethan knew he'd be whipped by her reins if he came any closer.

"Bye, Sean," Mandy whined miserably.

Ethan turned to Sean. "Since my loving girl won't be giving me warmth anytime soon, let's warm up with that bottle of whisky if Mandy hasn't already polished it off."

"Do you think the women will be safe riding alone?"

"Hell, nobody in their right mind would come near my girl!"

Sean nodded in agreement.

Chapter 8

It had been a week since Mandy spewed profuse apologies with the last of her lamb stew from a head that felt like a pincushion.

Blaming the offensive behaviour on alcohol, Colleen seemed to harbour no grudges about what was said; however, she asked whether her cousin remembered the conversation.

"Not at all," Mandy replied.

Colleen decided not to make her cousin aware of her revelation, feeling it best to 'let sleeping dogs lie'.

Puffy white clouds hung high in a pale blue sky as Sean headed out to Willowtree creek. Mandy was sitting on the checkered blanket reading her favourite book 'Scarlett Letter' when he approached. She didn't glance his way, and he missed that, her jumping up, waiting anxiously; and it made him feel like an old shoe.

Finally peering up, she patted a spot on the blanket.

"You really like that book," he said.

"I do and I see you've brought yours."

"I finished it so I thought you could read it."

"What's it about?"

"Great Expectations is about an orphan who despite his humble, lowly background becomes a successful gentleman."

"What's yours about?"

"Mine is about a woman who has an adulterous affair with a Pastor and has a child from that affair. The woman called 'Hester' is forced to wear a Scarlet letter 'A' on her chest as a constant source of embarrassment and shame. However, she doesn't wear it that way. She wears it almost proudly. Treats it more like an 'A' for able; able to raise her child on her own; able to shoulder the shame and hurt with dignity. It seems these books have something in common, though."

"What's that?"

"Both characters grow up without a father figure. My character gets to know her father when she's older. I think she may have understood her father in that short time better than I'll ever know mine, which saddens me. You're so different from him." She grasped his hand lightly. "You're affectionate and kind, supportive and loving, and I'm so grateful you're in my life."

"I'm so grateful for you, too. When will you allow me to meet him? Make our arrangement more proper?"

"I fear that if you meet him, I'll have to choose between you or my family. I could leave my father but worry for my mother. I think I bring some source of comfort and joy to her life, and if I were to leave, life might be worse for her."

"When my house is built, she could live with us."

"That would be so cozy. Your father, my mother, and the two of us together." Her voice was filled with humour despite that his offer was taken into consideration.

"Whatever it takes, Mandy. I love you."

"I love you, too," she said, stretching to kiss him.

They lingered, lip locked, until his stomach growled.

She pulled away, laughing. "I hear you're hungry."

"Yes, let's eat."

Abruptly, she asked, "What's your dream?"

Sean glanced up, stupefied. "My dream?"

Mandy nodded excitedly.

"Right now, it's to have a bite of that apple cobbler."

Clasping his hands, she whined, "I'm serious, Sean!"

"I'm seriously hungry, Mandy!"

He contemplated something profound or he'd never get fed. "Well, it's to find gold, have a house on one hundred and sixty acres of property, start a farm, and have lots of children running around doing all the work. What about you?"

Delicately smiling, she said, "You. You're my dream. Going through life with you by my side, smiling down at me, loving me, holding me, you're my dream."

Sean's coarse hands caressed her unblemished cheeks while his thin lips melded into the fullness of hers, until his stomach interrupted the moment again.

She pulled away thinking he could shake the trees with his loud bodily noise. "Better get into that basket before your stomach explodes!"

"Let me just find that apple cobbler and I'll be fine. We can get right back to kissing after that," he said, digging through the basket with fervour.

Mandy looked on in amusement as he tossed the sandwiches out, followed by sliced cucumbers, shelled peas, and sweet tea. She knew she'd never forget this day. She also knew that clearly the way to his heart was through his stomach.

As he munched on dessert, he considered asking about the betrothal before Montana, but he was her dream now so what was the point. He figured her father must have called it off, which was why Mandy was so afraid of bringing them together. Plucking a sandwich from the disheveled blanket, he decided to quell his voracious desire for her, at least for a little while. She was worth the wait.

****

That evening, Mandy was having supper with her mother and father when he glanced up unexpectedly.

"Where'd you get that necklace?"

She grasped it, realizing she'd forgotten to take it off.

Stumbling for the words, her mother interjected, "I gave it to her for her birthday last Sunday."

He nodded, gobbling the last mouthful of food.

"Henry, a man came by the house today by the name of Conrad Kors. He was looking to purchase our Hereford cattle."

Sitting back in the chair, he raised eyebrows in scrutiny, "How many?"

"As many as you'd be willing to part with."

"What'd he look like?" he asked, staring icily at her.

"I don't recall," Ellen Margaret's voice quivered, "told him to visit you in Virginia City."

"I'd give him all of my cattle if I were guaranteed that the land I held in town would be worth something in a year or two. But the truth is, gold has just been discovered in the Prickly Pear Valley, and miners are already scurrying up there. Bloody miners rape the land, strip it bare and move on to the next town," Henry hissed with much disgust.

"He was offering a hundred dollars a head," she said softly.

"Dammit, woman, are you deaf or just stupid?" Henry roared. "I have to hang on to these cattle! Can't go and rustle up any more during this damnable war!"

Before thundering away, he scowled at her despite that her saddened eyes never left his dirty plate.

A few silent moments ticked away before Ellen Margaret looked curiously at her daughter. "What's his name?"

Mandy peered up from her empty plate with cheeks rosy from awkwardness. "Sean Thomas," she whispered as if the log walls could hear and repeat what was said.

"Why haven't you told me about him?" her mother asked with eyes expressing great disappointment.

"I was afraid you might tell Father. Sean is a miner, recently come from Colorado."

"A miner, Mandy?" she asked, surprised.

"He's different, Momma. He's well dressed, educated, and very handsome."

"Be careful of a well-dressed man! Your father was a well-dressed man, very polite, handsome, and smart. A hard worker, too; already had his own ranch." Her face held a sad reminiscence. "He would take me out and make me feel so special. I had other suitors, but your father was very persuasive, almost persistent."

Mandy listened with great intensity.

"One night I was out with another man. Your father was on my Aunt and Uncle's front porch waiting for me to get home. He said that no one would ever love me as much as he would. There were subtle signs of jealousy and a temper, but I didn't pay them much attention. If your man gives you any feelings of doubt, don't ignore them!" she pleaded.

Mandy pondered her mother's sage advice. "Sean's been very kind and affectionate. When did Father change because I don't recognize the man you describe?"

"He changed when you were born. Imagine being jealous of a little baby. He was upset because I spent so much time with you. I had to nurse you and that wasn't easy because you were very fussy. You would cry and he would complain. Those first few months were very frustrating. He wanted me to attend Plantation socials, but I was too tired. Most times, he didn't return until the crack of dawn. One morning, he came home cursing and defiling..." she paused, "I was so wearisome, I ripped the shirt from his back."

Ellen Margaret shuddered at the memory.

"His answer was to bring in slaves. Mable, and her mother, Naomi, who just gave birth to Jacob, came to live with us. Thought I wouldn't mind having someone else nurse and keep you quiet. Didn't want to leave you, Mandy, but I did one night. When I wanted to go home, he grabbed my arm and said he would decide when to leave. After an indignant glare from his eyes, he walked away. It was very embarrassing for me!"

Mandy witnessed her mother reliving it all again with a look of shame and disbelief.

"I didn't understand how he could change so much!" her voice spoke frightfully. "His jealousy combined with that temper was a force unto itself. That temper will rage again if your father finds out that you're seeing a man without his permission. You better bring him around the house to meet your father soon," she warned matter-of-factly.

"He's a miner, Momma. Father doesn't seem too fond of miners."

"If he finds out you're seeing someone behind his back, it will not matter what his profession is! You'll never see him again!"

Mandy couldn't hide concern over her mother and over bringing Sean into this veritable turmoil.

****

The cool morning air was refreshing that first week of September at Alder Gulch. Sean asked his father if they could search the area that Mandy picked out, though he didn't mention it was her that picked it out. He just said that the spot felt right.

It was sometime in the afternoon, sweat beating off of their brows despite the cool air, that his father spotted it shining in the ridges.

"Stop!" Robert shouted amid the darkness of his son's shadow.

Sean tossed his shovel of gravel away and knelt by his father.

"Eureka!" he laughed, holding the golden nuggets in his hand. "I never said it would be easy or quick but when it happens, it sure feels great."

Robert grasped his son's shoulder, smiling heartily.

Sean embedded the moment to memory, laughing a sigh of relief.

"Let's find more before we lose light," Robert urged.

They came back into Virginia City, elated and tired. It was already dark, the town glowing in dim lamplight.

"Sean, I think I'll go to the saloon for a drink or two."

"I'll come with you."

Robert looked at his son in surprise. "Isn't Mandy performing tonight?"

"Yes, she is," he replied in earnest.

"Then go and tell her the good news," Robert urged. "I'll be along shortly."

Sean walked into the hotel and glimpsed the familiar sight of Mandy playing a cheerful tune amid Colleen's soprano voice before hastily climbing the staircase.

Twenty minutes later, he was cleanly attired and smugly seated with drink in hand. He decided to tell Mandy the good news first, though Ethan's inquisitive gaze made it hard to keep quiet.

When the ladies finished, both Ethan and Sean were standing and avidly clapping.

Mandy rushed over and thanked them for their thunderous applause.

When in reach, Sean grabbed and lifted her, whispering with blissful delight, "We struck gold today," he laughed heartily, "we struck gold!"

Mandy was ecstatic.

Ethan and Colleen were in a tight embrace, too. It had been a tumultuous week, but after profound apologies and sweet sentiments from Ethan, Colleen smiled at her beau again.

Sean was the happiest he'd ever been, waving Donevan over and ordering rounds of the finest bourbon with a warning that it best not taste like coffin varnish; or the gold would remain lining his pockets.

Staying firm with water, Mandy swore she'd never have another lick of alcohol.

"A toast," Sean announced, lifting his glass, "to Mandy's wise decision. May we learn from her example, except for tonight."

"Here, here," Ethan replied. "I say we raise our glass in a toast to the fellow who invented this nifty idea of toasting."

Mandy raised her glass in smug acknowledgement. "I believe it was William Shakespeare who first wrote it."

"Oh," Ethan moaned, turning to Sean. "I've done it now, haven't I?"

"Please enlighten us," Sean urged.

"I believe it was Falstaff who said 'Go fetch me a quart of sack; put a toast in it' from Shakespeare's 'Merry Wives of Windsor'."

"Most impressive memory, Mandy," Sean applauded.

Relief flashed across Ethan's face. "That's it?"

"Not really," Colleen interjected with a burst of bluntness. "The Wilkes family is known for dunking its stale bread in wine; it feels less like you're chewing on sawdust."

"Waste not, want not," Mandy replied. "Isn't that right my dear cousin?"

"Well, you surely didn't waste the wine last week."

"Another toast," Sean announced, "to letting bygones be bygones."

As the liquor flowed from arm-raising adulations, time slipped away and it had become dreadfully late.

Ethan would be escorting the ladies home despite Sean's mumbled protests to get Mandy safely to her door.

Walking to the carriage, holding hands, Mandy turned to Sean and asked diffidently, "Would you come to supper, tomorrow evening?"

Sean halted suddenly with softness in his glazed eyes. "Yes, Mandy."

"I'll make stew, with beef that is, and you can tell my mother and father what it's like to find gold," she beamed. "I'll confirm a time at the creek, that is, if you're not too busy digging up more gold."

"The gold can stay undug in the creek bed one more day," he smiled languidly.

As the lamps flickered their tiny flames onto the dark street, he kissed her, until Ethan coughed.

Mandy was so intoxicated with love she wavered and stumbled gracelessly into the carriage.

Colleen couldn't hold her abrasive tongue. "Are you sure that was water in your glass?"

"Hush up, Colleen!" Mandy snapped with sobriety. "Or you'll be digging up carrots by yourself next week." Turning to Sean, her dreamy smile returned. "I'll see you, tomorrow."

As the trio disappeared into black abyss, Sean contemplated joining his father at the saloon. He was tired though, and inebriated enough; and looked forward to the quiet bedroom if only for a little while. His father would probably come in stinking drunk, and as a result, end up snoring to the highest crescendo.

****

While Sean took unsteady steps to his room, Robert wasn't taking any steps to leave the saloon. Luckily his horse was close by to take his very intoxicated self to the hotel after jubilant libations.

When Robert entered the Golden Nugget, it was thronged with miners, some recognizable, even through a thick haze of smoke hanging in the still air. It seemed he was not the only one in a celebrating mood. Glasses were clanging, cards were shuffling, and money was jingling. He found a spot at the bar alongside a Frenchman and a Mexican. Tipping his hat to the bearded gentleman on his right, he said, "Evening."

"Bonjour, Monsieur."

"What'll it be?" Ned asked gruffly, whisky bottle already in hand.

"Whisky."

The Frenchman tilted his glass. "Santé!"

"Cheers!" Robert answered.

Minutes passed before Jacques Parmetier decided to break the ice, introducing himself, extending his hand.

Robert replied with a firm handshake.

The Mexican glanced over, saying, "O la," his voice deep and low.

Both Robert and Jacques acknowledged him with a simple nod. But Robert thought learning one new language was enough for tonight, besides the Mexican had a foul odour. Not that his was any better after being under the sun all day.

So he turned to Jacques, who said, "Je suis un commerçant."

Robert smiled.

Seeing no level of understanding, Jacques gently took Robert's empty glass and traded it with his own.

His dazed look remained, figuring more liquor would need to flow in order to understand the Frenchman's game.

Jacques took his pocket watch and slid it to Robert. "Pour vous." Then he removed Robert's hat. "Pour moi."

"Oh, you're a trader," he said, raising thick eyebrows.

"Oui, trader," Jacques replied.

Robert quickly snatched his hat back to cover matted, sweat stained hair.

"Eh toi?"

"I'm a miner," he intoned slowly, making digging motions in his open palm. "Ah hell!" he exclaimed, grasping a small nugget from his pocket.

"Mais oui, a miner."

"A very happy miner, today," Robert said, pointing to the ground.

"Aujourd hui….ah, très bon. Felicitations! Barman, deux autres whiskies," he requested, lifting two fingers.

Robert pointed to Jacques arm which was in a sling.

"Ah." Swatting his mouth several times, he made ah, ah sounds.

"An Indian."

Jacques nodded, mimicking a bow and arrow action and pointing to his wound.

"An Indian got you in the shoulder."

"Ah, oui. Et moi?" he described, lifting his gun and pointing it at the mirror. "Mais le sauvage s'enfuit." With pistol still clutched, his fingers precariously scurried along an open hand. "C'est tout."

"Put that thing away!" Ned blasted. "Or I'll have the Vigilantes run you out of the country!"

Jacques didn't need any further translation, nervously holstering his gun under Ned's livid glare.

Robert and Jacques continued their animated conversation, the steady pour of alcohol making it much more enjoyable. Jacques offered his new friend a cigar, and as he reached for it, their attention was caught by a commotion in the back corner of the room.

Three young men were talking in high pitched tones about the working women just arriving by stagecoach and rooming at the Merriweather Inn.

"I'll tell you what I'm gonna do to her!" Eddie O'Flaherty bragged, thrusting his pelvis off the chair.

Jacques waved them off as he lit cigars. He talked, through hand gestures, about his wife and baby in Quebec and his long absence away from them.

The saloon was virtually empty when Eddie approached, lifting a white Stetson from his beady head. "Hey…you want me get rid of these old timers, Ned?" his voice slurred.

Robert scowled at the young, impudent man.

"No, that's fine. Go on home," Ned answered curtly.

"Yeah, son, you best go home. It's way past your bed time," Robert intoned arrogantly before stuffing the cigar through his crooked smile.

Eddie glowered, reaching for his Colt Army forty-four until Ned warned, "Not here, not now!"

Hand still on his pistol, Eddie slowly stumbled away.

After a lengthy silent pause, Robert and Jacques decided it time to leave.

Once on the boardwalk, Jacques shouted, "Tabernac!"

A dark figure was atop his horse. The thief twisted in Jacques's saddle showing the whites of his eyes, brighter than the hat atop his head. His spurs dug deep and the horse leapt into a gallop.

Robert wasted no time mounting his chestnut Morgan and fading away.

"Son of a bitch!" Jacques cursed in his mother tongue stepping one heavy foot in front of the other. A distant clack, then another, stopped him dead in his tracks.

Lifting his gun, he resumed passing a long line of closed shops. The cloudy night shrouded him in full darkness when a horse whinnied, giving him direction until he kicked at a hard object.

"Thomas!" he cried warily. "Thomas, vous êtes là?"

Jacques's hands blindly found Robert lying on his stomach, unusually still, until trembling fingers seeped into metallic wetness. When Jacques tasted bitter blood, his shoulders sagged.

Mon Dieu!" he wailed, flipping Robert over. "Mon ami, je suis désolé!"

His head shook violently in shock and sadness.

Chapter 9

Sean's eyes opened to the plank ceiling. Thinking it too quiet in the room, he propped himself up to find an empty bed. Curious, he slid on clothes and descended the staircase. It's was a late morning on a Sunday; however, the dining room was busy. He caught Donevan heading out of the kitchen armed with platefuls of food.

"Donevan, have you seen my father?"

He slowed his step but didn't stop moving towards hungry, impatient patrons. "No, I haven's seen him since yesterday morning."

Moving towards the saloon, Sean anticipated rousing his father from a drunken stupor. Halfway there, he spotted the chestnut Morgan tied to a post, his head dangling uncharacteristically low.

Sean's pace quickened until he caught sight of a pine box resting on the boardwalk. Shaking in denial, he pounded and pounded on the locked door until a solemn man answered.

"That's my father's horse," Sean spoke gravely.

"Then that must be your father," the Undertaker said, turning and shifting his eyes to the man in the wooden coffin.

After a few slow steps, Sean's disbelief was shattered.

The Undertaker murmured quietly, "All I can tell you is I was awoken in the night with someone banging on my door just like you did. When I got downstairs, his body was on my front porch."

Sean took in his father's ashen face and dark clothes, untarnished by blood or bullet holes. "How'd he die?"

"Shot in the back," the Undertaker replied. "I'll notify our Vigilance Committee so they can start their investigation. Boothill cemetery is just northeast of here. I can arrange for a Pastor to say a few words if you like….."

His words became an incoherent mumble as Sean gazed out of the window with a fixed stare.

"You find any gold on him?" he interrupted sadly.

"No, there was nothin' in his pockets."

Sean headed for the door. "I'll get back to you."

With a heavy step, he moved towards the Golden Nugget Saloon.

Ned was drying up glasses when he approached, asking coldly, "Anything happen here last night?"

Ned looked up, surprised. "No, sir."

Sean's eyes were already on the swinging doors when Ned babbled, "Everyone left alive."

Clomping back, Sean grabbed fists full of collar, forcing the bartender's cheeks to burn redder than his hair. "Anything happen outside the saloon! Everyone leave alive there, too!" he jeered angrily.

"Nothin' happened here or out there!" Ned stammered, struggling to stay on his feet.

Sean's gait out of the saloon and onto the arid, dusty road was slow and deliberate as he hunted for clues, blood, and anybody with a guilty face. Merchants just opening shops and carting their wares onto boardwalks were pertly questioned.

By the time he reached his father's remains, he was filled with frustration and angst. Bowing his head against a silent and heavy chest, he clutched at the dirty jacket, tears poised to stain, when a church bell chimed. He promptly gave solemn instructions about the burial for next day, and put to pass the image of the man in the pine box that threatened to tear him apart.

Once his father's horse was back at the livery, his own was saddled for the somber ride to Willowtree Creek. As he rode, his heart remained burdened with regret, his mind tormented by the cowardly killing.

Mandy was sitting under the same willow tree turning the pages of a book and looking as calm and picturesque as the scenery around her. Grey backed waxwings were scattered along the fall grass scooping up dried berries.

He was set to spin his horse away when she peered up. Worry swept over him like a heavy shadow about how she would react. She could shake his composure and he could not shed his composure.

Peering up from a novel, her heart began to race. She could hardly contain herself with the knowledge that Sean had been accepted to supper.

"Sean," she spoke with a convivial smile that faded into creases of worry when he solemnly approached. "What's wrong? You are distraught."

Softly, he said, "My father was killed last night."

No screams or wails sounded from her softly parted lips, though her blue eyes stared in dismay. Clutching him tightly, her tears flowed into the fabric of his jacket.

He spoke briefly of the burial before pulling away gently, knowing his hands would be steadier panning for gold than holding the woman he loved so intimately.

She sensed he was in no mood to mourn, though she wished he would have.

As he mounted his horse, Mandy called out, "Sean, I'm here for you! I'll always be here for you!"

His pained eyes turned distant with a grim nod.

Mandy shivered in sorrowed grief as she watched the man she loved move away from her. With sullen steps, she returned home and remained sequestered in her room.

At one point, Ellen Margaret was clutching the doorknob, ready to turn, when she heard woeful cries.

The door finally creaked open when Mandy was summoned for supper.

"Where's this male acquaintance," Henry asked without glancing her way.

"His…he is unwell," her voice quivered. "I shall arrange for another time."

"Until that time, you're to stay away from him, and any other man. You hear me, Mandy?" He shot piercing eyes her way.

"Yes, Father."

****

The following morning, Colleen, Ethan and Mandy somberly arrived at the hotel. Sean was already seated in the dining room with strongly brewed coffee that did little to revive him from an enervating state. They, along with Donevan, followed the wagon carrying the coffin to Boothill Cemetery just outside of town. No words were spoken during the short procession to Robert's final resting place. At the gravesite, the Pastor's words were succinct.

"Even though I walk through the valley
Of the shadow of death, I fear no evil;
For thou art with me;
Thou anointest my head with oil, my cup overflows.
Surely, goodness and mercy shall follow me
All the days of my life;
And I shall dwell in the house of the Lord…"

After the service, Donevan and Ethan shook Sean's hand while Colleen gave a supportive hug. Mandy's arms were heavy at her sides as she grappled with his grief.

"Do you want me to stay with you?" she asked with a voice as light as the shade of her skin against the shimmering ebony dress.

"No, I want to work. I need to…work," he replied solemnly.

Mandy gazed forlornly at him, unable to summon words that might alter his blank stare at the austere mountains. "I will go, then."

She hesitated until the tears began rolling down her somber cheeks. Glancing back once, her heart sank while his stare remained transfixed on the impenetrable wall of rock.

When he was alone, he turned to the coffin. "I promise, Father, I will find out who did this to you, and my justice will be swift and merciless."

****

Three days passed. After Mandy played her final song at the hotel, she searched for Sean through the blur of smoke curling in the warm air. It was the first time she felt alone, so utterly alone.

The room was brimming with men shadowed in their dark jackets, talking, laughing, singing, and carrying on with their lives. Even Colleen, so smitten with Ethan, seemed to be away from her.

Feeling guided beyond her control, she slowly climbed the spiral staircase to his room. Her soft knock on the door was answered slowly.

Sean's sorrowful eyes reached out, and her heart throbbed. Moving to the bed, his gaze followed as the door creaked closed.

She sat staring at hands so delicately pale against the deep burgundy folds of her heavy dress when Sean approached. Peering at him, she saw only the man she loved hurting so much. Reason and propriety were cast aside when she kissed him. Her deep longing would not be denied anymore.

Sean saw desire in her beautiful face and kissed it, fervently parting lips.

Her smooth fingers brushed along his scruffy cheeks to stained collar.

He unbuttoned her dress while she loosened his shirt with cold and trembling hands that soon warmed against his firmly taut chest.

With trepidation, he touched her fast beating heart, the tips of his fingers an unnatural yet curiously enticing touch against the roundness of her firm breast. Pulling all clothing from her shoulders, he exposed the beauty of her long neck.

When she stood, the dress fell away to reveal an ivory laced corset and petticoats. With her gentle touch along the seam of his pants, the buttons were found and hesitantly pushed free.

With modest timidity, she watched as he unlaced her corset with intensely penetrating focus.

Once the undergarments and double strap shoes were peeled from flawless alabaster skin, he took the comb from her hair, freeing the tresses and easing her mind. With calloused, but kind hands, moving along slender shoulders, he traced the contours of her back to tiny waist. His kiss, both warm and beguiling, swiveled her, though she felt weightlessly guided to the small bed.

As his brawny, naked body lay beside her delicate frame, he felt a flushed cheek, his thumb running the rim of round and crimson lips. That curious touch travelled beyond her white neck to caress a small, pear-shaped breast. He felt her trembling with desire so his mouth encompassed what fingers had aroused, and were now delighting in the silkiness of her waist and hip. Deep hazel eyes pleaded to go on.

She answered with a tender kiss.

After suave hands parted submissively alluring thighs, he gently enveloped her small body, rubbing a coarse cheek against a soft one, and filling her with his hardness.

Through gentle thrusts, she felt this new sensation, at first pain, but slowly giving way to hot waves of pleasure. The tight muscles of his chest glided along firm breasts, sending shivers of bliss through her surrendering body.

No words were spoken. His thrusts became faster and she clutched at him, not knowing what would happen next. As gentle tears escaped her blue eyes, Sean shuddered.

Mandy reached her pinnacle of passion that erupted into…ecstasy. Holding him, his strong heart tapped lightly against her moist skin.

Sadly, she whispered, "I must go."

After she quickly dressed, her feet floated down the staircase to Ethan and Colleen. With eyes remaining downcast, she walked through the hotel doors to the carriage.

She thought, *I will never speak to anyone of this day; it will be ours and ours alone.*

She was deep in thought in the deep darkness of night, the entire journey home. Browning's poem came to mind expressing how she felt....

"How do I love thee? Let me count the ways.
I love thee to the depth and breadth,
And height my soul can reach.
I love thee to the level of every day's most quiet need,
By sun and candle-light.
I love thee freely, as men strive for right;
I love thee purely,
I love thee with a passion put to use."

****

The next morning Mable was serving Mandy and her mother an early breakfast when Jacob entered shivering off the cold.

"There's frost on the ground, Mrs. Ellen. We sure is lucky we brung in the tomatoes and cucumbers, yesterday."

Ellen Margaret agreed. "We're ready to start pickling the beans and beets. Please bring them in as well as the carrots, but not before you warm your hands and get some hot coffee."

"Yes, Mrs. Ellen. Thank you."

Mable poured a mug of the strong brew before smiling proudly at her hard working brother. They were very close, even closer since the move to Virginia City, sharing a room; however, they each had their own small bed.

Ellen Margaret eyed her daughter with curiosity. "Why so silent this morning?"

Mandy sluggishly glanced up from her lumpy oatmeal. "I'm just sad about tomorrow. It will be my last performance at the hotel and I dare say I will miss it." And she thought, *I will miss Sean, too.*

Ellen Margaret walked into her bedroom and returned with an emerald green ballroom dress draped over her arm. "I thought you could wear this."

Mandy looked up, eyes widening. "That's your favourite dress, Momma."

"Now it's your dress, Mandy."

"It's beautiful," she remarked as her hand moved along its silky softness.

"And it will look beautiful on you. I doubt your male friend will be able to keep his eyes off of you."

Or his hands, Mandy thought. A wave of shame slapped her face, cheeks feeling red hot.

"Is there something you wish to tell me?" Ellen Margaret questioned with great worry. "Has he been unkind?"

"No, Momma. He has been most kind."

"You want Mable to make you something else for breakfast?"

"No, Momma."

"Well, we might have to make some alterations to this dress. I know you don't care for hoop skirts or crinoline, so we may have to bring up the hem; but the waist should be fine. I used to be as slim as you."

"You're still slim, Momma."

"Go and try on this dress if you're finished poking at that oatmeal."

****

Over the next few days, most of Sean's time was spent at Alder Gulch. But every time he found gold, it was bittersweet. He always returned to the hotel long after the sun had set.

It was a Thursday. As he walked into the hotel, Colleen's singing filled his ears. He climbed the staircase until she announced it would be their last night at the hotel.

"We wish to thank you for your kind applause and would like to perform one of our favourites 'Auld Lang Syne' as our final song. Feel free to join in if you like."

Colleen glanced at her cousin in a happy sadness as she began to sing.

Sean perused the crowd of patrons and spotted Ethan watching intently. He hesitated, and the thought of not seeing Mandy for a while coaxed him into the room.

"Ethan," Sean stated soberly.

Peering up in surprise, he pulled a chair out for his friend while motioning to Theresa for two more whiskies.

"How you holding up?"

"I'm keeping busy at the gulch. Still finding gold," Sean uttered rather unpleasantly.

"Well, that's good. Have you heard from the Vigilance Committee?" Ethan asked cautiously.

"Stopped by late last night to say they have a suspect but wouldn't say who and hope to have him in custody by week's end," he answered flippantly while Theresa placed a shot glass within reach.

"Well, that's good to hear!" Ethan sensed a heavy weight of doubt for Virginia's City's lawmen, so he didn't comment any further.

The ladies finished the song to the most applause they had ever received. Colleen didn't know whether to take that as a compliment or an insult.

"Hey, how 'bout you sing one more! Give us a song from the south!" a burly man shouted out from the bar.

She shook her head while holding a contrived smile on her face.

"Are you a southerner or not? Come on! Don't be timid!" he goaded while other anti-unionists encouraged her, as well.

"Now, hush up, and I'm not timid!" she bellowed, turning to Mandy. "How about Old Folks at Home?"

"Why not?" she grinned. "What's Donevan going to do, chase us out of the hotel?"

The song began......

"Way down up-on de Swanee Ribber far, far away,
Dere's wha my heart am turning ebber,
Dere's wha de old folks stay."
All up an' down de whole creation sadly I roam,
Still longing fo' de old plantation,
And fo' de old folds at home......"

"Hopefully we're in a crowd of Confederates today," Ethan ranted nervously.

Sean was still thinking about the Vigilantes and the suspect they were searching for, wondering if the murdering son of a bitch was in the room.

When the song ended, boisterous requests ensued from an unappeasable crowd.

"How 'bout The Bonnie Blue Flag!" the bearded, pointy nosed Confederate man said.

"That's not your anthem anymore! Haven't you heard....your anthem's now Retreat! Retreat!" a lanky Unionist yelled, obviously unaware that most of the men in the room were loyal to the South.

The bearded man couldn't get to the lanky man fast enough before fists were being swung and glasses were being smashed against heads.

"Let's get the girls out of here!" Ethan hollered.

He grabbed Colleen while Sean took Mandy's hand as she desperately clasped her music sheets. When they reached the staircase, Mandy tugged him up the steps and towards his room.

Once safe inside, still trying to catch their breath, Sean looked at her oddly. "We don't have to…"

Putting two fingers to his lips, she whispered fiercely, "We don't have much time."

Her eyes welled with tears as she stretched to kiss him.

Sean couldn't deny the sadness he saw in them and stopped her.

"Mandy," he spoke softly, holding her tightly. "Not like this, Mandy…..my sweet Mandy."

She quivered, "When will I see you again? I won't be in town for a while, not with fall harvest."

He couldn't answer her until his father was peacefully laid to rest. And that would be when the killer was brought to justice or swiftly dealt with, so he held his tongue, pressing lips into her shaking forehead.

After drying her tears with his thumbs, he smiled lightly. "I will come to you. I just need more time."

She nodded somberly. "I'll be waiting….I'll wait for you, Sean."

Hugging him snugly, her corseted breasts pressed into the thinness of his white shirt while the music sheets scattered across the worn pine floor.

With head burrowed into the sensual darkness of her neck, he inhaled her essence.

Minutes later, she walked down the staircase, her hand nervously smoothing the unruffled emerald dress as it trailed against the steps.

Colleen and Ethan had already scurried through the tall doors, running to the carriage before they turned to find that they were alone.

"Where are they?" Ethan asked.

Colleen's face turned sour as she castigated her cousin, fuming, "Making a whorish decision!"

"I'll go back inside and get them," he rambled warily.

Colleen snatched his hand. "We'll wait here!"

She was pacing a blazing trail onto the dusty street, curtailing her desire to walk into Sean's room and grab Mandy by her upswept hair when she finally emerged from the hotel, lifting her shiny dress and gingerly moving around dark mounds. Colleen watched as the brilliant dress glowed from the light of the full moon.

When the wheels of the carriage started rolling, Colleen's boisterous and hushed tirade went directly into Mandy's ear.

"I hope you were looking at his gun collection and not doing what I think you were doing up there my dear foolish cousin."

She peered at Colleen with such anguish. "I just wanted to love him enough to take the pain and anger away. There's so much sadness in his eyes."

"Oh, dear cousin, you've got to let him figure that out on his own. I just don't want to see you get hurt, and if your father ever finds out what you've done, you will get hurt."

Mandy stared into the moonlit night, pressing her hands tightly together. All of her love, worry, and anxiety were solely for one man and it was not her father.

Chapter 10

Two weeks had passed since Robert's death, and Sean still dreaded the silence of his room. When dawn's first light broke through the hotel's small windows, he quickly dressed. With steps determined for the gulch, he was unaware of Donevan's gestures for attention.

"I've got a letter here for you!" he snapped abruptly. "I also need to know if you'll be paying for another month as soon as possible."

"I'll let you know soon," Sean replied listlessly, as he tore open the letter.

Dear Mr. Thomas,

I was very saddened by your father's death. He was a good man. I was with him a short time before he was killed. He rode after a man who was stealing my horse. I followed on foot, and when I found your father, he was already dead. The man who stole my horse was Eddie O'Flaherty. I cannot be sure he shot your father, but he was very angry with him. I am a coward and have fled Montana. I have a wife and child, and feared I would never see them again if I stayed. I am truly sorry for your loss.

With deepest sympathy,
Jacques Parmetier

Sean turned to Donevan with insistence. "Who delivered this?"

He hesitated. "It was just a boy. Not sure who he was….had long curly blonde hair."

"Then maybe you can tell me where I can find Eddie O'Flaherty?"

Donevan revealed a small, uneasy smile. "Won't be hard for you to find him."

Sean walked with a heavy step east along Wallace Street. Several miners skipped around his solid presence as they headed to the gulch. Reaching Vigilante Headquarters, he spotted a young man sitting on the porch, white Stetson shading his face while hands rested over a rifle on spindly legs. It appeared he was being scolded by an older gentleman, back rigid and finger pointed.

He glanced over, smirked, and lifted his hat until the looming man smacked it clear off his head while terse words continued to flow out of his mouth. Sean figured he just met Eddie O'Flaherty and would have to hook up with him when he was alone.

He continued to Pratt's mercantile and as he entered, a woman looked up from the counter. In a thick foreign accent, she asked if she could be of assistance.

"I wonder if your son is around," he asked coolly.

She appeared confused by his request.

"The one with long curly hair."

"He's not here, Monsieur. He's still in bed." She gathered her notebook and pen, and nervously walked to the end of the counter.

"Don't want to hurt him, Ma'am. Just want to ask a question, unless I should be asking you?"

She slowly turned around. "Speak quickly, before my husband arrives."

Sean got the information he needed from a desperately frightened Marie Claire. She admitted being well acquainted with Jacques Parmetier and felt he truly was not capable of murder. At the mention of Eddie O'Flaherty, she couldn't hide the fear in her face and begged Sean not to show anyone the letter.

Mr. Pratt entered the room and Sean instinctively smiled, saying his many thanks to Mrs. Pratt for her assistance. He tipped his hat and briskly left the mercantile for Alder Gulch where he would pull as much gold as he could from his claim.

When he arrived at the hotel that evening, Donevan caught his attention, informing him that Ethan was at the bar.

Sean went directly to his friend, who sat glumly staring at his mug a beer.

"Looks like you need another drink," he suggested flatly.

"No, that's not what I need," Ethan spoke somberly. "I need to know my friend's all right. I haven't seen or heard from you for a while and neither has Mandy."

"Last time I heard from Mandy, she said she'd be busy with fall harvest, so I'm letting her get her work done, just as I'm doing. As soon as I've pulled all of the gold from my claim, I'll go to her."

He motioned for two more beer as Ethan enquired about the Vigilance Committee.

"They're still investigating," Sean replied. "Seems their prime suspect has fled north and they don't appear to have any others." Sipping his beer, he glared at a vengeful reflection in the mirror. "That's a farce because I have one."

Ethan eyed his friend. "Who is it?"

"Eddie O'Flaherty," Sean admitted.

"Eddie…Eddie O'Flaherty?" Ethan stammered.

"You acquainted with the son of a bitch?"

"Everybody knows him. His brother's Frank O'Flaherty, one of our Vigilantes responsible for maintaining law in this town, complete with quick judgments and easy hangings. You don't want to mess with this kid."

"So I should just accept what happened to my father and walk away!"

"Do you really know he's responsible for your father's death? Maybe somebody else got to him. You said he was robbed. I can't see Eddie O'Flaherty robbing a man for his gold," Ethan lied emphatically as images of Sean dangling inert from a beam in the Hangman's building crept into his mind. "Already dug up his weight in gold last winter!"

"I saw the kid's face. He's responsible and I know it!" Sean howled.

"Keep your voice down." Ethan glanced at the burly men around them. "Think of Mandy. If you do anything to him, your future with her could be in jeopardy."

Sean was blinded by anger. He couldn't shake the smirk from his mind. Convinced that the low life, nefarious son of a bitch deserved to die, he figured all it would take was another smug look.

Ethan could see by his friend's loathsome face that his words were futile, but he had to try one final time.

"Sean, the last words I heard your father say was that he wanted you to marry Mandy, go make many babies, and have that big ass farm of yours. You go after Eddie O'Flaherty, you can forget Mandy, those babies, and that big ass farm. Those Vigilantes will hunt you down, stuff you full of bullets, or hang you in front of mobs of people." Ethan tossed money on the counter and walked away.

Sean glanced up from his beer and in the reflection saw Jeffrey Coates at the end of the bar. He immediately went over, offering Jeffrey an interesting proposition.

****

Over the next few days, Sean watched Eddie's movements, which were very predictable. The small, black haired, big-mouthed miscreant spent most mornings on the Vigilance Headquarters' porch, and most afternoons in the Golden Nugget Saloon playing Faro with what Sean saw were two other lazy rude-mouths.

One afternoon, Sean couldn't resist going in to see his old friend, Ned.

"What can I get you?"

Sean slid gold across the table. "The truth and a beer."

"I'll do my best," Ned said, eyeing the gold.

"That over there is Eddie O'Flaherty, and he was talking to my father, Robert Thomas, the night that…"

Ned interrupted as his hand crept over the gold, "Yes, but like I said everybody left alive and there was no shooting outside this saloon."

"Hey, Ned!" Eddie shouted through parted fat lips, "We need more firewater 'fore we go and welcome these soiled doves just arrived from Colorado. Oh hell, I come get it myself."

Eddie swaggered to the bar, smoothing back thin and wispy hair.

"Three more 'fore we hit the road," he uttered, squinting at Sean, "and one for him; looks like he just lost his best friend. Oh no, it's his father," Eddie smiled wryly. "My advice would be to go north, kill that French son of a bitch, and get your gold back. That is, unless you want the law to handle it."

Sean kept a cool stare on his beer. "And how much gold would that be?"

Eddie laughed as the glasses clanked together in his small hands for the gingerly journey to his friends' thirsty palates. Sandwiching his narrow torso between his cohorts, he slid the drinks their way. "Take advantage of my charitable nature," he mumbled, "fore I change my mind."

Eddie shifted his eyes from the cards atop the green baize to Sean's skulking body.

Sean waited patiently for the three lewd fools to lose their money to the banker and saunter out of the saloon. They weren't more than fifteen yards away when he cocked the hammer, snug in its holster, while awaiting the coward's reaction.

Stopping in his tracks, Eddie paused just seconds before he spun around quickly. A slug ripped through him before he could fire off a shot. Bewildered, he faltered to the ground. His two friends scampered away as Eddie's body pounded the dirt.

Sean marched over and kicked his gun away. He knew it wouldn't be long before Eddie drew his last breath, his hand useless in plugging a hole that gushed blood around splayed fingers. Besides, the suffering gave Sean an odd sense of pleasure.

He began walking away when Eddie cackled, "Took two shots to kill him! First one just made him moan. Second one shut him up for good!"

Another shot echoed throughout the town.

Sean felt retribution knowing Eddie suffered the same fate as his victim. The air seemed easier to breathe knowing his father's murderer was dead.

Even though this wasn't Sean's first time killing a man, this was his first time with a vengeful heart. The last time he held a smoking gun, he was defending himself after a poker game ended poorly in Denver.

****

Minutes before the shoot-out, Frank O'Flaherty was walking through the first floor of his two-storey building in the newer part of town. Wedged between a bordello and a saloon, he figured it the perfect location to the keep the riffraff at bay.

Staring at the heavy beam that supported his second floor, he wondered whether it would creak with the weight of any man who dared have a predilection for stealing gold rather than digging it out of Alder's golden stream. Images of Frank Parish, Boone Helm, and Jack Gallagher filled his mind.

On that bleak January day, tense faces were forever calmed and sullen eyes forever staring blankly, when their necks snapped from a beam of the old building that now housed potions to cure those with sickness in their minds and bodies.

Crates sat amid the centre of the new room. Frank climbed up and curled his fingers around the beam, bending knees and dangling feet. The squared pine structure was worthy of being a proper gallows, though he wondered if the need would ever arise again. Since the discovery of gold just a hundred miles away, it seemed unlikely folks would stay in Virginia City. It was a pity considering the room was large enough for two holding cells and had capacious meeting rooms just up the stairs.

He climbed the risers and veered towards a desk untouched by grubby fingers, coffee stains, or unfiled papers, at least not until now.

Arthur Wingham was poised into a chair suspended on two pegs that creaked under his weight while he skinned a green apple, his dusty boots propped up on a corner of the fine furniture.

Across from him, George Cross was polishing his Remington single-action with a cloth showing more black than white in its oily fibres.

"What the hell in tarnation are you doing?" Frank bellowed.

Arthur lurched forward in his chair with boots thumping the dusty floor and apple rolling to a sawdust ridden corner.

"We's just waitin' on news from Nevada," he stammered. "Word is Dolan's trial's bein' summarized today which means the hangin' should be duly executed by tomorrow. Don't wanna go far so's we can tack up and head out."

"Arthur, your shop is one block away, and the gulch is just a mile from here, George. I come get you if I hear any news. Go on now! Give my head some peace!"

"Reckon, don't see that happenin' with all the hammerin' and sawin'," George remarked, stroking the barrel of his forty-four.

"I'll have peace soon as I know your back is arched over a pan!" A long finger aimed at George, followed by Arthur. "And you're selling talc powder to grey haired ladies! Now git!"

Arthur grabbed his apple and wiped the pine's shavings from its pulp onto chaps while George plunked his gleaming barrel in its holster.

"I'm sure it won't be but minutes before Hilderman comes in here shoutin' Dolan's name," Arthur said, pointing his bruised apple Frank's direction.

"And it won't take but minutes to collect you!" Frank leered. "And take your rag with you!"

George ducked in time for the tossed cloth to smear the unmarked wall.

"Get the hell out of here!" Frank cussed.

"Someone didn't get his tender vittles this mornin'," George mumbled, scurrying down the stairs.

Frank ran his hands along the smooth surface of the mahogany desk, the first piece of furniture he had that wasn't hand hewn. It went well with the grandfather clock that loomed in the corner, generously donated by Sidney Edgerton.

His ears were adjusting to the thumping of claw hammers on iron nails and the ticking of the black arrow on white face, when a wheezing sound shuffled its way up the stairwell.

"Looking for Paris Pfouts," the wide-waisted man announced before coughing into a lace handkerchief.

"He ain't here. Conducting a private investigation in Nevada. Anything I can do you for? Name's Frank O'Flaherty."

"Jethro Tulley," he smiled limply under the weight of two rotund, ruddy cheeks. "I'm here representing Lizzie Crane, Jessie's Crane's grieving widow. You have a reprehensible hand in this peremptory deliberation and summary execution?"

"You're a little late. Jessie was hanged two months ago, fourth of July, I believe.

"You are unequivocally correct! He was charged with attempted murder on July fourth, and surreptitiously hanged on July fifth. I'm here to file a grievous complaint against this…this Committee on behalf of a wife and mother of two young children struggling to supply adequate nourishment and decent clothing in spite of this travesty of justice!" Jethro panted.

"Mr. Tu…"

Jethro cut in, "On what grounds did you have the wherewithal to make this unlawful judgment considering there was no malice prepense?"

His cheeks shook at the audacity.

"On my grounds, Mr. Tulley, and my grounds extend from Grasshopper Creek all the way to Prickly Pear Valley! Jessie Crane opened fire on a parade of patriotic townfolk, put women and children in jeopardy. Grievously wounded Neil Allen and damaged his livelihood."

"I spoke to the victim…uh, to the shopkeeper, and he suffered a minor flesh wound requiring three stitches. Admitted that he incurred rather minuscule damage to his mercantile: one shattered window pane and a slow leak in a hundred pound sack of flour," he said most assuredly.

Frank was poised to pounce when Jethro filled his lungs again.

"Furthermore, Jessie Crane was under the intoxication of noxious substances distorting his sense of right from wrong. I think the mitigating circumstances of this case were hardly sufficient to deem death as final punishment. This miscarriage of judgment is incomprehensible to my kin…uh, to my client and has led to debilitating consequences. Henceforth, I…"

"Mr. Tulley, your kin or your client should shed her black dress and mournful façade, walk the gulch a spell,"

Frank smiled brashly. "I'm sure there'll be more than enough men willing to take the place of Jessie Crane!"

"Is that your final answer or should I have the aspirations to seek this Paris Pfouts?" Jethro leaned in with sweaty palms resting on the gleaming desk.

"We stand together on this matter," Frank grumbled through clenched teeth, leaning in as he glared at the odious heap of flesh ready to exhale another ear-assaulting diatribe.

A drop of Jethro's salty perspirations trickled to the end of his nose, and dangled, finally plunging and oddly crackling before pooling onto the rich surface. A few seconds later another shot reverberated throughout the noisy street.

Arthur and George rushed up the stairs.

"Shots fired!" Arthur blurted out, "man lying on the road!"

****

News traveled fast throughout the town, and when Ethan found out who was shot, he went directly to the Donevan hotel.

His knock on the door was answered with a Navy Colt's three clicks.

"Sean?" he cried nervously.

"Come in!"

Ethan entered with eyes on the packed saddlebag and pistol, still cocked and locked in Sean's hand.

"So it's true," he said grimly.

"Kid pulled a gun on me; had no choice."

"What about the bullet to his head!"

"Wasn't dying fast enough!" Sean snapped.

"Won't be long before Vigilantes are at your doorstep, but I see you've already decided what you're gonna do!"

"There'll be no hanging, today. I'm gonna see Mandy before I lay low for a while, wait for the dust to settle, then come back to her if she wants me."

"Better go as far as you can. These Vigilantes have a long reach and are known for never giving up 'till they have their man."

"Best you stay here in case I have a run in downstairs. Don't want you involved." He shook Ethan's hand before swiftly fleeing the second story.

"Mr. Thomas!" Donevan hollered as Sean advanced to the front door. "Best you go out the kitchen. Five lawmen are coming up the street!"

Sean spun around and hurried through the quiet dining room. "Look's like I won't be needing that room anymore. Thank you for your hospitality!"

His decision to see Mandy was a foolish and desperate one. With a quickened pace, he reached the ranch in minutes, relieved to see it was relatively quiet.

After his knuckles rapped on the solid wooden door, a middle-aged woman hesitantly peered out. Ellen Margaret's resemblance to her daughter was unmistak-able. He could see where Mandy got her delicate features and intensely blue eyes however deepened by frown lines caused by years of discontent.

"Mrs. Wilkes?"

She nodded tentatively.

"I'm Sean Thomas. I'm here to see Amanda." He passed nervous eyes over his shoulder. "It's rather urgent that I speak to her."

The door opened to Mandy sitting at the kitchen table putting sliced cucumbers in a jar.

"Come in, Mr. Thomas. Can I get you some coffee?'

"No, thank you," he said, his demeanor suggesting a less than social visit.

Ellen Margaret eyed her daughter with tender concern until Mandy assured her with a slight nod and frail smile.

"Mable, let's take our coffee onto the porch."

When the door closed, Mandy ran to Sean, pressing her face into his warm chest and sobbing.

He gently pulled away and dried the tears from her pale skin.

"Mandy, I've done something I feel I had to do. Sit down, please," he said softly.

Taking her hands, he spoke of how he took the law into his own hands on the main street of town.

She felt sickened by what he was saying. Another sob threatened to rise up until she choked it down.

He divulged going north for a short spell but would return when tempers had cooled.

She turned away thinking she'd never see him again, never touch him again, never feel his warm affection again.

"Keep this, keep it safe for me," he pleaded as he placed the buckskin pouch in her hand.

Shaking, her voice trembled, "You may need it, Sean."

"I'm fine. I have money," he assured. "I promise I'll come back to you."

Pausing, he sighed, hoping his next words would be remembered for the days to come. "I love you," he whispered, his thumbs wiping more tears streaming from her watery eyes. His lips brushed hers, followed by a dry cheek against her moist one. "I have to go. I'm sorry, Mandy."

At the door, his eyes lingered on her once more, vowing to keep the memory of her in his mind, vowing that he would return, he will return to her.

Her eyes remained on the pouch clutched in trembling hands for if she peered his way, she would never let him go. As the door closed, a pang of melancholy pierced her heart like a knife. Her body shrugged in complete emptiness. Even her mother's tender, loving arms could not relieve the shaking in grief.

****

At the hotel, Donevan was being maliciously questioned by Frank O'Flaherty when Ethan quietly came down the stairs.

"He checked out this morning and didn't say where he was going!" Donevan stuttered.

"What room!"

Donevan glanced at Ethan. "Number four."

Frank signaled for Arthur and George to head upstairs before grabbing Donevan by the collar with both fists.

"He couldn't have left this morning 'cause he was too busy killing my brother this afternoon, you lying son of a bi…."

"He's long gone!" Ethan blurted out as the dark, long coated vigilantes squeezed past him. "Went east, so you best get your men…do what you do best…."

"Stop right there!" O'Flaherty barked with pistol pointed at Ethan's head.

Ethan glared with contempt. "Go ahead, shoot an unarmed man! Make the committee's sullied reputation even better!"

O'Flaherty struggled to keep the bullets from filling Ethan's body. "You don't go anywhere!" he threatened, "or you're just as good as dead, too! Stay close to that pretty blonde with the big voice, understand me!"

He nodded coolly as O'Flaherty's henchmen pushed past him to the shaded porch.

With anger pent up, Ethan reached for the swinging door.

"Don't do it, Ethan!" Donevan pleaded. "Don't give them any more reason to hang you, too!"

The door closed, but Frank's booming voice could still be heard. "George, fetch Langford and Williams! Arthur, grab the rifles and ammunition! We'll hook up at Stinkwater valley."

"What about Dolan?" Arthur asked.

"Let the elders tend to Dolan and push this Thomas into a corner if he's heading east. I'll form a posse and head north. Gonna make a big net, fellows. Catch the son of a bitch before nightfall. End this sooner than later!"

The Vigilantes dispersed amid whispers from the lingering townfolk.

Part 2

A new life

Chapter 11

Over the next few weeks, Mandy was just a shadow in the cabin. She only muttered words when spoken to and did very little to help with the many chores that had to be done before winter's first snowy appearance. She was consumed by personal grief over losing the man she loved, and nagging worry that he would be killed by the ever persistent Vigilantes. There wasn't any solace at the creek, any comfort in her books, any peace in her home, or any joy at her piano.

She felt uneasiness in her stomach, and as a result, had little appetite. A sallow complexion and dark sunken eyes were giving her mother great angst.

One night in a dream, she was walking along the mossy path of a verdant forest when, out of the corner of her eye, she saw something black. Her steps quickened until, through a clearing of branches, she witnessed Sean hanging inert from a tree, his face ashen and forever lost of emotion. The horror of that nightmare brought her to alert consciousness.

Tears streamed down her cheeks. "Sean," she wailed, "Please come back to me, Sean. Please, please come back to me, alive!"

Hugging knees tightly, her body shivered in anguish and sorrow.

It wasn't until the late hours of morning when she appeared in the kitchen, pale and listless.

Mable turned from the stove. "Morning, Miss Mandy. Making you some warm, comfortin' soup."

"I think I'll go for a walk to the creek."

"Best you dress warmly. Dere's already snow on da ground."

Mandy grabbed her coat, blanket and book, and dully walked out the door. She moved the pace of a tortoise despite a cold bitter wind that stung her cheeks.

At the trees, she sat atop the blanket with knees against her chest. Slowly opening Hawthorne's 'Scarlet Letter' with numb fingers, she tried to will Hester Prynne's resilience and strength into her being when an overwhelming feeling of sickness filled her with dread. It wasn't the first time she felt poorly, but it came on fast and made her feel very nauseous. She lied on the blanket, but worry and uncertainty made her feel worse.

Wandering to the creek, she splashed icy water on her face. A pale, emaciated reflection in the rippling waters reminded her of the sadness she felt eternally bound to.

While rubbing her churning stomach, she walked past little apple trees planted just last year and a row of fall squash that should be picked. Stopping suddenly, an unthinkable thought entered her mind. Naively, she shook it away, believing it just too improbable.

Once at home, Mable brought Mandy soup and touched her cool forehead. Just as she was about to speak her mind, Ellen Margaret entered the house with a strong gust of wind that scattered Mandy's loose music sheets to the floor.

"I say, that is one brisk fall day! Mandy, good to see you're up and eating." Ellen Margaret studied her daughter while unbuttoning a coat. "Are you feeling better?"

"My stomach's uneasy. It's been that way for the last couple of days," she murmured softly.

"Maybe you have a stomach bug?"

"I don't think so, Momma," her eyes watered. "There's been another change as well."

Mable and Ellen Margaret eyed each other with shock plainly written over their faces.

"How is that possible?" her mother asked, horrified.

Peering up, she mumbled, "It's very possible."

She thought, *very foolishly possible*.

No other words were spoken about Mandy's condition on that day. The gravity of it had to sink in. And once that did, all minds were on one person, the only person who would bring a mighty wrath.

****

Over the winter months, Mandy's condition stayed unknown to her father. Ellen Margaret felt it best to keep peace in the small home as long as possible. It was easy to do considering Henry spent most of his time in town. He began erecting buildings along Jackson Street. Some nights, he didn't even return for supper.

Ellen Margaret assumed he was off at the billiard hall, or playing poker; or God knows what else with someone else.

When he was home, Mandy hid her growing belly under layers of clothing and heavy blankets that were needed to keep her bones from rattling in the frigid air.

One night at supper, Henry mentioned a banker he'd been seeing quite often at the poker table. The young man named 'Rockefeller' came from a wealthy eastern family, was well educated, and would make a fine son-in-law.

Henry wanted to bring Mandy into town to have supper with him.

"Mandy, did you hear me?" he snapped.

"I'm under the weather right now, but perhaps next week," she spoke weakly.

"It's settled then. I'll set plans for next week," he announced, forking a mound of carrots.

It never ceased to amaze her how fast he could eat. When she was little, she tried to count how many times he chewed his food. She soon realized he didn't chew, just swallowed. That was why his voice was so amplified; he had a big throat.

Once the room was empty of his bold presence, Mandy shot despairing eyes at her mother.

"I will talk to you father in the morning. He has to be told and preferably before he makes supper plans with this young banker."

Mandy lay awake that night thinking about Sean. Walking to her window, she stared forlornly at ebony sky, wondering if he was staring at the slivery moon.

"God, please bring him back to me. I so want this baby to have a father."

Her hands felt the ceaseless kicking which she hoped would settle soon. She assumed she was projecting worry and sadness upon her unborn baby, and he was just expressing his discontent.

****

It was a bleak, blustery March day when Mandy sat at the piano leafing through sheet music. Unhappy with her choices, she stared at the keys and began playing random notes. An idea sprung from her mind like a flicker of hope.

Why not write a song that expresses my life? It will start out happy and turn sad when Sean flees the town. How do I write this stage I'm in now?

She dipped the pen in ink, drew lines across a blank page, and added notes. Peering at her belly, she realized that this was her miracle, a child made out of love. Her gloomy, melancholy state had to go. It had to reflect joy, happiness, excitement and courage. How else would she write a song she could share with her child and hopefully Sean one day?

The timing couldn't have been better for this new-found awareness when her father stormed in, blazing with anger.

She stood up, trying her hardest to be fearless.

He wildly blurted out, "I should boil your skin and scrub his touch off!"

"Do as you will!" she cried.

He thundered towards her.

She jumped back, noisily hitting random keys.

"Land sakes alive!" Mable blurted out, stepping into the kitchen from her room. "Dose beds keep gettin' harder and harder to make."

"Mable, get the hell back in your room!" Henry commanded through clenched teeth with eyes never leaving his daughter's fretful face.

Mable abruptly turned. "Yes, Master Wilkes."

"How could you disrespect me!" he boomed.

Mandy remained quiet and kept her face stiff, though not in the direction of her chiding father.

With a look of disgust, he spat out, "You bitch! If I knew you had such whoring ways, I'd have kept you under lock and key!"

The door slammed shut, rocking the corner cabinet, rattling dishes and cups.

Mandy collapsed on her bench. With shaking hands and abundant tears, she resolutely wrote her song.

Over and over, *joy, happiness, excitement and courage......joy, happiness, excitement and courage*, was all she could think.

It would take even more courage that night, at supper, when to Ellen Margaret and Mandy's surprise, he blurted out grimly, "Who's the father?"

Mandy peered solemnly at her mother.

"Who's the despicable father!" he roared, pounding angry fists on the table, sending a fork flying across the room.

"Sean Thomas," Mandy said quickly and quietly.

Henry glared at his plate, shaking his head, trying to conjure up the name from a swarm of Virginia City faces. Soon came his open-mouthed face of incredulity.

"The man who shot the O'Flaherty boy?"

Her head bowed in shame.

Henry jumped from the table, arm raised while Ellen Margaret held him back.

Mandy cowered. Her fear was as strong as his fury.

"Not only are you a bitch, you're a disgrace to this family!" He callously pushed Ellen Margaret away, heaved his plate into pieces, and his chair at the cast iron stove. "After all I've done for you, Mandy!"

She thought, *maybe I'm all that you say, Father. Maybe, I'm just like you....a disgrace to this family.*

"Henry, please!" Ellen Margaret implored.

His stout hand dug into soft cheeks while the other was poised to strike. "I hold you solely responsible for this! Your weak ways in rearing this child while I worked to provide for this family!"

When fingers released, his slap sent her into the table. Mandy was set to lash out, but her mother's head wagged frantically as the door rocked from its hinges.

Clutching her face, Ellen Margaret cried, "You must respect your father it you want to keep yourself and that baby safe!"

She felt Henry's temper had no bounds. If she fought back, she may not survive.

When he returned home late at night, he was loud, his defamatory words echoing across the grazing fields.

Stumbling into bed, he loomed over her, cigars and sweet alcohol pungent on his breath. His rough kisses were repulsive, so she pulled away.

"Come on, now. It's been so long. I need you tonight."

She squirmed with soft pleas, "No!"

He flipped over, mumbling under his breath, "We got to give that baby away. It just has to be……"

Without hesitating, she cried, "You touch that baby and I'll kill you!"

Henry's snoring filled the room.

Chapter 12

By mid-April, the air was still bitterly cold. The sun, though bright and shining high in the sky, produced very little warmth while Mandy and her mother cleared the vegetable garden.

Despite being of bulky size, Mandy worked hard with a resolute attitude despite her father's derogatory words. She learned to cook, do her own laundry, and make soap and tallow candles. When Sean came back, she would be able to run a household.

She took long walks encouraging and maintaining that state of mind depicted in her song, if only for the sake of her unborn child, whose endless kicking was a constant reminder of his presence.

After her back complained of too much bending, she waddled to the creek. The crisp, cool air filled her lungs and put a spring in her heavy step. This forested place of tall trees and harmonious birds brought such serenity to her. She went to the water and knelt to feel the steady ice-cold stream run through her fingers.

Alone with her thoughts, she moved along the creek's bank hoping the sound of the flowing waters would lesson the weight in her mind and in her growing body. At one point, she imagined floating her way to the Ruby River.

Thoughts of her baby slowly seeped in. What would he look like? Would he smile the way Sean smiled and melt her heart. How would he act? Would he be sensitive to his emotions and passionately intense, or would he be detached and aloof? Would he be like his grandfather, uncontrolled and explosive, or like his grandmother, giving and supportive? Mandy knew she was like her mother, good-spirited and kind, but her passion for life also gave her the sense to rage inside.

Recalling Sean's words about conflicts over land and rights, she felt the greatest challenge was the conflict one faced within himself; emotions were battled everyday but didn't have to be acted upon. She hoped and prayed her child would be able to handle his internal conflicts in a peaceful way.

A sharp pain yanked her back to the creek's edge. The feeling was eerily strange. Strange enough that she felt it best to turn around and go home.

Ellen Margaret glanced up as she neared the garden.

"I don't feel right," Mandy's face expressed confusion. "I have a cramp and must change. I'm going to change," she said flustered.

Her mother quickly followed.

As they entered the house, Ellen Margaret scrutinized her daughter. "Maybe your water broke. How bad is your cramp?"

"Not terribly……awful," she divulged while moving to her bedroom. "Just uncomfortable."

Ellen Margaret and Mable cast anxious glances her direction.

"Maybe, I did too much walking. It seems to have subsided," she assured.

"You may wanna fetch da doctor," Mable suggested before resuming peeling potatoes.

"I'll wash up and get changed," Ellen Margaret spoke with urgency.

Mandy entered the kitchen with a serene smile. "I'm sure it's nothing. I'm just going to have a glass of water and sit down."

"Uh-huh. You just tell me when dat nothin' feelin' is somethin' feelin' again," Mable said comically as she left the kitchen for a pail of water to boil on the stove.

Her rambling continued outside. "I half expec' dat baby to pop out on da kitchen floor. Jacob!" she hollered. "Get da carriage hitched to da horses! Miss Mandy's havin' her baby! She just don't know it yet!"

Ellen Margaret reappeared. "You sure you're fine? No more pain?"

"No, Momma, look!" She stood up spreading arms until her face hastily grimaced.

"I'm going to get the doctor. Go lie down!" her mother ordered in a shrill voice, bolting past Mable. "Be back as soon as I can with the doctor!"

"Dat baby gonna be here before you get back," Mable smirked.

And he was.

Mable had helped her mother deliver babies and knew it could take a few hours to a few days. Mandy was blessed with a short labour, but not without its tearing pain, her headboard forever marred by sharp nails.

Through tears of euphoric relief, she thanked Mable for not having to deliver the baby alone.

When Ellen Margaret returned with the doctor, Mable came out beaming.

"Well, Miss Mandy sure is lucky. Dis baby couldn't wait. Say hello to your beautiful little granson."

She passed the infant no more than the length of her arm from wrist to elbow to his surprised grandmother.

The doctor went in to see Mandy. "I see you couldn't wait for me either," he said with amusement.

Because the baby was so small, skinny, and lethargic, Mable figured he was early. Mandy figured it was because of all the exercise he did in the womb.

His eyes, when open, were a deep blue; and he had a head full of silky dark hair.

The doctor motioned for the baby to be brought into the bedroom. After a quick examination, he looked at Mandy with kindness. "He seems fine and healthy; however, when babies are born early their organs may be underdeveloped. I want you to keep him warm and well fed for the next few weeks. I will come back soon to check on his progress."

She put protective arms around her sleeping infant son, promising to make him grow strong and healthy.

While keeping him warm and comfortable would be easy, feeding him was much harder. He would nurse and fall asleep a few minutes later. She would often have to wake him by tickling his tiny feet or tapping his soft cheek. He also didn't cry much those first few weeks so she'd wake many times in the night to feed him or ensure he was sleeping safely.

On one damp spring night, she rocked him gently and considered a question she would never have asked before. What is a human life worth? With all of the privations that could befall a person: working a new land, disease, war, hunger, and inclement weather; is a human life worth so little?

As he slept peacefully swathed in doting arms, Mandy's body felt a warm glow at the touch of his wispy hair.

"You're worth everything to me," she cried lightly. "I will love and protect you 'till the day I die."

She held him as tightly as she could, knowing how vulnerable he was in frailty, in absence of a father, and in a home of instability.

****

"What are you going to call him?" Colleen asked, admiring the newborn lying on the bed in his cloth diaper kicking tiny feet.

Mandy yawned. "I thought maybe I'd call him Henry Robert Wilkes. Maybe father will like that. The Henry part, anyway."

"I don't know why anyone wouldn't love this baby. He's beautiful and so quiet."

Colleen's brother, Tommy, was standing nearby and hadn't said a word until he gawked at Henry Jr. moving like an upside down frog.

"That baby has lips like a duck and legs like a chicken!"

Colleen gave him a stupefied look.

"Tommy!" she shouted. "He'll get bigger and his head will grow around those lips. You're pretty small."

Tommy winced, knowing he was small for thirteen. "I just want him to get bigger fast so we can go fishin' together."

Colleen gave him a soft smile which was rare, assuming it must have been due to her happy news. She beamed, "In six months, Henry Jr. will have a cousin!"

Mandy gave her a warm embrace.

"Henry Jr. was born on April fifteenth, was he not?" Colleen asked apprehensively.

"Yes," she replied, kissing his unwrinkled little forehead. "Around four o'clock. Why?"

Colleen expressed sorrow. "That's the day that….that Abraham Lincoln was killed."

Mandy cried in disbelief, "No, Colleen, say it isn't true! For all that he has done, this is how he's treated? Is there no sense in this world?" She was profoundly saddened.

"Sometimes, life seems senseless. Then I look at this baby and see hope. I see hope in your son." Colleen cradled her cousin's trembling shoulders.

"You'll never forget his birthday, Mandy," Tommy piped in. "Why don't you call him Lincoln?"

"Are you slow, Tommy? This child's got enough on his plate without a father, and a grandfather who," Colleen hesitated, "who's owned slaves. Sorry, Mandy. My brother can be as dumb as a stump, sometimes."

Tommy was given a cursory glare. With face reddening, he vowed to stay taciturn for the rest of the visit.

"You know if you ever need anything, anything at all, you come to me, Mandy. He's a beautiful boy and will bring you much joy." She hugged her cousin tightly.

****

For the next few weeks, Henry Jr. was just heavenly. He barely cried, fed better, and slept throughout the night. By the sixth week, everything had changed. It was as if somebody tapped him on the shoulder and said 'you know you don't have to be content anymore. You have a voice and should exercise it.'

He used that voice to get his mother's attention, especially at night. Though the rooms in the log cabin were separated by walls, they were not sound proof at all.

Many nights, Henry could be heard complaining and stomping his crabby self right out the front door.

His grandson's crying fits inspired him to put into action plans to build a two-storey house. He sold a property in town for good profit so he could get the lumber to begin construction. The new home would be built in front of the cabin. Mable and Jacob would be given the log dwelling and get much welcomed privacy.

With Henry busy building, times were very peaceful. Since he didn't go into town, he stayed relatively sober which was a blessing for Ellen Margaret. He would be seen for the traditional few minutes at supper. If he stayed any longer, he had something to say; and Mandy dreaded those nights. She would rather remain his imaginary daughter for the rest of her life but that would not be so on this night.

Henry Jr. was asleep as he was during most of their suppertimes those first few months.

Henry spoke of his grandson for the first time. "That child lives under my roof and I provide for it, that child lives under my rules, understand?"

Mandy thought about how her father said 'understand'. It wasn't a question, but a statement with no feeling, just implication.

Her father continued, "That child will need a lot of discipline considering who his father was, or is, if he's still alive. Understand what I'm saying, Mandy?"

There was that word again. She felt like screaming out, *I understand what you want to do!* But eked out a simple nod instead. She didn't want to hear another 'understand' coming out of his harsh mouth.

"Pardon me?" he snapped.

"Yes, sir, I understand," she relented.

"Furthermore," he warned, "that child is to be kept....hidden. Anyone in town finds out you're an un-married mother…mother of a child from an outlaw…I'd be ruined and this family'd be destitute! No one must find out. You are solely responsible for keeping that child within this property. We have over four hun-dred acres! That should give you and the child plenty of room to live comfortably."

He slowly rose from the chair, his cold eyes never leaving Mandy. "And once in a while you could say how grateful you are."

She peered at him with a trembling smile. "I'm always grateful to you and all that you provide."

"Obviously not!" his eyes expressed bafflement. "If you were, I wouldn't have a bastard under my roof!"

"Let's not forget why we're here, Henry," Ellen Margaret spoke reticently.

His hand flew across the room, stinging her face and shattering a glass. Tiny shards scattered across the table as wine oozed along his plate.

Henry stood threateningly over his wife. "Let's not forget whose land this is, whose house you're living in, and whose plate you're eating off of!" he seethed with boiling rage.

When the baby's crying began, Henry turned to Mandy. "And let's not forget your grave mistake." His tone was ominously chilling.

The front door shuddered, its hinge noisily dangling from a loose nail in the wall.

"Go and comfort your son," Ellen Margaret said miserably while wiping shards of glass onto her plate.

"Momma, I'm so sorry," Mandy wailed.

Oh Mandy, she thought, *the worst is yet to come when he strolls in that door late tonight.*

****

It took months for Henry Wilkes to complete his two-storey home. He and Jacob built it without any help, even though there were offers.

One clear and sunny June day, Billy Calhoon and his wife, Judy, were riding in their carriage to the Wilkes ranch. Judy had some freshly baked butter tarts resting on her lap.

"What are you going to say when you get there?" Judy asked nervously.

"Now, don't worry my dear," Billy asserted. "I'm gonna play it naturally; say I'm admiring his work."

"Maybe you should just come out and ask him if he needs help. Who doesn't need good Christian help nowadays?" she spoke cheerfully.

"I have my own way of doing things, so let me do it my way, please honey."

"I know, Billy. I just don't like to see you out of work."

"I told you I have another job lined up. Should start in a few weeks. We can manage until then."

His confident words comforted Judy.

The property of the Wilkes ranch was massive. No other ranch could visibly be seen from their front pasture.

Moving along the dirt pathway, Billy tugged on the reins when he reached the barn.

Henry sighed deeply when the carriage approached. He didn't care for interruptions while he was working, let alone be it from people he didn't recognize.

Billy met him halfway, introducing himself and extending his hand. "We attend church with Ellen Margaret."

Henry remained closed-mouthed, nodding gruffly.

"We heard that Mandy was back in town and wanted to welcome her back," he spoke sincerely.

"Well, just wait here."

Henry trudged to the house, testing the loose hinge again. "Ellen Margaret!"

She woke from a nap to his loud booming voice, replying sleepily, "What is it?"

"Get up! You've got church folk here looking for Mandy. Get rid of them," he snarled.

Henry stomped away, leaving Ellen Margaret to trail behind. He proceeded directly to the new house and almost ran into Billy.

"Mr. Wilkes, I was just admiring your work. You have a good, solid foundation."

Henry nodded to his nuisance.

Sensing his need to get back to work, Billy asked, "Would you be wanting any help building this house? I've been working in Virginia City for the past year now. Am just between jobs and could lend a hand."

"Well, I get more than enough help," Henry said pensively, "Jacob! How much I pay you to build this house?"

Jacob appeared and looked to Henry, who indicated by raising steely eyebrows that it was fine to answer.

"Master Henry, you pay me five cents a day to build this house for you," he said appreciatively.

"Fine, Jacob, get back to your work." Henry glared at Billy. "That how much you get paid to work in town?"

"No that's not what I get paid," he said in earnest.

"I see. Best get back to work."

Billy tried to hide a despondent face. "Thank you for your time."

Set to hammer in a nail, Henry had a change of mind.

"Mr. Calhoon!" he barked. "Know of Donevan Hotel!"

Billy turned, smiling, "I'm familiar with the place."

"Stop by Monday morning and speak to Donevan Langtry about adding more boarding rooms."

"Why, thank you. I will and good day."

Henry showed his sly smile, knowing how important it was to protect his powerful reputation.

Billy approached the ladies, tipping his hat. "Good day, Ellen Margaret."

"It's a pleasure to see you again, Billy."

"We best get going, Judy. Don't want to keep these kind people from their work."

"Thank you for the butter tarts," Ellen Margaret remarked brightly. "Frankly, you are the best baker in town, Judy."

"You're welcome. I do hope to see you in church on Sunday," she smiled sweetly, walking to the carriage.

When the Calhoons were a safe distance away, Billy inquired about Mandy.

"It seems she's not back from her Aunt's. I guess Mr. Crane's sighting of her by the creek was wrong; although, I could have sworn I heard a baby in that house. How was your conversation with Henry?"

"He's a kind, considerate man. I may be helping Donevan Langtry expand his hotel, and that would keep me busy for a long time," Billy announced cheerfully. He didn't tell Judy that Henry paid Jacob what he would call slave wages, figuring that was water under the bridge considering Henry's kind gesture.

Chapter 13

The leaves of the cottonwoods were turning a vibrant yellow when the Wilkes home was finally finished. Henry's house was impressive with a wide pine front door that opened into a comfortable hallway. To the right was a dining room, and to the left, a parlour with the piano and huge fireplace. A straight step staircase led to three bedrooms. The ample kitchen was at the back of the house. Every room had planked pine floors and casement windows.

Ellen Margaret was so happy, she smiled and kissed Henry. He never kissed her back, but he didn't push her away either. She hoped their lives would be better in this house, feeling much like it was a fresh start, that is, until Henry Jr. squawked in Mandy's arms.

Her father walked away.

"Do you like this house?" she asked, gently bobbing him up and down.

He smiled, pointing his little finger inadvertently upwards.

"Yes, let's go see your very own bedroom," she said, carrying him up the wooden stairs.

Henry kept tinkering with small details in the house like the trim, painting, and wallpapering, so his heavy presence was deeply felt. With his moods so unpredictable, Mandy felt like she was walking on eggshells. She sensed her mother felt that way too even though she never admitted it. Mandy also didn't care for the way he treated her mother, with such coldness and lack of respect. Secretly, she hoped he would have another job outside of the home soon. Alone with her mother, they would laugh, talk, and give Henry Jr. oodles of attention.

There would be very little laughing and talking on this day. It was a damp and rainy afternoon when Henry chose to wallpaper the dining room. As he unrolled a sheet and began to paste it, the previous sheet gradually peeled away from the wall. With wide, thick hands he slathered on more paste and impatiently smoothed out the lumps. The unruly paper curled over his head, when at noon, Ellen Margaret walked in with his meal.

"Dammit!" Henry exclaimed.

"Henry, why don't we get Mr. Leslie to hang the paper? He's offered on several occasions."

"You lazy, stupid woman! Mr. Leslie has the biggest mouth in town. Everybody'd know about Mandy and that bastard by sundown!" Ripping the paper off the wall, he madly shredded and tossed it at her face. "We'll go with paint!"

Grabbing his plate, he thumped out to the porch.

"Momma?" Mandy cautiously approached. "Why don't we paper the wall?"

Ellen Margaret wiped the paste from her rosy cheek. "I hate that striped paper. The room was starting to look like a barber shop. Let Henry paint the wall. We can always add paper later."

Henry's cranky mood didn't improve by supper time.

"This is the third time you've served me stew! I'm sick of it!" Flinging his plate in the air, Mandy watched as brown bits of beef, carrots, and potato, slowly slid down the newly un-papered wall.

"And another thing!" he howled, leering at the pie Mable made for dessert. "I don't want to see another damn pie, or cake, or bread, until the cost of flour has dropped. The town's shortage has forced Pratt to charge one hundred dollars a sack! I won't be surprised if we get a knock on that door asking for rations!"

His boots thumped down the hall, followed by the sudden bang of a door at the helm of Henry's forceful hand, rattling the broken supper plate like an uncontrollable shiver.

"Why don't you leave it for father to clean up," Mandy said in a rather crisp tone.

"I don't want it to mark the wall. It's just best to get it wiped up now. Go and tell Mable to stop baking with flour until the price is no more than ten dollars a sack."

Mandy grabbed the warm apple pie and cut herself a big slice. She would make sure there were no left over pieces for him when he came home late and loud.

That night, when she said her prayers, she pleaded for him to find work away from the ranch.

Her prayer was answered within the week when he starting letting out his precious stallion, Jackson, to sire mares at distant, neighbouring farms. He also spent more time in town planning a cattle drive from Arkansas. If he did that, he'd be gone for months.

Until then, Ellen Margaret would have to be content with the odd evening when Henry didn't return from Virginia City. On one such occasion, Mandy was having breakfast when her mother came into the kitchen looking fully rested and happier. She took a seat in the warm kitchen as Mable passed her a hot bowl of oatmeal and toasted bread.

"Momma, I didn't hear Father last night. Did he come home?"

"No, Mandy, I hope nothing happened to him," she said with vague concern while spreading huckleberry jam on her toast.

Just as she was about to take her first bite the door opened and closed quickly.

"Sorry I didn't make it home last night," Henry said, ambling to the cabinet for a mug and passing it to Mable. "There was a boxing match between Con Ovem and Hugh O'Neill, 185 rounds! Lasted over three hours! I've never seen anything like it. Got so late, I stayed at the Merriweather Inn," he divulged, grinning like a cat that just ate the canary.

Ellen Margaret's smile was effervescent. "That's fine, Henry."

"Make it up to you tonight," he said haughtily. "I won't go into town."

Henry Jr. began crying for his breakfast.

"On second thought, maybe I should go into town," Henry spoke hastily. "It might be the one night Morgan Terrence plays poker, and I can settle some of my loans; that is, if he can tear himself away from that silly game, Faro." His head shook with contempt. "Anybody gonna shut that thing up?"

Mandy dropped her spoon and bolted out of the kitchen.

Ellen Margaret's eyes remained on her breakfast. Another boxing match couldn't come too soon!

****

When Henry Jr. was eleven months old, he started walking. Talking soon followed. Mandy couldn't wait to teach him to read, play piano, and go to Willowtree Creek.

He was developing his father's smile with two tiny impressions in his cheeks that warmed Mandy's heart. That smile always reminded her of Sean; however, she did her best not to dwell on him for too long. The only time she freely pondered his image was at the piano. She would play songs, letting sadness and unfulfilled desires flow through.

Henry Jr. had his mother's eyes and exhibited a sensitive nature at a young age. He was afraid of the dark and would often wake in the middle of the night. When his grandpa spoke loudly at supper, he would jump and be nervous.

There were peculiar quirks, as well. Henry Jr. would cry in fear if Mandy approached him with candlelight. It was as if he'd been burned, but she'd never been close enough to harm him with flame.

One day, Henry brought home a wooden carved Indian mask which was said to ward off evil spirits. He ostentatiously hung it in the dining room across from his grandson, sitting in his high chair. From the moment the mask was placed on the wall, Henry Jr. fixated on it and wailed.

"Why the hell's he crying?" Henry bellowed.

"Father, I think it's that mask," Mandy replied gently.

Henry eyed the mask, then his grandson's tearful face. "He'll have to get over it. The mask stays!"

Mandy shot a worried glance at her mother, who proceeded to get up and switch places with her. Henry Jr. sat propped on her lap, his little eyes frantically searching, but soon calming, when the mask couldn't be seen. It disappeared the next day.

Henry acted like a rabid dog, spewing saliva while growling that he wouldn't have supper until it was found.

Mandy peered at her mother to find a subtle smile.

Ellen Margaret figured Henry could stand to miss a meal or two.

As soon as Henry Jr. could walk the distance, his mother took him to Willowtree Creek. No sooner than he mastered walking, he was running. He loved to run just like she had as a child, and it would come in handy in the future.

They would be gone the entire afternoon, eating, playing, and fishing, the odd times.

Dashing to her atop the blanket, he would always rest his head upon her lap. She would bend to kiss him, his skin clammy from sweat.

He liked to catch butterflies, put them in jars, and watch them fly. But they would always be set free before returning home.

"If we don't, they'll die," Mandy said softly.

Gazing at his mother, he showed a sensitive seriousness well beyond his years.

Ambling along the bank of the creek, she thought of something he could collect that wouldn't perish.

He picked up a small rock that was jagged and reddish-brown.

"Henry Jr., why don't you name it and bring it home?"

He beamed at his momma. "I'll call him Sharpy."

"That's a wonderful name," she smiled brightly. Soon after, a poem formed in her mind…..

A warm little hand touches my face,
You smile and I know my place.
You are a gift from God, my child,
Ever so affectionate and mild.
Whether on the run,
Chasing butterflies in the sun,
Or scooping slimy frogs up from their wooden logs,
Soft tears I slowly cry,
For a motherly love that will never die.

****

One damp summer morning, a man draped in black appeared on a horse in front of the fenced property. Other farms had dotted the valley; however, the Wilkes property and its acreage still gave itself seclusion.

The new house, with clapboard siding and green shudders, hulked over the log cabin while two men dwarfed amidst the massive barn, busily working on a tool.

Halfway between him and the men, a child popped up from the tall, green grass. Sean watched as the small child chased after a moth or a butterfly.

Henry Jr. glimpsed the stranger, pausing a few seconds before curiously walking towards him.

Sean couldn't make out the boy's face as he trudged through the long grass in his little white shirt and suspendered britches.

Suddenly a voice cried out, "Henry Jr.!"

One of the men from the barn advanced briskly towards the child, hands on his hips. "Henry Jr."! he shouted in a deep, commanding voice.

Henry Jr. stopped and bolted towards the tall, lanky man, who kept ranting his name. He was scooped up and held tightly.

"Henry Jr., don't want you running off, 'specially towards strangers. You hear me?" Tommy spoke firmly.

"Yes, Tommy, I promise. When are we going fishin'?"

"Just as soon as I'm finished fixin' this plough with your grandpa." Tommy held Henry Jr. until the dark stranger rode away. "Run to the kitchen and ask your momma or Mable for a pail of water," he ordered before squinting at the darkening sky.

Henry never glanced up. He was too absorbed in getting the plough fixed before the rains came. Gloomy black clouds were rolling in while the air was still, almost foreboding.

By the time Sean rode into Virginia City, light rain had started to fall. The ground soon became small muddy puddles but he barely noticed. He was so conflicted by what he saw. Had Mandy married and bore a child so soon after he fled Virginia City? She promised she would wait for him. He wondered if the boy was his, though doubt weighed heavy in his mind.

Upon arriving at the spot of Ethan's hardware store, Sean discovered it was now a butcher shop. Disgruntled and thirsty, he proceeded to the Golden Nugget saloon.

Dismounting, he quickly tied his horse to the post and lowered his hat over eyes that took in the empty street before entering the drinking establishment.

Moving directly to the bar, he didn't recognize Ned, but Ned recognized him instantly.

"What'll it be?" Ned spoke warily.

"Two whiskies," Sean replied in a low voice, eyeing his hands over the smoothly polished counter.

Ned grabbed the bottle and nervously filled two shot glasses. "Paddy!" he called. "Goin' in the back for more whisky! Keep an eye on the room."

Sean's thoughts were torn over whether he should return to the Wilkes ranch. He had to see her, talk to her, and admit that he did return earlier, but that the Vigilantes were everywhere: the creek, the mountains; that they were relentless in their pursuit. Respite only came when the lawmen were executing a hanging, or dredging their gullets in fiery liquor, or having a romp with a whore. Once they were finished, it was back to the chase. No one could be trusted for he was a marked man with a high reward for his capture, dead or alive.

Pounding back his last shot, he searched out the bartender.

Meanwhile, Ned had high-tailed it to Vigilante head-quarters. Upstairs, Michael O'Flaherty was sitting alone and rubbing his temple as he glanced at the stock prices on the first page of the Montana Post.

"Where are the Vigilantes?" Ned asked bleakly.

Michael looked up, eyes red, half-shut, "In Helena, stringing up horse thieves. I just needed a quiet place to hang my hat. Baby cried half the night. Why?"

"Sean Thomas is sitting at the bar," Ned's voice quivered.

Michael leaned smugly into his chair. "Best go and get the son of a bitch. Be a nice surprise when the boys get back."

"You sure you're up for this?"

"I hear this malefactor's been living with squirrels and jack rabbits in the shadows of the mountains these past years. I'm sure my Colt can coerce this reprobate into coming peacefully. If not, I can summon my draw, fastest this side of the Missouri."

He put on his jacket, spun the cylinder of his single-action to find five beans in the wheel, fed the sixth and strode out the door.

Sean began feeling uneasy about the bartender's lengthy disappearance.

Paddy sauntered over. "Would ye like another, lad?"

"Get me a bottle of whisky for the road; make it fast!"

Walking out under a portentous sky, the torrential downpour made deeper pools in the street. Quick lightening lit up the eastern part of town and thunder soon followed. Sean turned to his horse and hastily untied him.

While shoving the bottle in his saddlebag, a deep voice cut through the noise of the storm.

"Sean Thomas, I'm Michael O'Flaherty! I aim to take you in, see you tried and hanged for the murder of my brother. Turn around nice and slow with hands in the air!"

Sean wouldn't be hanged. He'd rather die with a quick bullet to the heart than be paraded around town and hung from a cottonwood tree.

A fast countdown began...three, goodbye Virginia City.....two, goodbye Mandy.......one. At one, and the clap of booming thunder, he swiftly pivoted, pistol raised and cocked. A bullet tore into his left shoulder as his shot blasted into O'Flaherty's chest. Lightening continued to brighten the blackened sky when Sean's horse bolted, threatening to run away. He snatched the reins while Michael stumbled, pistol dangling from his curled finger.

Ned watched in horror as Michael fell onto a bed of muddy earth. Figuring it high time to be a hero and claim the reward, he darted for his gun.

Sean mounted his frantic horse and rode past O'Flaherty, whose eyes vacantly stared while water streamed into his mouth.

"You never win with a cross draw, you fool!" he muttered under his breath, glancing at the empty holster on Michael's left side.

Ned reappeared with a twelve-gauge and locked on to the dark moving figure. With one quick 'click' and the pull of the trigger, a spray of buckshot released, and then another, emptying both chambers. Ned's sodden eyes blinked profusely to see Sean slump in the saddle as his horse galloped out of town.

Chapter 14

The following day, Ethan rode out to the Wilkes ranch desperate to talk to Mandy. Rushing to the front door, he ran into Jacob.

"Where's Henry?" he asked with anxious eyes roaming the pasture.

"Why, he out back scything the hay."

"Good."

Mandy was in the kitchen with Mable making jam when he entered.

"Ladies!" he called out.

"Why, Ethan, what a surprise?" Mandy smiled, wiping sticky hands on her apron.

After a warm hug, he enquired about Henry Jr.

"Why he was just here, wasn't he Mable? Trying to eat up all our huckleberries before being crushed into jam. Come to think of it, we're missing that big bowl of huckleberries."

"I have to talk to you," he said with urgency, "privately."

Mable turned from the stove, offering to find Henry Jr. She untied her apron and walked out the back door.

"Sit down," Mandy suggested pleasantly.

He pulled a chair from the table. "Mandy, something happened in town……"

"Momma!" Henry Jr. cried, running from the parlour looking desperately pale.

"What is it? Having trouble breathing?"

He shook his head, holding his stomach. "I feel sick."

"Where's that big bowl of huckleberries?"

Suddenly, Henry Jr. threw up.

"It's right there, Momma!" he shrieked, pointing to Ethan's lap, looking fearful. "I'm so sorry…."

"It's fine, Henry Jr.," Ethan replied calmly, taking Mandy's dishtowel and flicking mangled huckleberries from clean pants.

Mandy flipped up her apron and dried her son's tear-stained face. "Just don't eat that many huckleberries at one time. That's just too much for a little boy."

"I'm not done, Momma!"

She quickly spun him away as more berries spewed from his little mouth.

Ethan was still wiping his pants when he leapt off the chair to avoid the purged mounds.

"Think I'll come back another time. You have your hands full, Mandy. We'll talk another time."

"Take some jam," she offered while rubbing Henry Jr.'s tummy.

"Another time!" he urged, dashing to the front door.

"Why don't we fill the tub for a bath which should soothe your tummy?" Mandy recommended. "But let me get a bowl first, just in case you have more berries to come out of that tummy."

"I'm sorry, Momma. They were so yummy!" His blue eyes watered again.

"Maybe a handful, but a big bowlful is not so yummy for your tummy."

She sat him in a chair before going out back for a bucket of water.

The door slammed again, too soon for it to be his momma. Henry Jr. peered down and prayed it wasn't his grandpa for he'd surely be angry with the mess he made.

"Why child, you feelin' poorly?" Mable asked with concern.

His sigh came through purple lips. "Made jam on the floor."

Mable walked around the table to see what he'd done.

"Henry Jr., it's too bad you couldn't aim it in da bowl, for we could've served it to your granpa for supper," she said slyly.

He looked up in awe before giggling and showing deeply stained teeth.

Mable got all serious, kneeling down beside him. "You tell your granpa I said dat, I'll beat you mysef."

"I won't tell him. I'll never tell him no matter what."

She nodded, smiling. "What we gonna do with dat sweet tooth of yours."

Henry Jr. grinned widely, dimples showing. "Give me more berries?"

Mable's head shook in disapproval, grabbling the bowl and scooping crushed berries from the floor.

Henry Jr. smiled the entire day envisioning his grand-pa shoveling mounds of floor jam into his mouth.

It wasn't until suppertime, when his smile went as sour as an unripe berry. Mandy was in the kitchen taking a bowl of buttered beans from the counter when Jacob entered, out of breath.

"Mandy, there's something I must tell you," he whispered with urgency.

"Let's go out back," she replied.

Henry entered the kitchen, his step heavy and pro-nounced. "Where is everyone?"

"Mrs. Ellen be right down with Henry Jr., and Mandy…she's speaking wid Jacob about da garden and summer seeds," Mable lied while walking bowls of food to the dining table.

Mandy entered the kitchen, pale and distraught. News about Sean's appearance in town and the gunfire that had erupted while he was fleeing stabbed at her heart as she sank heavily on the chair.

Ellen Margaret came into the warm sunlit room and sat Henry Jr. down beside his mother. She then walked around Henry's brooding figure at the head of the table while he scooped boiled potatoes onto his plate. When she sat, she took in Mandy's morbid expression. She became even more alarmed with Henry, glowering at his grandson, who was quivering like he'd just been caught with his hand in the cookie jar.

"Henry," she spoke calmly, passing him the beans. "We've been busy today making jam."

"Hmm," Henry grunted as he shook away the bowl of greens and continued cutting his meat like he was sawing at a bone.

"Mandy has news about the cows," she said, hoping to cut the tension in the room.

"Yes, Father," Mandy spoke in hushed tones. "Two calves were born this morning, both healthy."

"Henry Jr., your tummy still hurting?" his grandma asked while he picked at candied carrots.

Shaking his head frantically, he began stuffing great mouthfuls into a fretful stomach. His grandpa's smoldering eyes made him feel bad about his behaviour earlier in the day.

Mandy was too engrossed in her own sorrowful sadness to realize her father knew about the town's upheaval and was casting heinous eyes at the wretched offspring just a few feet from his grasp.

That night, harrowed grief followed Mandy like a heavy shadow up the risers and into her bed. The night sky seemed filled with her unsettled woes as distant thunder rumbled while a strong, moist breeze puffed her curtains to line the ceiling.

Suddenly, the air was scooped from the room, sucking the drapes to dance whitely against the starless sky. The door creaked open and she curiously peered up from her damp pillow. A metallic light flickered once, then twice, illuminating a shadow at the end of her bed.

"Sean?" she whispered with trepidation. "Come to me, Sean."

The house shuddered when the sky roared, but the shadow remained unwavering as he moved to her trembling being. She quickly clutched him to her bosoms, so afraid he would disappear amidst the blinding light. Her kiss was urgent, needing, longing, for the familiarity of his touch, to strengthen the memory of him. Scratching the thin, white fabric from her slender shoulder, his kisses played softly on her skin while the wind cowered when light appeared, flashing vibrantly.

"Please, help me remember," she wailed desperately.

Hands moved over a veil of cotton with foreign fingers exploring the contours of her breasts, dip of her stomach, and bones of her hips, until he reached the gown's hem. The cotton puffed up and his cool touch awakened the fine hairs on her skin but made the blood boil from her veins. Heat flowed from inner thighs to inner passage, a throbbing ache coming in waves, swelling and stretching her bones as the shadow loomed up and down. Then liquid, warm liquid, as a fine weight fell over her body.

"Please stay," she beckoned.

The curtains flapped into the room, and the door thrust closed. She turned to him, lying beside her, and slid hands into black wetness that flashed red.

"Sean?" she cried, pulling on sharp chin to find a face full of skull: empty sockets, high cheekbones, pearly teeth. Her piercing scream rattled the walls, waking everyone including the mice from there cozy planked domains.

****

Meanwhile, Sean was struggling to stay on horse and muddy trail when he entered Helena, cold and in pain. Under a cloudy midnight sky, he sat hunched over his slow and mechanical horse.

He must have been a sight for sore eyes when he entered Amelia Boudreau's parlour.

"Why, Mr. Thomas, it's been a while." Taking in the sight of him from top to bottom, her hazel eyes noted the rigid body and torment on his deathly white face. She had seen a lot of stiff men enter her whorehouse but the look of torment concerned her.

Sean remained silent.

"Sarah!" Amelia bellowed. "Sean Thomas is here." Giving him a steely glare, she threatened, "If you bring any trouble to this house, I'll cut it off. You hear me?"

Sarah came running in, smiling, until she saw Sean's condition. She quickly led him to her room.

Stumbling to the bed, his last bit of strength was extinguished.

"Sean, what happened?" Sarah asked.

But he was already drifting, careening for the mattress of straw.

Sarah's screams filled the room.

Sean heard voices but couldn't move. Sarah was speaking to a man, his voice unrecognizable.

"Well, he's lucky. Bullet through the shoulder and buckshot to his lower back, which has left one bloody mess, but hit no vital organs," the doctor informed, wiping sweat from thick arched brows. "His vest has more holes in it than Swiss cheese, and he's lost a lot of blood, which is enough to kill a man. He won't have energy anytime soon. So if you're free, Sarah, I'm always willing," he said, licking his salty lips with a look of hunger too apparent on his perspiring face.

"Doctor Culpepper, go home to your wife," Sarah ordered, quietly shooing him from her room.

She glanced at Sean with love in her heart, and hope in her mind, that he could see her as more than just a common whore. His paleness and frailty made her worry that he would never recover and take her away from this vile profession.

Clutching Sean's laudanum, Sarah thought of Amelia's wise words to squirrel away money for rainy days. If she didn't, when she was either too sick, or too old for whoring, ending her life with the bottle in her hand was a dire possibility.

His eyes opened for a brief moment.

"Welcome back to Helena. Welcome back to me," she whispered, kissing his lips.

Lying down beside him, she felt his unusually cold body and prayed he wasn't a moribund man, for when he asked, she would be his wife. Holding him closely, she would keep him from death's door; she would make him forget about that other woman. However, Sarah didn't realize that, despite being blemished by smallpox during childhood, her face resembled Mandy's in the soft glow of her candlelit room.

Sean would place coin in Sarah's hand just to watch wavy hair fall free on slim shoulders and hear Shakespearean passages from full lips. She was able to sneak in kisses, hugs, and gentle caresses, but nothing more. This time would be different. After she cared for him so well, he'd want her, make love to her, and marry her.

He'd been tucked in Sarah's bed in and out of consciousness for four days when Amelia felt it time to speak to him, entering without warning.

"To what do I owe the pleasure?" he said weakly.

"You've got the owe part right. You owe me four days accommodation."

He reached under the pillow and tossed her a pouch.

"Take what is owed and leave me alone," he winced.

"Sarah will be happy to know you're up. Maybe she'll get the rest of you up, too!"

Sarah entered with a bowl of warm water, smiling tenderly. After water droplets ran from a cloth, she brushed his pallid forehead. When he didn't object, she sponged along the lean muscles of his neck and shoulders, skirting the wound that would eventually form a scar. When his chest was slick with wet, her lips dried the dampness, moving beyond his navel.

Sarah felt his tension melt away. Her treatment would be stronger than any medicine, to help him heal, to help him forget his past.

Even though she took to sleeping beside him those last few nights, he put up no struggle when she touched him, loved him. Still in considerable pain, she was a comfort in more ways that one. He liked that she was accommodating; any man would. But she tried too hard, and it stifled him. He finally got wind that she was moving beyond her brothel walls to a more permanent situation.

Sarah opened her door to find him sitting on the bed, dressed and eager to go. He patted a spot, and she meandered over.

"I appreciate all you've done for me these past days. I probably wouldn't have survived." Taking her hand, he placed coin in the palm before closing it.

It was not refused.

"I love you," she said with a maudlin face.

"I know, I just…..I'm not ready for anything serious. I shot somebody back in Virginia City, and I reckon they'll be coming for me if they aren't already here."

"We could go away together. I'll go with you right now," her eyes pleaded.

"It's too dangerous. Stay where you are. I'll come when the time is right."

"When will that be? A year? Two years?" Sarah implored.

"I don't know. There are men out there, want to put a bullet through my skull, or hang me from a tree." Sean walked to the door. "Being on the run is hard. I sleep whenever I can, wherever I can; always looking over my shoulder; never knowing who to talk to; or where I should go, north, south. It's not a life for a woman, let alone a woman I deeply care for."

"Oh, Sean!" She came rushing, holding him tightly.

"I've got to go." Turning the knob, he pulled away.

Walking through the parlour, he bumped into Amelia Boudreau.

"That time, Mr. Thomas?"

"Ms. Amelia, it's been a pleasure as always," he smiled appreciatively.

"Well, rumour is, your reward is now at two thousand dollars, dead or alive. It's a good thing my business is very profitable. The fact that you're neither average in looks, intelligence, or size," she purred with lascivious eyes that followed a finger along his chest to the waist of wool trousers, "has also worked in your favour. Others in this town won't care so much for those features, so I advise you to go north, way north. Stop in to see my cousin, Katherine, at the Wayward Hotel in Fort Benton. She's a good pain reliever. Then go smuggle whisky up to Canada. I hear it's very profitable. Bonne chance!"

"I thank you for uplifting words and sound advice."

****

When Frank O'Flaherty entered Virginia City, he went directly to the Undertaker. His brother, Michael, was laid out in his tailor-made suit, the same black suit he was swathed in when he said his vows in the town's Methodist Church.

Frank recalled the exuberant joy on his brother's face that crisp fall day, very much like the countenance he had when Frank left town for a hanging in Helena. Michael had just become a father and, after much liquid jubilation and magnanimous stomach purging the next day, was advised to stay home. Frank didn't want any stalling or whining, especially from his kin.

In Helena, Frank had just paraded Amos Milner through a crowd of six thousand onlookers, pistol to his breast, ready to still any trouble that might hinder the convicted man's final walk to the gallows. The hanging was quick: taut rope, snapped neck, dangling feet, and crowd dispersing without any hoopla. He was heading to the most accommodating whorehouse, until Arthur Wingham's younger brother approached, stretched over his black mare. The horse was sleek in sweat, mouth drooling, foam splotching the copper ground.

Frank's desire for a fair-skinned, big bosomed harlot to work out his knotty kinks wouldn't be satisfied. Instead, he'd be spurring his horse hard, fueled by a stabbing pain that knifed at his heart over losing his younger brother, and seething rage at envisioning Thomas holding the smoking gun.

Michael didn't deserve his fate. Frank cursed Eddie's name along the hundred mile journey home. His youngest brother was trouble the moment he drew his first breath, while his mother was drawing her last. He was a sickly child and as such, was treated with kid gloves despite that he should have been disciplined with firm hands. When their father was absent freighting for weeks on end, Frank took the switch to Eddie on several occasions. But when their Da returned, pity for the ailing boy returned, as well, and Frank was harshly reprimanded for causing wounds that oozed and festered.

Eddie seemed impervious to pain, yanking scabs from his bony elbows and knees just to watch the blood bubble up like ripe red currents. Frank thought he should have acted in Shakespearean plays the way he hammed up his hurting to astronomical proportions.

Countless times, Frank envisioned his strong hands around Eddie's scrawny neck, shaking the meanness out of him.

It was a night in late December when Frank reached the end of his rope as Eddie appeared, stumbling up the porch stairs.

"You're shit-faced again," Frank spoke in a low, dispassionate voice.

Eddie jolted and desperately clung to a wooden railing to steady wobbly legs. He glanced into a dark corner and squinted to see grey smoke swirling from the stem pipe.

"I thought you was Da for a second or two. Sounded like him, smelt like him," he slurred. "Jesus, it's cold out here. Gone is the day when you have to wait up for your baby brother. I know how to find my room," he pointed. "Besides, Corinna gonna be cold in bed without you. She's already too rigid around the edges, though she makes a decent peach pie."

"I want you to stay away from Alec Carter!" Frank warned. "He's wanted for killing the Dutchman."

Eddie smiled wryly. "Alec didn't kill that kid. He don't have the stomach for it."

"How about Yeager? Man just gave up the road agents responsible for robbing Peabody & Caldwell's stagecoach. Bannack's own Sheriff Plummer, Ray, Stinson, Wagner, all wanted."

"That liver-bellied coward! Red woud rat on his ma to save his hide." Eddie hugged the post while his head spun wildly in the frigid air.

"Don't matter. He'll hang along with the others. When he squealed, I worried your name would spew out of his mouth, too!"

"You work with too many men you gotta split what you take too many times. Those fools gonna be hanged, for what, twenty-five dollars a piece? Hardly worth it, now is it? Besides, too many loose lips in the bunch, all talk…no show," Eddie stammered as his frosty breath faded into black night." Swallowing heavily, his stomach was forced back down below jutting ribs.

"How much you steal, Eddie? You been gambling every night. Don't ever touch the tin can. Where you getting it from? Sure ain't the gulch."

"My back's too broke for bending, and my skin's too thin for shoveling. I's just been lucky. But I go to the gulch tomorrow. I's sure my luck'll change."

"If you're committing highway robbery, Da's turning in his grave!" Frank scowled with disgust.

"Da ever knew you let his killer git away scot free, he'd strip the O'Flaherty name from you! Let the law handle it, little bro. Ain't that what you said!" Eddie spat out. "Let the law deal with that Winslow bastard. Man no less than shove Da's gold pocket watch in my face; let it dangle in the sun; blind me as it ticks back and forth."

"Law would have handled it if he wasn't found dead a week later, frozen stiff with a bullet in his brain!"

"Justice is blind, Frankie. You know you's just a boot-licker. You think you's stepping up being a vigilante. Your asprations! They's just gonna turn a blind eye on you, too! You's just a democratic, Irish sod. Best you go back to the gulch, git your hands dirty, too!"

Frank raised his pistol, now ice cold, and glowered at his brother pathetically creaking the floorboards with shifty legs.

"Frankie, let's git in the house. Can't feel my hands and I gotta take a piss. Come on, Frankie. I promise I'll sift through the alders with you. Just git me in the house."

Frank stuffed the cold piece in the waist of his pants and walked to his unsteady brother, fully ashamed of weakness and a familial sense of obligation.

Chapter 15

It had been weeks since that stormy night and Henry Jr. still slept huddled under his protective sheets and quilt for fear the beast would be awakened. The storm's groans had sent him running to his momma; however, he became mesmerized by the sudden twists and turns of her covers. They reminded him of a flying object his grandma created out of sticks and rags.

He imagined her floating out of the window tangled in those floating sheets until her ragged screams sent him cowering to a corner of the room. He was crushing his ears with little hands when the beast appeared.

The ogre lunged over his momma, head snapping up and down as if he was devouring her. His grandma appeared with flickering light and the beast illuminated even larger on the far wall. She was cut down when the beast's large arm charged like scythe shearing hay, the light smothered by her gown. When the beast bellowed, Henry Jr. realized it was his grandpa. Scurrying to his room, he cloaked himself in blankets until exhaustion claimed his fretful state.

The next day, he watched her feverishly scrubbing blood from her gown and sheets, knuckles raw against the washboard in the basin he would soak in on Sundays when it was too cold to venture out to the creek. At one point, he touched her shoulder to make sure she was real.

She peered up with saddened eyes. "I have to believe, Henry Jr., that he's still alive…he is alive," she nodded, smiling delicately, before returning to her scouring as pink water swirled along the edges of the tub. He watched as the stain faded, hoping his memory of that night would fade, as well.

She glanced up again, finally cognizant of his pasty face and fearful eyes.

"Oh Henry Jr., it's just a woman thing," she assured. "Momma's fine."

He peered at the house with doubt. His grandma was still in her room and his grandpa was nowhere to be seen.

When night fell on the home, Henry Jr. prayed, as he did every night, that the storms would never return to awaken the beast again. But, he soon discovered that the beast would be summoned even if a storm wasn't brewing over the house.

****

It was a chilly October morning when Ellen Margaret came home from church complaining of chills and a painful headache. Mandy kept the fire going in the parlour to lift the dampness from the house while her mother took a long nap.

By supper time, she was feeling much better and thought she could read to Henry Jr. that night as she did most nights. Before he picked a book, he wanted to show off his newest rock.

"Gramma, look! It's smooth and has shiny flecks like the side of a trout."

"Well, you're right, Henry Jr. It's a magnificent rock. What are you going to call it?"

"I think I'll call it Speckles," he said, petting it.

"What is Speckles like?" Ellen Margaret asked, curious about his thoughts.

"Speckles is friendly. He doesn't fight with the other rocks. He listens to everything I say. He's my best friend."

"Speckles sounds like a wonderful friend. Bring your book over. Grandma's getting awfully tired."

He brought over a book called 'Play Day Book, New Stories for Little Folks' and propped himself on her lap as she sat in the rocking chair.

"Which story would you like me to read?"

Henry Jr. glanced at the table of contents, already understanding most of the words on the page. "The boy who wanted to see the world."

Ellen Margaret finished the short story and held him a little longer. "Henry Jr.?"

"Yes, Gramma."

"Do you hear Grandpa late at night?"

"Oh, yes. He's very loud," he admitted honestly, his wide eyes expressing fear.

"You stay away from Grandpa when he's like that. You stay in your room," she said as her gentle fingers moved through his soft hair.

"Yes, Gramma. I won't go near him."

By the next evening, both she and Henry Jr. were sick with high fevers. Mandy and Mable took turns trying to cool and comfort both grandmother and grandchild. Mandy also convinced her father to procure some Dover's powder from the drugstore to ease their coughs that had developed.

While Henry Jr. seemed to improve over the next week, Ellen Margaret's condition weakened. The fever persisted while her breathing became laboured.

When she manifested livid lips and fingernails, Mandy felt a deluge of dread.

Before Henry headed to town, she asked him to fetch the doctor. Several hours later, he arrived alone.

After examining Ellen Margaret, the doctor gravely told Mandy that she had pneumonia and her heart was failing. He felt that nothing more could be done but control the pain with opium. He handed her cough syrup with laudanum.

She looked up in confusion.

"It's for your son. It will help with the cough and wheezing which should subside in a few weeks. If it doesn't subside or gets worse, send for me right away."

Mandy never left her mother's bedside. She continued to cool her with a dampened cloth while delicately holding her hand. Her mother never spoke again. As she took her last breath, Mandy pleaded for her not to go.

When the room went quiet, her tears flowed. Grief at the loss of the woman she loved so much was so profound. Her mother, sage teacher, and saving grace, had departed this world, leaving Mandy with such loneliness and isolation, she didn't hear Henry Jr. run into the room.

His sad little voice cried out, "Gramma, wake up. You're making Momma very sad. Gramma?"

Mandy reached for her son and held him so tightly, he got scared. Peering at his grandma, he expected she would wake at any time. When Mandy said she would never awake again, he released his tears.

Late that night, Henry came home and moved to the glow of lamplight on the kitchen table. Mandy was sitting on a chair with eyes staring blankly and body completely worn out when she said that her mother was deceased.

"I'll see to funeral arrangements in the morning."

"Jacob laid her out in the dining room if you care to see her." Mandy's words were barely a whisper in the quiet kitchen.

He stopped briefly at the doorway.

Her wish for a comforting hug or sympathetic word would go unfulfilled as his steps continued up the staircase. Collapsing into her arms, she allowed the last of her tears to flow from sorrowful eyes.

****

It was a quiet funeral at the home. Tommy attended with his father Clarence while Colleen and Ethan Holden appeared with their two children. Mandy quietly arranged for Pastor Kennedy to say a few words. When he arrived, she purposefully avoided her father's glare.

The Pastor's words under the willow tree were such a comfort to her, speaking of hope, which she would cling to in the weeks to come.

Henry Jr. was deeply quiet. He didn't like the idea of his grandma being all alone in the ground. He loved her and wondered who would read to him at night and ask about his pet rocks now that she was gone. Who would give him special treats and smother him with kisses and hugs?

Mandy peered at Henry Jr., whose sad eyes tore at her heart. She picked up her little boy and carried him to the house, never wanting to let him go. She couldn't deny that she feared for herself and her child. Her mother was a protective shield against her father's uncontrolled tirades, and now that shield was gone. She hoped she would be strong enough to ride the waves of his hurtful words and actions.

Henry remained quiet during suppertime with eyes focused on the food atop his plate. His supper routine never changed after Ellen Margaret died. He ate quickly, put his plate in the dry sink, and went to town within a span of mere minutes.

Mandy created a routine for Henry Jr., and over the next few years, he flourished with the stability. In the first few hours of the day he tackled printing, reading, and math. Bible study and piano lessons came next. After a meal at noon, they would stroll to the creek when the weather was good for science and exercise. She was his personal teacher, though he wasn't always the willing student. He was a natural at reading but hated printing and piano, surprisingly enough. Exercise was his favourite subject.

The only time she allowed herself moments alone were before supper at the piano while Henry Jr. played in his room. Mable continued to cook the family meals however Mandy was by her side from time to time.

Once every couple of weeks, it was laundry day; and it was a full day. Mandy knew it was time when her father would bellow at the top of his lungs for clean shirts. She despised laundry day. Henry Jr. loved it because it meant a day of playing at Willowtree Creek.

Jacob would carry the large wash pot out to the creek and set it atop a fire. Once water was added and very hot, Mandy and Mable would soak the clothes.

Henry Jr. was stripped to his bare skin and allowed to spend a lingering morning in the cool, shallow waters holding his breath while he splashed after frogs and fish, or searched for a new rock friend.

His little clothes were washed in hot water, scrubbed against the washboard with lye, rinsed in the creek, and hung on tree limbs touched by the sun's warmth so that they would be dry by the time he came out, skin wrinkled and cold just like his mother's hands.

On this laundry day, he ran around the lush forest chasing little white moths until he was seduced by a fat bee drinking its golden nectar from a deep blue wildflower.

After their picnic, Mandy made him sit on the blanket and read for a spell. She looked up in surprise, saying, "Henry Jr. what is that on your face?"

"I don't know," he replied vacantly.

"It's a scowl, and you do not scowl at your mother EVER!" she spoke crisply. "Do you understand me?"

"Yes, Momma," he replied sullenly.

"You read two of those play day stories NOW!"

He walked away with a sly smile. He could read two of those stories in a few minutes.

"Make that three stories!" she announced suddenly.

Henry Jr. couldn't understand how she did that. It was like she could read his mind. Even though he may not have liked doing it, he always did what he was told. When he was finished, he quietly left the blanket to go deeper into the forest. Every laundry day, he attempted to go a little further away from his mother's protective eyes.

"Mable, do you think people can change?" Mandy asked while stripping her soiled dress and tossing it in the pot.

"I spose when dey get older, dey can mellow out some," Mable answered honestly.

"And how much older is that?"

"Don't know, Miss Mandy."

She glanced at the blanket to find it empty.

"Henry Jr!" she shouted. "Henry Jr!"

She moved toward the edge of the winding creek.

"Where's dat boy got to?" Mable asked.

"I'll continue into the forest. You follow the creek a spell."

Mandy finally found him peaking into the hollow of a giant cottonwood tree.

"Henry Jr., what are you doing?"

Spinning, he blinked at her, starkly white against the verdant trees. "Come and see. They're so small and cute."

"What are they?"

"I don't know. They're furry and have pointy ears."

Mandy peaked inside the hollow. "Henry Jr.," she quivered, "these are wolf pups."

Hastily scooping him up, she ran from the den, getting a few yards before a wolf snarled at her, fangs exposed, clenched in anger. Instinctively turning her son away, she slid him to the ground, begging he stay close behind. She returned her fearful glare at the wolf and slowly crept away as it growled and snapped at her.

"Momma, I'm sorry!" he screeched, clutching the elastic of her silk bloomers.

"Henry Jr., you must stay quiet to protect yourself, to protect your momma!" Her soft steps continued backward. Gripping a loose branch, she whispered harshly, "When I say run, you run the direction we're heading right now. Not towards the cubs and not towards the angry wolf!"

When the wolf pounced, she screamed, "Run, Henry, run!"

Swinging the thick branch, she hit the animal in the snout. The wolf's whimpering filled the quiet forest as Mandy fled to her son. Swiftly scooping him, she ran until she was atop the blanket.

Through gasping breaths, she told Henry Jr. not to go near baby animals, especially wolf pups. She explained that their mothers would attack anyone who was seen as a threat, and that even though he was small, Henry Jr. was one of those threats. She squeezed him so much that her rapid heartbeat thumped in his ear.

He muffled into her warm, softly covered breasts that he would never go near baby animals, and that he would always be quiet to protect her. His arms tightened, pressing his face further into the white cotton, relieved that it didn't run red.

That night at supper, Mandy felt it best to warn her father about the pups by the creek.

"How did you find them?" Henry asked.

"Actually, Henry Jr. found them and warned me."

"Is that so…did you touch them?" Henry interrogated his grandson with a critical glare.

Henry Jr. nodded but said, "No."

"Did you touch the pups?" Henry asked in a booming voice that shook the lamplight suspended over the lengthy dining table.

"Yes," Henry Jr. replied nervously.

Henry walloped the back of his little head. "That's so you'll remember never to lie." Then he walloped him, again. "And that's so you'll remember never to touch wolf pups again. You could've gotten your mother killed!"

Henry Jr.'s tears flowed amidst sharp sobs.

"Stop crying!" Henry roared.

"Come, Henry Jr.," Mandy spoke softly.

"You will stay seated, Mandy!" her father shouted. "Go to your room now, boy!"

Henry Jr. ran while his grandpa resumed sawing at roasted beef.

"Father?"

"Not a word out of you," Henry threatened. "If I catch that boy lying again he'll get the switch. Lying will not be tolerated!"

"I'll just get Henry Jr. ready for bed."

Henry snatched her arm. "You'll show me where that bitch and her pups are. They must be taken care of. Let Mable see to the boy."

Mandy nodded, hoping it wouldn't take too long. All she wanted to do was comfort her son.

When she returned, she climbed the stairs to find he was already sleeping in his bed. Lying beside him, she gently stroked his hair. "I know how you feel. I know exactly how you feel," she said sadly. "It will change, though. You will get smarter and faster, and it won't be so bad. It's not so bad." She kissed his soft forehead and quietly left the room.

****

Henry was still trying to organize a cattle drive. One had just been arranged two years prior, but he was left out. He thought about breeding horses but wanted to fill his pasture with more Hereford cows.

One morning, Mandy was washing up dishes and encouraged Henry Jr. to shell peas and put them into piles of ten. It was always helpful incorporating learning with a chore, and it would be needed while Mable helped Jacob with summer planting. However, every time she turned to see her son's progress, he was munching on peas.

"Henry Jr., how many piles of ten do you have?

"Ah, two, almost."

"You eat anymore and I won't have any for supper."

"Yes, Momma," he said, popping another pea into his little mouth.

The front door slammed, followed by his grandpa's familiar shuffle. Henry Jr. instinctively rolled the pea off of his tongue and onto the table.

"Would it kill you to offer me water from time to time?" Henry grumbled with a wipe to his broad sweaty forehead.

"Sorry, Father. I was just cleaning up the kitchen," Mandy replied uneasily.

Henry took a hard stare at his grandson rolling peas along the table.

"What's he doing?"

"His counting," she answered, toweling her hands.

"Why doesn't he count seeds as he puts them in the ground; make him more useful?"

"Henry Jr., go help Mable and Jacob with the planting."

He kept eyes on his mother until he got past the kitchen table and out the door.

"What's to eat, Mandy?"

"I made you a sandwich, Father. Want it now?"

"You made me a sandwich?" Henry sneered.

Jacob and Henry Jr. looked up from a row of seeds, expecting the sandwich to come flying out the door.

"You know I don't eat sandwiches! What the hell, Mandy!" he shouted as a plate shattered.

Mable bolted for the kitchen.

"Come on, Henry Jr., keep puttin' the seeds in the soil," Jacob coaxed as Henry Jr. slowly moved nervous eyes off the door.

Henry came out of the kitchen, fuming, "Since I'm not getting food anytime soon!" Thumping over to Henry Jr., he grabbed his arm harshly. "It's time for you to work in the barn!"

Henry Jr. flashed a fearful face to Jacob, then his mother.

Desperate to stop him, she cried, "He's just a little boy!"

"He's the same age I was when I mucked out stalls. It's time for him to learn some chores, and he sure won't be learning them from you!" he roared, yanking his grandson toward the barn.

She began to follow, but Jacob halted her. "Miss Mandy, I'll go keep an eye on Henry Jr."

"No, Jacob," she hesitated. "Continue your planting. I'm sure he'll be fine. He's obeying his grandfather and he'll be fine," her voice assured with an unsteady gait to the kitchen. "He hasn't done anything wrong."

"Neither did you," Jacob said under his breath.

Mandy figured it was inevitable that Henry Jr. would spend time with his grandfather alone, and that it would be better during the daytime when he wasn't so ill-tempered. She naively hoped that they would bond with each other.

Henry had different intentions for his grandson. He felt it time the boy started working instead of sitting around playing the piano and reading all day. Another lazy family member wasn't needed in his house. He also felt his grandson needed discipline and strict rearing so that he'd never turn out like his father. Thrusting a shovel at Henry Jr.'s hand, he told him to start scooping manure and straw into the wheel barrow.

Henry Jr. did as told rather cautiously while his grandpa towered over him with arms crossed.

"You know, boy, I think you're the first bastard child of Virginia City," he blurted out with a smirk.

Henry Jr. peered up, unsure of whether that was a good thing or a bad thing. He returned to his shoveling but became very timid at the closeness of the man with the strong, fierce hands. As time went on, the shovel got heavier and heavier as bits of dirty straw fell to the barn floor.

"Watch what your doing! You'll traipse it into the house!" his grandpa snapped.

When Henry Jr.'s hands got shakier, he dropped a shovel full of muck. His grandpa grabbed the shovel before smacking him in the back of the head.

"Come back when you have more muscle!" he bellowed.

Henry Jr. cowered at his grandpa's angry voice. Running to the house, his eyes stung. Mandy was still in the kitchen preparing a proper meal, unaware he had ascended the stairs, climbed into bed, and was sobbing into his pillow. He was so sad and confused. Why was his grandpa so mean to him? He figured he must be pretty weak for his grandpa to be so angry.

That night at supper, Henry surprised Mandy by announcing he was going to head a cattle drive from Arkansas. He'd been corresponding with an old acquaintance who was interested in driving one thousand Hereford cows into Montana. Henry sold the Donevan Hotel to finance the trip, expecting a pretty penny from the sale, but was dissatisfied. Property values had softened since easy mining had played out. He presumed he'd be gone from the ranch for at least a year.

Henry Jr. was having trouble forking the ham atop his plate when he heard his grandpa's news. Glancing at his momma, he smiled while grabbing a piece with his fingers and stuffing it in his mouth. His face nearly splattered the plate after the swift smack to his head.

"Maybe the boy could learn to use a fork while I'm away!" Henry hollered. "And you will have to run this ranch while I'm away. Can you handle that, Mandy?"

"Yes, I'm more than capable of running this ranch while you're away," Mandy answered with conviction and hopefulness.

Henry seemed convinced and decided to set out in late-July.

The time went so slowly for Henry Jr., who had mastered his days of the week as he counted down his grandpa's departure from the ranch. When that day finally arrived, he watched from his bedroom window until his grandpa and the wagon led by oxen were no longer visible. Bursting out of the house, he ran past his mother to the barn.

"Henry Jr.!" Mandy shouted out while following his footsteps.

He was found petting Jefferson's soft velvety nose, saying, "He's gone now. I'm gonna feed you, brush you, and take you for long walks."

"Henry Jr.," she interjected. "That's a lot of responsibility for a six year old boy."

His smile disappeared as the horse nuzzled his ear.

"But if you listen to Jacob and follow his orders, you can spend more time with Jefferson."

He beamed at his mother before squeezing her tightly.

"And continue to practice your grammar, or you will not be GOING anywhere but the kitchen table."

Chapter 16

A few weeks after Henry's departure, Jacob brought in mail from Virginia City. Mandy perused the letters with a tiny glimmer of hope there might be one from Sean. Glimmer faded and a sickening feeling ensued when she saw a letter written by Eliza Sherman.

Moving to the kitchen table, she pondered opening it. Confident her father wouldn't be walking through the front door anytime soon, she mustered her courage and tore at the seal. It seemed her father was in contact with the woman. He kept it a secret that Matthew Sherman, who was once his best friend, had died leaving his pretty little wife a widow.

Mandy surmised that her father was going to comfort Eliza, as he had done many years ago, when her husband was still very much alive. Eliza wrote about how thrilled she was with Henry's plans to visit her. Mandy's tears flowed as thoughts of that fateful night at Matthew Sherman's dining table came into full focus.

Mandy was sweetly staring at Jeffrey Sherman, he her senior by two years, with determined hazel eyes amid thick wavy lashes, dirty blond hair, and beautiful full lips that curled so handsomely when he smiled. She didn't notice how his father, Matthew, bore eyes into Henry until words started snarling out of his mouth.

"How dare you!" he pointed in anger, "how dare you sit at my table and eat my food…so comfortably while you've been….." He looked at Eliza in repulsion.

Mandy was confused.

Ellen Margaret was embarrassed.

Matthew turned to Henry, shaking with fury. "You get the hell out of my house and never show your face near me again! There isn't any county in Arkansas where I will find you, you hear me!" He slowly rose with fists atop the table. "I will blacken your name and reputation, and as God is my witness, despise you to the day I die!"

Henry's face was beet red, jaw unnaturally rigid. Squeezing Ellen Margaret's arm, he dragged her away with Mandy ashamedly following. She glanced at Jeffrey, sitting dumbfounded, still as a stone.

It wasn't until Mandy's parents were alone in their bedroom when Ellen Margaret lashed out at her husband.

Mandy never heard her mother speak in such a shrill tone. It reminded her of a wounded animal desperately trying to free itself from a trap. Glass was broken; Henry's voice was muffled; but it was Ellen Margaret's woeful cries that tore at Mandy's heart. Putting hands to her head, she sobbed uncontrollably. She wept for the man, who just before supper, kissed her hand profusely and professed his undying love for her.

All hope was dashed when the next day Henry announced that moving west was the right thing to do. He used excuses, never the truth, that it was necessary to go. Besides, Ellen Margaret had no choice. Her parents were deceased. She had no money of her own, and he never let her forget that.

"I'm your provider," he would say, "and you'll do as I say!"

"Momma?" Henry Jr. called softly.

Mandy's memories of that day vanished when she gazed at her concerned son.

He got so sad when he saw her crying, his lower lip started trembling.

"Oh Henry Jr., come give me a hug, my sweet angel," she begged, wiping her eyes.

"Momma, Tommy's here to take me fishin'," he muffled into her calico dress. "I don't have to go. I can stay with you."

She pulled him away. "You go fishin'…you go fishing with Tommy. Momma's going into town, going shoping." *With my head held high.*

****

At Willowtree Creek, Tommy and Henry Jr. sat quietly on a big rock, as they often did during their fishing expeditions.

"Tommy, what does bastard mean?"

He took his time to answer. Despite being slow, he knew the meaning of the word. "It means a boy without a father."

Henry Jr. nodded, figuring his grandpa wasn't lying. He just didn't like his tone when he said it, and said it often with a pernicious smile. Thinking back, Henry Jr. couldn't remember a time when he called him by his proper name. He was always boy, or child, or bastard. Maybe if he changed his name, his grandpa would use it.

Henry Jr. spent that afternoon conjuring up a new name; a name that exuded strength and courage; one that would make his grandpa proud.

What about Stonewall…. named after Thomas Stonewall Jackson, one of the best Confederate commanders, hero and leader of the South?

His momma said grandpa admired Stonewall Jackson so much that he gave his stallion that name. Maybe if Henry Jr. had a name like that, his grandpa would forget about all of the other ones.

A smile lit up his face as his mind moved to horses.

While Henry was gone, Mandy would teach her son how to ride a horse. Henry had six thoroughbred horses. Jackson was his stallion, chestnut brown and powerful. Mandy didn't care for his unpredictable temperament so she kept Henry Jr. away. The broodmare was Virginia and the arduous journey west turned her into a crotchety, old nag. Of the remaining horses, Jefferson was Henry Jr.'s favourite. He loved riding the bay horse. Mandy opted to ride an iron gray mare named Carolina.

Mandy loved it when he said, "Giddy up, horsey! Giddy up, Jefferson!"

They never moved faster than a walk along the property or to Willowtree Creek. Though Mandy had galloped through Little Rock County, she did very little riding in Montana, so her confidence in teaching Henry Jr. was very low.

Once they were at the creek, Henry Jr. would usher Jefferson to the flowing waters, cup water in his small hands, and feel the roughness of Jefferson's tongue. He so enjoyed being with Jefferson, Mandy felt uneasy. When her father returned, he would be torn from that horse. The bond the two were creating was going to end in plenty of tears and sadness.

Henry Jr. would walk Jefferson along the creek's edge, introducing the horse to a new rock friend or a frog he just caught off a slippery wet stone.

Mandy would yell over, "Don't go in that creek with your shoes on!"

But it was too late, most times. He would come over, pants dripping, shoes squishing, as his mother asked him where his common sense was.

Henry Jr. would shrug his shoulders and say he didn't seem to have any of that sense.

One day, while heading back to the ranch, Henry Jr. did something that nearly scared her to death. He said his silly 'giddy up' and kicked his heals into the horse. Jefferson took off like a shot with him gripping the horn of the saddle, screaming for help.

"Hold on, Henry Jr.!" Mandy cried, desperately trying to catch him.

It was Jacob, running from the barn, calling out, "Whoa, Jefferson!" He grabbed the loose reins with his left hand and Henry Jr. with his right.

"Henry Jr.!" Mandy screamed, climbing off her horse and grabbing his arms.

He peered up, smiling, "That was fun! Let's do it again!"

"No, no, no!" she wailed, shaking him. "We don't kick in our heels, or we never go riding again. You hear me?"

"Yes, Momma," he replied unhappily.

"I'm going to make soap. You can help me."

Henry Jr. glared at Jacob, his expression pleading intervention.

"Miss Mandy, I could sure use help in the barn."

She turned to her little boy, who was pleading, knees firmly on the ground.

"You listen to Jacob and don't go on Jefferson anymore today."

"I won't I promise," he said, running to the barn with Jacob closely following.

Mandy entered the house and a quick glance at her reflection in the hall mirror sent out a giggle.

"Mable, I must brush this bird's nest before we get started!"

"Take your time, child. Just collectin' da scrapes," she answered from the kitchen.

When Mandy was seated at her vanity, her wild hair was released from wayward pins to fall around a rosy complexion. Lifting the dark tresses over her ears, a tune of long ago filled her head, followed by the magical night that she would never forget.

She was eyeing her fan, every blade scrolled with a different bachelor eager to spin her around the dance floor, when he appeared. Her friends sighed dreamily when his smooth steps entered the ballroom. But she just smiled demurely, because she was his betrothed, if only in secret.

"Miss Amanda," Chuck Odden drawled. "I do believe it is my turn."

She flicked her fan closed and began a slow dance with an even slower, stiff-footed gent while her eyes fixated on Jeffrey Sherman. Jeffrey, ever sociable, was too mesmerized in conversation with his friends. Then he did what he predictably did at all ballroom galas: walked out into the night air.

It irked her that he didn't wait for the obligatory twirl to end, take her in his arms, and thrust the fan away.

Instead, she would go searching him out like they were caught in a game of hide and seek.

She gave Chuck her speediest curtsey and bolted to the landscape of looming oaks, peeking under the dark umbrellas, and finding nothing but cobwebs and dewy leaves.

Frustration set in, and she was just about to leave when she saw grey smoke billowing from a wide trunk.

"Jeffrey?"

His lanky body wound around the tree, and she was thankful for the shading of his eyes, so sultry when they locked on her, as if she was clothed in transparency, skin prickly, trembling.

"I feel like you're evading me," she said softly. "I haven't seen you in weeks. Not even at the Military Leap-Year Ball; made a pie with pecans."

Jeffrey chuckled lightly.

"Mable made the pie," Mandy confessed quite peevishly.

"Well, I didn't expect you'd be there. Rumours were swirling that cholera had touched your ranch. That your....your slaves were sick and you were tending to them."

"That's right, but I don't believe it was cholera," Mandy assured.

"I could care less about your culinary delights and even less about your…your sympathy to slaves!"

"Well, Jeffrey…."

"Amanda, these Ni…Negroes can be replaced. They're just human livestock. I know your Mammy was important to you, but she died, and there's no reason why you couldn't have perished from that blight, too."

Mandy's gentle smile faded into a light scowl.

"Now, now…don't you hide that radiant smile from me; it shines an iridescent lightness that renders me speechless. My heart takes a peculiar kind of flutter around you. Only settles when your dazzling eyes, so much brighter that the stars on a moonless night, gaze upon me."

Jeffrey's sweet sentiments were softening her. If he touched her, she would be a pile of supple mush he could mould to his liking.

His hand curled around her soft cheek while his eyes dove into hers. "Amanda, the day is drawing close when I hold you in my arms and guide you in a dance through life." His lips hovered over hers but never touched.

Jeffrey was a gentleman of propriety, and was also distinguished, to her belief, as the best dancer east of the Mississippi.

"I do believe they're playing our song, my prima donna."

He gently escorted her to the grand ballroom shimmering in crystal chandeliers and soft candlelight, as the waltz flowed softly to their ears. With back rigid and proud, Jeffrey closely led Mandy's trusting, submissive body with light and airy steps around a swell of swooning ladies and envious bachelors. They were the king and queen of this civil war ball. Mandy's tiara was just a pearl comb with hand sewn flowers; however, it was her dress, a silk weave of delicate pink, that flowed sublimely as she turned and glided along the polished floor.

"Miss Mandy," Mable whispered.

She turned with saddened eyes. "I was just working the knots in my hair and I just…got to thinking about Jeffrey and our last dance." Her sigh withered as a tear ran down her cheek.

Mable took the brush and ran it through tangled locks. "Nothin' wrong with a sweet memory."

"That's just it, Mable. The last words Jeffrey spoke to me were…harsh, in Little Rock, just after that horrible dinner. He said, with coldness in his eyes, that 'I should pray for my salvation every day.' My friend, Elizabeth, was clutching his arm flashing a sickly sweet smile. I wanted to slap it away and tell her he was mean-spirited, rude, and uncaring; that I naively fell for it too. He spoke of…he treated slaves unkindly,' she divulged with sobriety. "I'm sorry, Mable. But it was the dance that put me in such a spell. It made me feel so special, so important inside. I'd never felt that way in all of my life."

"Oh, Miss Mandy, his words, his actions, they're not yours. Just remember the dance."

Mandy clutched Mable's hand and held it to her damp cheek. "Makes me pine for Sean, even more."

"Just remember the dance. Let the rest fade away."

Noises stirred Mandy to her bedroom window where Henry Jr. was seen stroking Jefferson's shiny coat.

"I try to keep the memory of him alive, everyday," her voice quivered. "I try, every day." Leaning her forehead against the cool glass pane, Jacob came into sight and rushed to Henry Jr., whisking him and the horse back to the barn.

"What's his urgency," she mumbled. Then she caught glimpse of him, horse charging up the path strong and fast, rider tall and darkly clothed.

She scampered out of the house with Mable at her heels. Running along the tall grass, she cried, "Sean!"

The man turned and tipped his hat. "Ma'am, I'm Frank, Frank O'Flaherty," he smiled.

Mandy was rendered speechless, her body coiling against Mable's solid frame.

"I'd like to speak with Mr. Wilkes regarding his property holdings. Haven't seen him for some time," he remarked, glancing about the place with a heavy stare. "Should I be worried?"

"Mr. Wilkes is out of town conducting cattle business," Jacob spoke judiciously. "Mrs. Wilkes is tending to the farm just fine."

"I see," Frank replied smoothly. "Well, I guess I'll just have to wait for his return. In the meantime," pausing, he reached into his pocket, "here's my card. I can be reached at this location during the day, unless I'm off chasing troublemakers and hanging them," his voice spoke ominously. "Please knock on my door if you require any assistance, Mrs. Wilkes."

He tipped his hat before hoisting himself and swinging a long leg over the saddle. "I wish you good day," he announced over squeaking leather as his solid stature took a deep seat, "and please don't hesitate stopping by when you're in town."

Loping his horse along the stone path, Mandy shivered into Mable's protective arms.

"Can I come out of the barn now?" Henry Jr.'s small voice cried.

It would be the only time Henry Jr. asked to be away from the horses. Throughout most of the winter, he meticulously cared for the thoroughbreds: brushing them and untangling their manes, cleaning their stalls, and bridling them for walks along the crunchy snow.

Mandy had the hardest time getting him to sit long enough to finish his schooling and piano lessons. She acquiesced most days to his annoying pleas just so she could have peace and quiet while she cleaned, or sewed, or played the piano.

By spring, Henry Jr. was quite comfortable getting Jefferson to walk, stop, and turn amongst the cows in the front pasture. For his birthday, Mandy bought him a cowboy hat and made a chocolate cake. He thought it was the best birthday ever and wished secretly that his grandpa would never come home.

****

Mandy had her own secret wish which brought on a curious itch that had to be scratched. She rode into town with grocery list in hand, but stuffed it into her purse as she entered the unfamiliar mercantile.

Minutes later, Frank entered the building and was quickly accosted by its shopkeeper, Tom Harwood.

"There's a woman waiting for you upstairs. She's awfully purdy."

"My wife?" Frank asked quizzically.

"Ah, no. This woman is of a…..finer material. I mean…she's less caustic. Well, she's just…."

"I understand, Tom. Go on about your day and keep your feet off my steps, unless I give you the signal." He whispered, "Privacy with a potential witness is of utmost importance unless it's deemed worthless of my time."

"Ah, yes. Mum's the word." Tom fingered his lips.

"I am coming in loud and clear because the last time I nearly put my foot through the floor."

Tom winked. "Yup. Everything's okey-dokey."

Frank nodded with much doubt. His eager feet took giant leaps until he reached the second floor, very pleased to find Amanda Wilkes facing his desk. Her slim figure draped in a snug-fitting mauve dress made her most attractive. Her romantic implication with Sean Thomas made her simply irresistible.

"Mrs. Wilkes?"

She turned with a delicate smile across her flawless face.

"It's a pleasure to have you stop by. Can I help you with any matter?"

"Possibly," she said, standing.

"No, please…sit." Moving swiftly to his chair, he proceeded to clear any impeding papers hindering full view of her. "How may I be of service?"

"Mr. Wilkes has been gone for some time now, and I'm getting a little anxious. He is considerably older than…he is of a mature age, and I worry for his health."

"I see, and you would like me to round up a search party for him?"

"Do you have a lot of experience searching for people?"

"Well, my searching extends mainly to low life criminals disrupting the good citizens of Montana, but I'm sure I could find innocents as well. How far would I be looking?"

"I received a letter from St. Louis, Missouri, and that was two months ago. Have you ever not found anyone you were searching for?"

Frank leaned back in his chair as Mandy clung to his words like a dog eagerly awaiting a bone. "I know of at least two cantankerous individuals who've eluded my capture, but they will soon be pursued again. You see, Mrs. Wilkes, I find these malefactors tend to stay close to the scene of their crimes, rather foolishly." He tapped his heel against the dusty floor.

"Take R.C. Rawley for instance; an inside spy for thieving marauders Stinson, Forbes and Lyons, he scurried from Bannack on a blustery winter's day. Returned months later in tattered threads looking like a lone chicken on a wet day," he chuckled apathetically. "Kept shooting his mouth off and uttering threats, that is, until his tongue stopped wagging at Hangman's Gulch. And now, Bannack's a peaceful and safe town." Frank's heel knocked on the planks again.

Tom scooted up the stairs, pleased that his memory worked quick as lightening. "Frank, Arthur's waiting for you at the…at the hitching post? Says it's time to get a move on."

"Fine, Tom," he answered sharply. "Tell him I'll be there momentarily."

Tom nodded while scratching his balding head.

"If I do search for Mr. Wilkes," Frank began. "I'll be forced to call off my search for a man who's committed at least two grisly murders. I'll need some time to think about it. Could we discuss this over lunch, tomorrow?"

"Thank you, Mr. O'Flaherty. I appreciate your assistance with this matter…"

"Please, call me Frank," he said, outstretching his hand. When she offered hers, he felt her softness and imagined, ever briefly, every fingertip sliding down his bare chest.

She stood, swallowing back the disdain she had for herself. The man, with indifferent eyes amidst a face of large features, sent a wretched feeling throughout her body. But her mind pushed on, screaming that it might keep the man she loved, alive.

****

During the summer, Henry returned with two hundred and fifty Hereford cows. The men he hired to drive the cattle stayed at the ranch another week to help with the branding. Henry spent most of his time in the barn or out in the pasture, so Mandy warned her son to stay clear of him and he obeyed for the most part.

One night, Henry entered the kitchen just as supper was being served.

"Men have all gone into town," he informed while dousing hands in tepid dish water. "I will join them later.

They will have supper here tomorrow night, though, so let's make it a feast."

"Yes, Father," she replied happily.

Mandy offered a bowl of steaming new potatoes while he stared blankly at his grandson.

"You never asked me why so few cows were brought to Montana."

"I'm sorry, father. Why so few cattle?" she asked while stepping around him with a serrated knife and proceeding to cut the kernels from her son's cob of corn.

"Mandy, will you stop mollycoddling that child!"

"Father, while you were gone Henry Jr. lost his two front teeth."

Henry paused a moment, the scowl seeming frozen on his face, until he forked a mound of green string beans into his mouth.

Henry Jr. kept his eyes permanently planted on his plate, stabbing every kernel carefully. No food would ever go astray in his life again.

"The war has devastated Arkansas," Henry began. "Homes burnt to the ground, land ravished, much of the livestock killed or eaten by the armies that swept through the counties. I offered twenty dollars a head and got what I could." He popped another potato into his mouth.

"We'll make do."

"I spent time with Eliza Sherman. Poor woman lost her husband and son, Jeffrey, in the same year during the war."

Placing her fork and knife down, Mandy looked resignedly at her father. "How kind of you." Then it dawned on her. "Jeffrey Sherman?"

Henry nodded gravely. "Fought at Hill's Plantation near Cache River in Woodruff County; died just months after we left Arkansas."

"That's not far from our County," Mandy cried.

"We have to make things right," he said with hard-staring eyes shifting to his grandson.

His words fell on deaf ears as she tried to grasp that Jeffrey Sherman was dead.

"You met Mr. Charles. Best drover I've ever worked with," he said before ravenously gobbling a chunk of rare steak.

"Yes, he seems rather pleasant."

"Mr. Charles doesn't have any children." His knife pointed Henry Jr.'s direction.

"That's unfortunate," she mumbled softly with somber eyes never leaving her plate.

"He's offered to take Henry Jr., to Arkansas."

Mandy stopped chewing, panic and shock paralyzing the movement of her mouth. Glancing at her son and his empty supper plate, she realized he had developed a rushed habit of eating too. "Henry Jr.?"

"Did you hear what I said, Mandy!" Henry barked.

Her eyes stared in disbelief. "Henry Jr. belongs here with his mother…. and grandfather."

"This is your opportunity to start fresh, find a husband and have legitimate children. Give Mr. Charles that boy!"

Mandy's head shook.

"What the hell does that mean?" he charged.

"No," she whispered crisply.

Henry leapt from his chair and squeezed Mandy painfully. "You will give the child to Mr. Charles!"

She turned to her son, sitting bewildered, knife in hand.

"Go to your room, Henry Jr!"

He sat frozen as his grandpa pressed strong hands into his mother's small arms.

"You heard your mother, now go!" Henry boomed.

He released the knife and bolted from the kitchen, crying by the time he reached the stairs. Leaning against his bedroom door, it closed while his heart pounded against small ribs.

Kneeling, he prayed, "Please don't let him send me away! Please don't let him send me away. Please make him stop hurting my momma!"

Loud voices echoed throughout the house.

"I will never give Henry Jr. away! I will never give your grandson away!" she howled.

Henry's grip threatened to snap her bones. "You will do as I say in my house! That boy will always be a bastard....."

Mable came sauntering into the room with eyes focused on the dining table.

"Sorry I'm so late. Just lost track of time," she said, noisily scraping wasted food from one plate onto another with a dirty fork.

Henry callously pushed Mandy away, but his blazing glare tore into her just as painfully, revealing how much she would truly regret not giving up her son.

After the front door slammed into its frame, Mable hurried to Mandy's side.

"Go calm youself, den go to your son."

Mandy rubbed bruised arms, shaking her head.

"You've got to stay strong for Henry Jr.; you've got to stay strong. Dry your tears and go to your son."

"He'll never take him!" she wailed, trembling. "He will never take my son!"

"We won't let dat happen, Mandy," Mable spoke reassuringly.

In her room, Mandy's hands ran furiously across the pine vanity, breaking a glass dish that held the pouch of gold. Clutching it to her breast, she envisioned taking Henry Jr. to Helena; however, this wasn't her first time contemplating the bold move, and it wouldn't be her last.

After her cheeks were dried and the nuggets safely hidden in a dresser drawer, she moved to his room. He was already lying on the bed, knees bound to his chest. Wrapping her arms in a protective embrace, she snuggled a weary face into the silkiness of his hair.

He pressed her hand between his head and pillow, never wanting to let it go.

"I'll never leave you, Henry Jr., I promise," she vowed. "I'll never leave you and you'll never leave me."

While the hired men stayed on at the Wilkes ranch, Henry Jr. never left his mother's side. She invited the men to supper every night, so she wouldn't be alone with her father. The morning they departed for Arkansas, she stood beside her son, smiling and waving.

Henry turned to his daughter with a ghastly scowl before heading to the barn.

Chapter 17

The warm sun streamed through Mandy's window as she pinned back her hair with a wide-toothed comb. A lingering glance reflected a plain complexion, except for her eyes. They seemed to betray her, exuding a delicate weakness that had to change. And between those eyes, she fingered the deep creases that must have resulted from her fallible ways.

She saw no point in fancying herself up, with so little time and so little need considering her confines, but her face had to show strength and defiance to protect herself and her son.

Since her father's return, she had only seen Frank O'Flaherty twice and he didn't need to see her any prettier. His intentions were blaringly evident, despite that his advances were kept at bay; however, she wondered if Sean would recognize her on the crowded street and shine his dimpled smile with welcome arms.

"There's no time for daydreaming," Mandy said lightly. "It's time to get on with my day."

She moved to Henry Jr.'s room, eager to rouse him. When she opened the door to find an empty bed, she hastily worried, calling out his name.

"We're in da kitchen, Miss Mandy," Mable replied.

He was eating his oatmeal by the mouthfuls when she approached him.

"Henry Jr. did you see your grandpa before he went into town this morning?"

"Only for a little while," he mumbled. "But he wasn't in the barn, Momma. He was out front acting kind of grumpy and rubbing his head saying words that didn't sound….nice."

"What did he say?" she wondered.

He took a minute to remember. "I know…he said 'shit can't hitch this fukin' horse to the carriage'."

She stared in open mouthed surprise, trying to decide how to respond.

Henry Jr. stared wide-eyed, knowing those words were bad.

Not wanting her little boy spewing profanity, she came up with an idea. "Well I know a word that is a combination of two bad words. I'll let you use that word if you promise not to tell anyone it's a bad word.

Henry Jr. was intrigued. "What is it?"

"Shuck," she said proudly.

"How do you spell it?"

"S-H-U-C-K"

He gazed at his mother. "Shuck, shuck, shuck."

Mandy laughed. She thought he was so cute and would stay cuter if he didn't have a cussing mouth.

Henry Jr. loved to hear her laugh and wanted to hear it more often.

The next day he made her laugh again, though this time at Willowtree Creek while resting on her lap, her gentle hands running through his short dark hair.

"Henry Jr. what do you think is our most important sense?"

He genuinely answered, "It's sleeping, Momma."

She laughed. "I think I know what tomorrow's lesson will be about." She laughed again.

With curious eyes, his fingers twirled the satin ribbons of her cotton dress. "Momma, did my father make you laugh?"

"All the time," she answered without hesitating. "He could be really funny. He was…he is a really kind, gentle man, and I miss his smile everyday. You smile just like him, Henry Jr., and it's a beautiful smile."

"Do you think he'll ever come back?"

"Everyday I pray he'll come back and take us in his arms, that he'll take you fishing in this creek; and that we'll laugh, play and love each other," she said with a sudden feeling of being watched. Scanning every cranny of the wooded place, she hoped it was him; and that he'd eventually wind his way to her.

She shook away the possibility, gazing at Henry Jr. with a pleasurable smile of that wondrously beautiful time, knowing it only played in her mind.

The next day, she taught Henry Jr. about the five senses and what she believed was the most important sense 'touch'.

"Why, without touch, Henry Jr., I wouldn't feel your warmth when I held you in my arms. Imagine how babies would suffer if they didn't have their mother's loving touch."

Nodding, he knew touching his momma in soft cottons and satiny silks brought comfort and security.

"Now pull out your Bible and turn to Deuteronomy."

Flipping the pages, he got to what he called, "Doodooronomy." He giggled and assumed she would too.

But the laughter didn't come because it wasn't right to make fun of the Bible. Mandy made Henry Jr. write a letter apologizing to God, thinking it could kill two birds with one stone, by making him remember to take the

Bible seriously, and improving his printing and spelling which were incorrigible.

He sulked when she handed him blank paper with a stern face. Thinking deeply, he dipped the pen in inkwell and printed.....

Dear God,

I'm sory for makin fun of the Bible. I onle wanted to make my momma lafe again.

By the way, I have been praeing evry nite for grandpa to go away agan so I can ride Jeferson. He is stil here.

Amen,
Henry Jr.

Mandy read the letter and didn't know whether to laugh or cry, so she just criticized in a schoolmaster's tone that his illegible spelling needed much work.

****

During a morning lesson at the piano, Henry Jr. was practicing a song about a little birch canoe when Mable approached, announcing the beets were cooled and ready to be sliced and pickled.

"Henry Jr., practice your scales while I get my work done."

He sighed solemnly. "Yes, Momma."

"If you get tired of that, you can help me preserve these beets."

His head shook sullenly while tapping the keys.

"I wish that he loved playing like I do, Mable. He's more passionate about catching frogs."

"He's a boy, Miss Mandy. He wants ta do boy things."

Suddenly, the parlour went silent of his playing.

Mandy angrily stomped over to find the room empty.

"Henry Jr.?" she called, rushing to the hall as the front door closed.

Briskly, she caught up to her father leading Henry Jr. towards the barn.

"Where are you going?"

Henry turned with a heavy stance. "Boy needs to know how to shoot a rifle."

"I think he's too young," her voice trembled.

"He needs to be able to protect himself and his mother. Come along," he demanded, stretching an ominous hand.

Nervously taking it, Henry Jr. kept a fast pace to his grandpa's wide steps, his mother trailing behind, that is, until Henry spun around and unkindly ordered her back in the house.

Henry Jr. was led to the farthest outside wall of the barn where old bottles had been lined up on wooden logs for target practice. His body twitched uncontrollably when his grandpa busily rammed ten bullets into the chamber of the rifle, levered it, aimed and fired.

The bullet whizzed and shattered glass, causing Henry Jr. to jump fretfully, effectively eradicating his twitching.

Henry scowled in disgust. When he enveloped his grandson's little body, he forced a small hand on the barrel of the rifle and the other on the trigger. "You rest the stock of the rifle under your arm," he advised firmly. "Then you aim and shoot."

Henry Jr. began shaking in fear. He didn't like the sound the rifle made, or that his grandpa was so close.

"Aim and fire boy!" he roared, his powerful breath forcing the hairs to stand on Henry Jr.'s neck. "Now!"

Seconds passed before the rifle was jerked out of small hands and into his small head. Henry Jr. bolted to the house, fearful he would do something else.

Mandy heard the door slam, followed by fast and little footsteps up the stairs. He was crying in bed when she walked in the room.

"Henry Jr., what happened?" she asked, as he faced the wall. "I won't leave till you turn around. Talk to me!"

He flipped over, his cheek glistening red and swollen.

"What happened?" her voice crackled.

"The rifle hit me when it went off," he said as honestly as he could.

She felt that was plausible. "Want me to get a cold cloth?"

"No," he said, turning away.

"If you need me, I'll be in the kitchen," she spoke softly while her hand smoothed the creases of his shirt.

When the room went empty of her presence, Henry Jr.'s quivering resumed. His grandpa's ferocious temper scared him to death.

****

Tommy came by the next afternoon showing concern over the purplish bruise on his cousin's cheekbone.

Henry Jr. gave an awkward smile, mumbling that it looked worse than it felt.

They found their favourite spot on a cool September afternoon at the creek. Tommy let out his line in the cold, clear waters. "You need protecting, Henry Jr.?"

"No, I'm fine," he answered solemnly.

"You have me, though. I'll watch over you."

Henry Jr. felt safe when Tommy was around because he was gentle and kind, but also because his grandpa wasn't so mean. However, Tommy didn't live with them and when he left, his grandpa's animosity returned.

When four trout were hooked, Henry Jr. proudly brought them home. After Jacob cleaned and filleted two of them, he brought one to Mandy's sizzling frying pan.

Since Henry was in town, it would just be her, Henry Jr., and the fish. As they were sitting down admiring his catch, her father unexpectedly walked in.

"My supper plans were cancelled. Morgan is ill. Mandy, get me a plate and some cutlery."

She promptly did as asked.

"We're having fish tonight," she said staidly. "Henry Jr. caught it with Tommy, today."

Mandy placed the food on his plate praying it wouldn't end up on the wall. Glancing at her son, she found wide-eyes staring at her father.

Henry took his cutlery and shoveled in big mouthfuls, staying peacefully quiet.

Henry Jr.'s curious stare stayed unnoticed.

It wasn't until his plate was cleared when Henry said, "I haven't had fish since before you were born, Mandy."

She assumed that he was placated by a happy memory of long ago.

Henry stood, slid his plate into soapy water, and motioned he'd be in the barn.

"You caught a tasty fish, Henry Jr.," Mandy smiled.

He smiled back, dimples showing, eyes twinkling.

"I made apple pie for dessert. Want a piece?"

"Can I have Grandpa's piece too?" he asked eagerly.

"No," Mandy replied swiftly.

Chapter 18

Saturday came. Mandy and Henry Jr. went to visit Colleen and her growing family. The weekly afternoon visits became a ritual and comfort to Mandy after her mother died.

Colleen had four children. Patricia was the oldest, followed by David, Matthew, and Audrey. Henry Jr. had a fondness for Patricia because they were closest in age, and she was a tomboy. She wanted pants. She wanted pants so badly so she could play hide and seek, or cowboys and Indians, and not trip over a dress.

Colleen adamantly opposed it. "Girls were not meant to wear pants."

One night, the topic of 'pant' safety came up.

"Momma, it's dangerous for me to run in a dress. I might trip and fall on a log."

"Then don't run," Colleen replied.

Patricia had a pouty look until she peered at her father, who smiled and winked. She knew she'd get those pants, thanks to her doting father, and she did, though she had to promise to put on a dress at supper time.

When she saw Henry Jr., she was beaming with joy.

The two cousins shot out of the house through the back field for the forest of spruce, aspens, and ponderosa pines. They would go into the trees for hours and make weapons out of sticks and sewing thread, then fight over who would be the cowboy.

On this day, Patricia would be Jesse James and Henry Jr. would be Geronimo.

"Hold your horses, Patsy," Henry Jr. said. "Jesse James robs banks. He doesn't go after Indians."

"Well, let's say Jesse James robs a bank and gallops through the plains into Indian Territory where he runs into Geronimo; or, we can just play battle at the Alamo if you'd rather be a Mexican and I could be Davy Crockett."

Henry Jr. submitted. He never said no to Patricia for she was his favourite cousin. The rest of them still sucked their thumbs.

Hiding behind trees, Patricia's wooden pistol poked out while Henry Jr. struggled to get a crooked arrow on a less than taut bow. Henry Jr. was the Indian, so he would eventually be lying on the ground with massive gunshot wounds. He overplayed the pain and suffering on his face, taking his time to play die. When he played dead though, he didn't move.

Patricia ambled over and nudged him with her foot.

"Killed him dead with my six shooter," she exclaimed, blowing on the tip of the stick.

Play time ended when Colleen yelled, "Supper time!"

Henry Jr. flew past Patricia. He was faster than her even though she had her pants on.

Before the mob of children arrived for their supper, Colleen and Mandy talked.

"How are things with your father and Henry Jr.?" Colleen asked with eyes focused on hands cubing potatoes.

"He doesn't seem as nervous around Father now. Maybe it's because he's older," Mandy replied while munching on a carrot. "Or maybe it's because he's faster.

He told me he plays a game with Father; calls it cat and mouse."

Colleen glanced at Mandy as she towel dried her hands. "How's that game go?"

"The cat tries to catch the mouse but the mouse is too fast."

Mandy recollected playing that game with her father. He would try to slap her with a furious hand, but she'd dodge it; and his arms were too short. It gave her confidence, and she hoped that was how her son felt.

Colleen didn't care for that game because she knew that cat could swallow that mouse if he wanted to. "Be careful. Henry Jr. will grow to be a man. Your father's not setting a good example," she declared.

"I don't have a lot of choice," Mandy grumbled, contemplating her predicament. "I just hope Henry Jr. sees more good in me than mean in his grandfather!"

Disgruntlement oozed through her pores, and Colleen feared it would linger through supper. "I'm making stew, with beef, just for you."

Mandy glanced up, her unhappy mood fading. "Does it come with sweet wine?"

Colleen smiled, clutching her cousin's arms. "Only if you promise not to drink the entire bottle."

"Maybe just a little sip," Mandy suggested as thoughts of Sean entered her mind.

"I think he'd be fine with that…just fine," her cousin remarked, turning to the stove with watered eyes. "Best get cooking, or we'll be crunching on potatoes and stabbing bloody meat."

"Not to worry," Mandy laughed softly, "Ethan will eat it under any circumstance."

****

Henry Jr. was up in his room when his mother started playing her sad music. He wasn't up for that, so he scurried to the kitchen and scooped up a handful of sugar for Jefferson. His grandpa was in town until supper time, or so he thought.

Slowly, he opened the barn door. "Shame you have to be cooped up in here on such a nice day. If Grandpa'd just let me take you out, you could get some exercise," he said as Jefferson licked the sugar with his raspy tongue.

No sooner had the words flown from his mouth when his grandpa startled him, shouting, "What in blazes are you doing?"

"Oh, shuck," Henry Jr. mouthed under his breath. Mustering his courage, he faced him.

"What are you feeding that horse?" he snarled. "Answer me!"

"Nothing! There's nothing in my hand!" his voice trembled, palms outstretched.

While Henry reached for the switch, his grandson bolted past him.

"You bastard!" Henry cussed. "When I catch you, I'm gonna strip you and whip you red!"

Running through the back field, Henry Jr. frantically climbed one of the apple trees.

When his grandpa reached the tree, he doubled over, panting, "You've got to come down sometime."

Henry Jr. was thankful his grandpa was so winded otherwise he could have stretched out his arm and easily clamped onto a little shoe. Then the willow branch would have been in full force.

The last experience with that particular punishment was still fresh in Henry Jr.'s mind. His grandpa was brushing down Jackson in the barn when he slowly approached, his wobbly hand holding a plate of pie.

Glancing over, Henry shook his head. "You're trembling like a little mouse. Come here and give me that pie."

Henry Jr. tiptoed forward, but when his grandpa's reach came near, the plate fell.

Glaring at the crumpled dessert on the dirty barn floor, Henry approached him, the smell of alcohol pungent on his breath. "Pick it up and put it back on the plate you clumsy child."

His small hands scooped up the sticky mess mottled with straw and clumpy dirt as his grandpa took hold of the switch.

"Hold that plate straight, boy," he commanded while rolling up Henry Jr.'s sleeves. Then he swatted until the skin reddened and tears welled up in his sad, blue eyes. When finished, Henry forced the white sleeves down, told him to compose himself, and go to bed.

Henry Jr. was prepared to sit in the tree all day and night if he had to. He didn't feel like the switch today.

His Grandpa lingered, glowering, while trying to catch his breath, until finally, he turned and thumped away.

A smile of relief formed as Henry Jr. leaned back in the tree. His back touched a branch but when it started slithering, he realized it was no tree limb. A shiver went down his spine, lifting the small hairs on his arms as it began hissing. Lunging for another branch, it snapped. His arm broke his fall, and the fall broke his arm. Biting his lower lip, he stopped himself from screaming as blood dripped down his chin. Waiting until his grandpa was out of site, he took the furthest path to the house.

Mandy took him to the doctor in Virginia City, covered in blankets to ease his shuddering from the shock and pain.

"Well, it's broken," the doctor said. "There's too much swelling to make a proper cast. He'll have to come back in a couple of days. In the meantime, he keeps it in this sling as still as possible. You're welcome to add some warm compresses to bring down the swelling. Give him laudanum to help him sleep and apply this comfrey if he'll let you touch it. I'll see you in a couple days, young man," he smiled.

Henry Jr. wanted to punch it off his face. He was angry, very angry.

At supper, that night, no words were spoken.

Henry Jr. learned to eat with his left hand which was a challenge. At least he didn't have any peas to contend with.

Every now and then, his grandpa looked his way with an empty stare. Henry Jr. assumed he'd had enough punishment for one day.

Mandy stared at her plate, wishing she'd never planted the apple trees. When she tucked him in at night, she gave him a bag of candy. "You want one now?"

Shaking a cranky head, he frowned at his swollen arm.

"Can I get you anything else before I go?" she asked, set to kiss him.

Turning away, he didn't want any of her sympathy; he didn't want any of her love either, for it would melt away his anger. He just wanted to lie in a sulking mood.

It was the first time she saw fury in his face, and a shadow of doubt crept into her mind that somehow her father was responsible. "If you ever have something to tell me, I'm always here to listen." Pausing, a few silent minutes ticked away before she left the room.

That night, Henry Jr. dreamt of the snake. It had somehow gotten into his bed and slithered along his body. He woke up frightened and hurting. Grabbing the bag of candy, he shoved in a mouthful, praying it would make him feel better and hoping it would take his mind somewhere else; but it didn't.

By the time Mandy took him in for the cast, it was less painful; and the swelling was gone. But after the cotton bandage was wrapped around his arm, smeared with a warm mixture of glue and starch, and splinted, the aggravating pain had returned. The whole process of making the splint, hardening the cast, and re-wrapping with a clean cloth, seemed to take forever in his mind. He thought maybe the switch would have been the better punishment on that day.

As they walked out of the doctor's office, Mandy tried to cheer him with the upcoming visit to his cousins.

That only made him unhappier because he would have to run around with the cast, or worse, not run at all. It got much worse when he said he had to use the outhouse, and wasn't looking forward to wiping with his left hand.

"Henry Jr.," Mandy said with lightness in her voice. "Let's go get you some more candy. I'll even let you pick it out."

When they walked out of the store, Frank was leaning against the hitching post swatting away flies with his newspaper.

"Well, well, Mrs. Wilkes, pleasure to see you this fine afternoon. And who is this?"

"This is my son, Henry Jr.," Mandy swallowed.

"It looks like you took a bad fall. Does it hurt much?"

"Uh-huh," Henry Jr. replied, snapping the tip of his mint stick and crunching loudly.

"I see your momma's using sugar medicine to keep you happy." Frank glimpsed a demure smile on Mandy's attractive face. "I wonder," he thought aloud, "if we could meet again. I'm leaving town, soon, for Helena, but thought maybe we could chat. I've just found one of my elusive outlaws; trial should be summarized end of this week."

Mandy bit her tongue to curb an insatiable need to know if it was Sean. "I suppose that would be fine. I'll meet you in town, though, tomorrow."

Unable to hide his lecherous grin, Frank was grateful she was distracted when the outlaw's offspring tugged on her slender arm. "Good!" he announced, jolting the boy off of his mother. "Meet me at Rosie's, say noon time, and I'll fill you in on the details. Nice to meet you, little man," he said, firmly shaking Henry Jr.'s left hand.

"Who was that?" he asked when out of earshot.

"Just a friend," Mandy replied pensively, "just a friend. And please don't tug on your momma when she's talking."

"But, Momma, I'm about ready to mess my pants!"

"Oh," Mandy shrieked, clutching his good arm and bolting to the nearest outhouse. "Why didn't you say something?"

About ready to reply, Henry Jr.'s attention was swept away as his mother weaved around wagons, horses, and their brown mounds.

****

On Saturday, Mandy and Henry Jr. visited Colleen and the rest of the Holden clan. While Patricia showed concern over Henry Jr.'s broken limb, Mandy showed relief that, after yesterday's plates of Irish Stew at Rosie's, and Frank's helpful hand to replace a napkin that had fallen from her lap, his big lips did not spew out Sean's name.

"Guess you won't be running for a while, "Patricia observed glumly.

"Are you kidding," Henry Jr. replied. "Give you ten seconds…then I'm gonna find you!"

No broken arm was going to stop him from playing. What it did stop him from doing was playing the piano. That was the one good thing about breaking an arm.

However, Patricia and Henry Jr. did end up playing one tune that afternoon. He used his left hand while Patricia used her right. They giggled and made lots of mistakes but were having too much fun to be criticized.

Mandy hadn't seen Henry Jr. laugh so much, so she stayed pretty quiet even though hearing the piano being played so poorly was making her cringe.

Chapter 19

Weeks passed and by the full heat of summer, Henry Jr. had healed enough that he could go without the cast. He was happy to be back with two healthy arms for fishing, swimming, and chasing his cousin.

Everyone seemed to be in fine spirits, including Henry. He had made acquaintances with Peter Warren, who was interested in developing some of his vacant properties along Jackson Street. The three men, Henry, Morgan Terrence, and Peter Warren, were growing quite close.

One afternoon, Mandy was pounding carpets on a rope line when he approached.

"Mandy, I'd like you to go into town today to get the food supplies from Pratt's and a few bottles of whisky. I'm feeling poorly today."

She eyed him with concern for he never felt poorly. He was always strong and unwavering, reminding her of a stone wall that no storm or strong wind could penetrate.

"Let me just finish cleaning these carpets."

"You'll go now!" he commanded. "Mable will finish this work. Horses are already hitched to the wagon; be on your way."

Mandy walked briskly to the house. "Mable!" she called once inside the hallway.

"Yes, Miss Mandy?"

"I'm going into town," she smiled. "Keep Henry Jr. in his room until I get back."

"Will do," Mable nodded with a glance up the stairway to his closed door.

In his room, Henry Jr. sauntered away from his pet rocks and wooden toys lying on the floor to peruse a book his mother had just procured. He was just about to read the first page of a whale of a tale called 'Moby Dick' when the door crept open. A grin formed, but soon vanished when his grandpa walked in for the first time.

"Your room is untidy!" Henry scowled, thrusting out a heavy hand. "Come with me."

"I'll clean it up," he said with nervous eagerness. "And I'll wait for Momma."

"Your momma's gone. Don't make me ask twice, boy."

Hesitantly, he extended his little hand and was taken down the stairs through the hallway. He shot fearful eyes at the kitchen but couldn't find his voice.

Mable was still humming in the kitchen, kneading dough, when Jacob called out to her.

"I'm in da kitchen," she mumbled. "Where else would I be?"

Jacob carried in Henry Jr., shaking profusely, his eyes in a dazed stare.

"Good Lord!" she cried. "What happened?"

"Get some towels and whisky," Jacob ordered. "Be calm, Henry Jr., breath! You're fine now!"

He was still trembling when tears began to flow.

"What the hell happened, Jacob?" Mable wailed as she wrapped him in a towel.

"I found him in the barn and his grandpa was none to happy. Punished him again and wasn't quiet about it neither. I thought you was spose to look after him!" Jacob stammered.

"He was in his room when Mandy left," she admitted while filling a glass with amber liquor.

They looked at Henry Jr., and felt deeply sorry for the boy, so pale, so frightened.

"Henry Jr., were you in your room when your grandpa found you?" Mable asked.

A little nod came through his wheezy breathing as he choked back more tears. Jacob brought the whisky to his mouth in little sips.

"Oh child, you've got to find your voice and call out to Mable. You've got to find your voice!" Taking him in her arms, she stroked his wet hair.

"Jacob!" Mandy called. "Are you in here?"

He looked to Mable, who hastily shook her head.

"I'm in the kitchen, Miss Mandy."

"Well, I've had the best afternoon," she said, entering the kitchen with a huge smile. Her happiness slid away when she saw Henry Jr.'s dreary face. "What happened?"

"Mandy, Henry Jr. went to the creek and slipped on a rock," Jacob lied. "He's fine now…just scared."

'You sure you're fine?" Mandy asked, gently placing fingers on his warm head and pushing back hair to find a newly formed bruise.

He nodded, a small "uh-huh" escaping his closed mouth, but the sadness and fear remained in his deep blue eyes.

"Let's go get you changed," she spoke forlornly. "Jacob, the food supplies are in the wagon."

She was just about to carry him when he hastily said he'd walk on his own.

Mandy hesitantly took his hand as he jumped from the table and led her up the stairs. Doubt seeped into her mind as she glared at his pants, dry as a bone. She had seen that look in his eyes before and knew in her heart that this was no accident. Her instincts screamed for her to take him away. She knew she should have reacted sooner.

Jacob faced Mable, whispering, "How long do we lie to Mandy?"

"Dat boy will be taken from her if she fights back. She cannot fight dat man and she has no choice but to stay. We must do better to protect Henry Jr.!"

"Why does he punish him so badly?"

"Because he's a bastard. White people hate deir bastard children," she said tersely. "You's just too young to remember, Jacob."

"Remember what?" he exclaimed.

Mable sat heavily in a chair with shoulders sagging as memories about her life before the likes of Henry Wilkes flashed in her mind.

"Sit down, Jacob."

"I don't want to sit down. Say what you got to say quickly! There's food to be brung in."

"My father left da plantation long before you was conceived. Master Whitehall was our master den and he loved our momma. She was pretty and smart. Served all da fancy guests dat dined in dat big white plantation house."

"I don't remember him."

"You wouldn't. You was just a little baby when Master Henry took us away. Master Whitehall was cruel to his slaves except for Momma. He was none too afraid to whip da men and none too afraid to bed da women. Momma felt strange bein' taken care of so fondly by him.

Felt so special, she asked him to be more considerate to da other slaves."

Mable sadly poked at her worn hands. "Master Whitehall didn't like Momma's words, so he cut her face to remove her beauty, her enchantment over him. He den took her to bed and you were born nine months later."

Jacob was stunned, his words of denial trapped in his open mouth.

"As soon as Master Whitehall saw you, he said you had to go. Did you ever wonder, Jacob, where you got dose eyes da colour of amber?" she asked, swirling her finger in the bourbon.

He stood silently, his back against the wall.

"Master Henry appeared lookin' for a nursing slave, and Master Whitehall gladly offered us. At least we stayed together, and Master Henry's been fair to us. He don't care if his slaves are bastards, but dat little boy…all Henry sees in dat boy is his father, and it fills him full of hate!" Mable cried. "How did Henry Jr. get so wet in da barn?"

"I saw a bucket of water. Maybe he just fell into it. That's the best lie I can come up with right now!" Jacob replied heatedly, snatching the glass from Mable and draining its contents before storming out the back door.

Mable lifted the bottle and let the poured, contemplating what she could cook up to give Henry eternal rest.

****

The following morning, Mandy suggested Henry Jr. bathe at the creek since it was laundry day.

"Could I just have a bath in the kitchen with Mable?"

Mandy was surprised. "I guess it would be fine but a quick one."

"I like it when she gives me a bath and tells me stories about you in Arkansas," he lied.

The back door creaked open and Mable sauntered in with a basket of vegetables.

"Will you give Henry Jr. a bath while Joseph and I set up the big wash pot?"

"Sure will, Miss Mandy. Let me get da wash basin."

Once water was heated on the stove and poured into the round tub, Henry Jr. stood naked behind the kitchen table.

"Water's ready, child. Don't want it to get cold."

"Is it hot?" he asked cautiously.

"No, it won't burn you. Come away from da table. Come to Mable," she said, holding her hand out softly.

He shuffled from the table.

"What is it? Why so shy around Mable?'

He was acting too quiet, too hesitant, for a boy who loved the water.

"Turn around, Henry Jr.," Mable said warily.

Slowly he turned to reveal giant red welts on his legs.

"Oh child, come here. Dis water won't hurt you. It'll just soothe."

Stepping into the small wash tub, he bent knees into his little chest and looked pensively at Mable. "Tell me a story about Momma."

"What do you want to hear?" she asked, dampening the cloth and moving it along his slender back.

"I want to know if my grandpa hit Momma like he hits me."

She stopped her gentle scrubbing and looked directly into his sensitive eyes. "Yes Henry Jr., he hit your momma when she was young."

He nodded. "And she's fine now. She's fine now."

"Yes, Henry Jr."

"Then, I'll be fine. I'll be fine," he sighed, shoulders relaxed, feeling better.

Mable felt sickened. She worried about the boy who suffered two punishments too closely together and prayed it would never happen again. She hugged him tightly and whispered, "My smart little boy, stay close to Mable child, stay close to me."

****

Over the fall and winter months, Mandy pondered leaving while Mable and Jacob watched over Henry Jr. like parents of a newborn baby. It was a blessing when Henry spent even less time at the ranch. His supper appearances became very infrequent, and when he was around, he paid little attention to his daughter and grandson. That suited Mandy just fine.

In early spring, Jacob entered the kitchen lugging a sack of flour. "Still cold out there," he complained, rubbing his frigid hands.

Mable passed him a mug of coffee.

"That should be more than enough flour to make Henry Jr. a triple layer cake," Mandy smiled.

"Miss Mandy, I have somethin' for you if I can get these stiff fingers into my pocket."

When he pulled out the letter, Mandy's heart skipped a beat.

Jacob oddly shook his head. "Didn't get it from the Post Office."

Mandy was too focused on the letter and tearing it open, Jacob's words an incoherent mumble. Her perplexed face confused her audience.

"Miss Mandy, is it your….friend?" Mable asked.

"I have to go into town," she muttered. "Jacob, please hitch the horses to the carriage?"

"It's awfully cold out there," Jacob warned.

"Then saddle a fresh horse. I have to get a gift for Henry Jr."

Stuffing the letter in her hand, she set a course for her mother's armoire. This occasion required conservative attire. Frank O'Flaherty didn't need any more enticement. He was already too friendly with his long fingers.

Within the hour, hood of a cloak draped over her head through the sparse mercantile, Mandy took light steps to Frank's office.

"Amanda," he smiled, gliding over and delicately placing his hand on the small of her back to a spindle chair.

"Can I take your coat?"

His lewd smile indicated that he wanted to strip it off.

"No, thank you," she smiled delicately. "I'm still chilled."

"Let me remedy that," he said, promptly moving to the wood-burning stove. "It's been months since you've graced my presence. How are you fairing?"

"I'm keeping well, Mr. O'Flaherty."

"Come now, I think we're past the point of formalities. How's Henry?"

"He's fine…just a typical boy."

"I didn't mean your son. How's your father and his cattle business?"

She reticently gazed into cold, analytical eyes. "He's doing fine; cattle are fine."

"Well, I'm happy to hear everything's just fine."

"Your letter mentioned some new developments," she spoke abruptly.

"Now that's what I like in a woman....comes straight to the point, brevity."

Reaching into his breast pocket, he pulled out a letter and placed it on the tidy desk. "It's an eye-opening read from Sean Thomas. Just a month old."

Ethan Holden's name was scribbled on the linen envelope marred in dirt, dried blood, and fingerprint smudges. "How did you get that?"

"His mail's been inspected for years. Post Office was alerted about his aiding and abetting a reckless, marauding outlaw, and they've been most co-operative. Would you like to read it?"

Reaching for the letter, her hand was quickly clasped. "Not here," he said, his thumb pressing into the white knuckles of her hand.

The letter was stuffed into his jacket pocket just as swiftly as her hand was pulled from his wanton clutch.

"You mustn't blame Ethan, though. He wasn't the one who snitched on everyone close to Thomas. It was Donevan Langtry. Man has eyes like a hawk. He figured that particular trait would earn him a substantial donation to his hotel expansion fund."

Frank laughed with incredulity.

Lowering eyes, Mandy regretted her indiscretions were too public. Her cheeks burned warmer than the room.

The skin tightened around Frank's fisted knuckles.

"Donevan spilled the beans about your affection toward this unsavoury character through broken teeth. The only real question I have is whether you have any affection for me?"

Bewildered, her head shook when he interjected, "You see the letter gives a good direction for my next search. Just have to form a posse and we'll be good to go. I could, however, stay in town if I had a good enough reason to stay." His yearning eyes roamed over every inch of her body. "I've taken a room at the Donevan hotel, now called Melrose boarding house, while I ponder my next move. Will be there until tomorrow afternoon."

Sauntering over, he placed a firm hand on her back and exhaled, "Number four."

The words echoed in her ears as she moved through the mercantile to Tom's counter.

"Do you have detergive soap?" she spoke lightly.

"No, Ma'am. All I have is Rosin soap."

She clutched the soap and disappointedly searched for coin.

"But I could try to order some," Tom stammered, wishing he could appease the sad lady as she ambled away. "If you's willin' to wait."

When she arrived at the house, Mable approached, and was given the bar. "Well, I'm sure Henry Jr.'d be delighted wid yellow soap."

"Mable, prepare a bath," she said despondently while moving up the stairs.

"Yes, Miss Mandy. Are you ill? Miss Mandy?"

When night fell on the Wilkes ranch, Mandy tossed and turned, sleeplessly dreading a morning that would come to soon.

****

At the break of dawn, fully cloaked with hand on the knob of the door, Mable interrupted her silent departure.

"Miss Mandy, where you off to so early?"

"I have to find a gift for Henry Jr."

"You already done dat! You forget showin' it to me months ago. Henry Jr. don't need any more presents! He needs his momma to watch over him. If dis has anything to do with your male friend, leave him be. If he's haf the man he's said to be, he can take care of hisself!"

"Mable, go back to the kitchen where you belong!" The door slammed her decision final.

The journey into town was a blur. She didn't take to memory the climb up the winding staircase, either. She just knew that her life would be forever changed when her soiled knuckles rapped on the door.

"Ma'am," a voice called out. "Ma'am?"

Mandy turned to see a woman staring strangely, sheets draped over her arm.

"The room is empty," Theresa said. "The gentleman left with a posse of vigilantes early this morning. There's been a shoot-out in Fort Benton," she informed with alarm. "Two men dead!"

Mandy darted out of the hotel and drove her carriage through the centre of town. Her horses whinnied when she tugged tightly on the reins directly in front of the Methodist church.

Pastor Kennedy was surprised to find every pew wasn't empty when he hobbled in with an armful of kindling.

"Ma'am, service doesn't begin for another hour," his breath puffed misty white.

Concern for the unmoving figure overwhelmed his usual ritual of warming the room first.

Sitting across from her, he peered under the heavy hood.

"Amanda?"

Her ashen face remained lowered, eyelashes clumped together in icy wetness.

"Been a long time," the ecclesiastic said. "It's good to see you. How are you keeping?"

"I'm afraid I've done things that are not right in God's eyes," she confessed.

"I see, and you've come seeking guidance."

"I come seeking forgiveness of my sins and for the sin that I was just about to commit. I miss my son's father so desperately I'd do anything for him to return to us safely. But the price…."

"Have you prayed for his safety?"

"Everyday, but I fear it's not enough. A man offered a glimmer of hope that he would be unharmed, but the price for this is just too dear."

"Can this man be trusted, like your trust in God? Be careful of wolves in sheep's clothing. This town was forged from greed and material desires. And now that its source flows empty of golden riches, people are desperate for anything else they can get their hands on."

His words rang too true through her numb ears.

"Pray for your forgiveness, serve the Lord in every capacity, and put your own house in order with God's will."

Mandy trembled out a soft nod.

"Now, if I don't get that stove filled with wood, I'll have every one of my congregation rattling their teeth and stomping their feet through my service, just like you are now."

She smiled stiffly, though her heart was warmed and her mind stilled by his divine words.

****

Sean was perched atop a high peak as he watched O'Flaherty and his men scouring the foothills of the mountains. He cupped his hands around warm breath cursing his fate in Fort Benton. Hightailing it out of town before a snowfall, he shivered from the dampness, but was grateful that it blanketed his tracks as he watched black figures stamp muddy prints in the white slush.

His journey would continue north, slow and steep, after O'Flaherty's posse grumbled their way southeast.

Once on flatter ground, he entered a small meadow of pristine snow, believing he was beyond any danger. A succulent smell reached his nose just as a shot blasted past his ear.

The horse bucked; Sean's body was too stiff and weary for the sudden vertical shift of his saddle. He struggled for cover behind a tree while his gelding made wide galloping circles.

"I can still see yah!" a woman shrilled. "Come out with your hands up or I'll shoot your horse!"

Sean rubbed his hands together warm, glanced at his useless pistol, then swung around to face the woman draped in fur.

"Take your piece and toss it my way!" she yelped.

"It's empty; no threat to you!" he answered.

"That's bullshit. Now throw out your piece with delicate fingers or I'll blow you apart!"

Sean eyed her face, rosy and weathered with time, figuring she was well past her best shooting years.

He was wrong, jumping, when a blast skimmed his pant leg.

"Do you wanna dance, Mister?"

When his pistol was safely tossed away and collected by the mountain woman, she led him to another woman tending to a fire with fowl roasting on a spit in front of a ramshackled cabin.

"Got company! Pull out the china, Sadie."

Sadie looked up and was the mirror reflection of her sister, until she smiled showing a handful of teeth as brown as his chestnut gelding.

The shooter slid back her fur hood to reveal half a right ear missing. "Sit!" she ordered. "What we gonna call you?"

Sean was so busy eyeing the browning turkey, he didn't hear her, until her rifle jabbed him in the ribs.

"Call me, Sean."

"Boy, I ain't seen hungering eyes like those since a Chinaman tried to get into my ruffled drawers! You do as I say, and I'll let you eat. Lord thundering Jesus, this fire's hot, Sadie!"

"Don't I know it" she answered, fanning the folds of her dress. "Flip the turkey, Lizzie!"

"Don't get your knickers in a knot."

"Ain't wearin' any knickers, Lizzie. The hole in the crotch just kept growin' so bad it only cover two hips.

Sean could vouch for that, turning away from the flash of black thatch under her flapping dress.

"Fire's so hot, he blushin' too!" Sadie chortled.

Lizzie perched her boot on a log and inspected his colt's empty chambers. "So's you ain't lyin'! You'll live through this meal."

"Don't say much, do you?" Sadie asked.

"Turkey smells good," he commented.

"That's 'cause it's cooking over alder logs, stuffed with Chinese herbs. I git it right under the skin and let it brown on all sides, right Lizzie!"

"Ah, hell. I git to flippin' it straight away, Sadie!"

"Don't blaspheme in my presence. You know I'm older 'an you. Take you over my knee and spank you with my Bible!"

"Older by five minutes, and you touch my with that thing I'll set your hands on fire again!" Lizzie eyed Sean. "Sadie's a pious Christian. I'm an impious atheist."

"Lizzie believes God just let Kansas bleed."

"Let's not bring up Kansas or you'll bleed." Lizzie pulled on the leg of the turkey and it easily pulled away from its carcass. "Supper is served!" She bit into the dark meat and its juices ran down her chin.

Sadie appeared a little more refined, slicing the breast apart and passing it along on a tin plate to Sean.

"Careful you don't set your dress on fire!" Lizzie warned.

"Don't you take one more bite, Lizzie Hopkins. I aim to say grace!" Sadie said, devoutly determined.

"What's that you wanna do to your face?"

"I know's your hearin's just fine!" Sadie barked. "I'm gonna say grace!"

"Then speed it up. My leg's gettin' cold!"

"Heavenly father, thank you for all your blessings on this blessed evening…."

"Hell, if I had any more blessings on my doorstep, I'd be frozen to it," Lizzie pointed with her turkey bone.

"Oh, quit your caterwaulin'!" Sadie pleaded. "Lord, please forgive my sister, Lizzie. She's beginnin' to lose her common decency in this woeful place. And, thank you for bringin' a man to our table…oh, firepit. Amen."

"So what the hell you doin' in a forest filled with savage Indians and wild animals without bullets!" Lizzie blurted out.

"Well," he chewed quickly, "had to make a hasty retreat from Fort Benton. Had no time to procure bullets."

"Are you in some kind of trouble, Sean?" Sadie asked with concern.

"You could say that."

"Well it's lucky for you Sadie's such a fervent Christian. Eager to save sinners of all kinds, ain't that right?" Lizzie snapped the wish bone and began picking her teeth with it.

"Pray the Lord for forgiveness and he'll grant you absolution," Sadie spoke as if in a trance.

"Sadie's done lots of forgivin'. Forgave the border ruffians who swept into Kansas and killed our father, Herbert. Forgave them for tryin' to soil her, though I shot back and they plum blasted my ear off, takin' half my hearin' with it!" Lizzie exclaimed, pointing at what remained.

"Don't forget, I forgave them for takin' our best hooch, too. Stuffin' a rag in it, lightin' it, and tossin' it through the window of our little home," Sadie informed.

"How could I forget? Nearly died! Watched your hands go up in flames 'till we crawled through a hole in our floor. My pappy dug that hole so that when the tornado came, we oughten been blown away. Where was we?"

"Saving Sean from a sinful life."

"Oh, yah! Sadie can save your soul but I can read your palm. Only cost you a bald eagle coin."

"You want a dollar to read my hand?"

"Tell you your future," Sadie enticed. "That's how we got these Chinese herbs. Ain't that right, Lizzie?"

"Yep. Did a hand job on him!"

"I won't have much of a future without any bullets," Sean said matter-of-factly.

"Lizzie will do it for fifty cents."

Sean dug into his pocket and pulled out three silver dollars. "Son of a bitch," he muttered under his breath.

"Lizzie can make change."

She dove into her buckskin pouch and pulled out two Dominion of Canada twenty-five cent notes. "I'm sure it's the same penny for penny."

"What's he gonna do with that?" Sadie asked.

"Surely the bank can change it," Lizzie replied.

"Why would the bank wanna do that? Who's gonna take that money in Fort Benton?"

"I'm not going back to Fort Benton to find out." Sean shook his head with certainty.

Lizzie dove back into her buckskin pouch and pulled out two liberty seated quarters. "I knew I oughten to have taken this funny money." She scooted close to Sean. "Give me your palm."

He outstretched his hand and she licked it. "You got a bit of turkey juice left over. Want not, waste not!"

Sadie walked over with a candle.

"Can you hold it steady, Sadie, so's I can see the lines?"

"It's not me. It's the wind."

They huddled close together, the smell of smoke and sweat pungent in the air, until downwind Sean nearly bowled over from the tang of urine and feminine secretions.

"Let's see here," Lizzie muttered. "This here's your life line and it's long. It's very long considerin' you're in danger. And this is your heart line….oh, look, Sadie, it forks at the end."

"Oh, my!" Sadie swooned over Sean with amorous eyes. "You're a good catch."

"And this here's your fate line and it's well-marked. You're honest….a real straight-shooter!"

"In more ways than one," Sean answered forthwith. "Does it say anything about children?"

"No…but this line here says you'll have a happy life when you're older."

"That's what my hand says? Well that'll help me sleep nights," he said sarcastically.

"It also says you've made good judgments in your life," Lizzie said affirmatively.

Sean chuckled.

"How many men you shot didn't have a gun pointed at you?"

He yanked his hand away.

"It's time for some hooch, Sadie."

"We's originally from Kentucky. My pappy was a swarthy looking fellow, too swarthy lookin', my mamma said. Sadly, the negro blood ran stronger than the white blood in his veins, so we moseyed west, figurin' Kansas was a safer place to be."

"Bleedin' Kansas," Sadie sighed.

Lizzie popped a cork and offered Sean a taste. "Most often, it's made with corn, but works just as good with taters, too."

He washed away every taste of turkey with a burning gulp.

"After our house was a pile of ash, we headed west to pan for gold. All we turn up is rock and dirt. Walked into a land office wantin' property to farm. Bunch of black suits laughed their heads off."

"They sure did," Sadie nodded sadly.

"Told us to come back when we had husbands. I lifted my rifle and told 'em I could farm better 'an any man on any land."

"That's what she said," Sadie reconfirmed.

"One of 'em promptly laid out a map, got his pointy pen, closed his eyes and stabbed at this piece of land." Lizzie stretched her arms wide. "Now that I been here a while, what with the shallow soil and lack of light, mushrooms grow best in these parts. Horses like it, though. Good grass."

"Amen. Horses like it," Sadie spoke softly.

"My Matilda's sure takin' a likin' to your gelding. What kind of horse is that?"

"That's a Morgan," Sean answered solemnly.

"What you call him?" Sadie asked.

"I don't. My father would whistle for his attention."

"Why don't you call him, Morgan?" Sadie offered, passing him the jug.

Sean washed away the memory of his father. "You have any trouble with Indians in these parts?"

"The odd one or two tribes been this way. Shoshoni and Nez Perce didn't give us a lick of trouble. Not fond of the Blackfoot, though; were rough on me, 'till Sadie came out of the cabin, her face covered in chokecherry juice. She'd been fixin' to make jam when they showed up. Took one look at her, jumped back ten feet, and scampered away."

"They thought for sure I was covered in pox. They don't like the pox," Sadie confirmed with a simple nod.

As the jug passed too rapidly between so few hands, Sean's head began to spin too rapidly.

When his soft snores filled the quiet meadow, Lizzie went rifling through his pockets.

"What yah doin'!" Sadie cried. "Leave him be. I have plans for those hands!"

Lizzie gave her sister a stupefied look. "I want the rest of those bald eagles, then I'm splitin' him in two."

"I want him to bring stones over and build us a proper fireplace, so's we can cook indoors…not get smoked out."

"He's never gonna stay!"

"Yes, he will. I prayed to the heavens above for him this thanksgivin' and here he is."

"Oh, Sadie, look at the stars. Great Bear is high in the sky," she pointed. "Spring up, fall down."

"You've read his lines," Sadie cried desperately. "They's the best lines we's ever seen. He's a good man, Lizzie!"

She tossed her head, but couldn't deny the hope she saw in his right hand.

They dragged him into a corner of their one-roomed shack and draped him in a tattered wool blanket.

Sean lifted the lid of one eye and watched as the two sisters slept in each others arms, wrapped in fur, on a bed of dried needles and leaves.

Opting to stay until the snow melted, he dragged over stones and cut logs while the women fed him wild game smothered in Chinese herbs. When the fireplace was completed and the wide holes within their logging filled, he snuck out under a black sky with his pistol.

He would be heading southeast to Fort Benton and the nearest mercantile for lead bullets. After that, he'd set his sights for Virginia City.

Just before he was ready to mount his gelding, he threatened, "You buck me off again, and I'll shoot you dead!"

****

On Henry Jr.'s eighth birthday, Mandy asked Mable and Jacob to join them for supper. She made a vanilla cake this time, though, with sweet butter cream icing.

Henry Jr. was eating his second piece when Mandy spoke of his special day.

"Did you know that this is the day our dear President Lincoln passed away?"

"No, Momma. Who was he?"

"President Lincoln was responsible for ending slavery, which gave Mable and Jacob their freedom."

His face expressed confusion. He thought they were always free to do what they wanted.

"Before the war, your grandpa owned Mable and Jacob, and they weren't paid for the work they did on this ranch. They were not free to leave when they wanted to. Now that has all changed. Mable and Jacob could find other work and leave this ranch by their own choice."

"Amen to that!" Mable blurted out, eyeing her crusty hands.

Jacob eyed his sister with curiosity. "What's that sposed to mean?"

"It mean I could git out of dis kitchen!"

"What would you do?" Mandy asked with worry.

"I could write a cookin' book. Everybody know how good I cook in Pulaski County. Always sayin' to me, 'Mable how you get your pastry so tender and flaky? How you make dat omelet,' what you call dat omelet?"

"A puff omelet," Mandy replied somberly.

"Dat right. A puff omelet," Mable said indignantly. "Dey say 'how you make it so light and fluffy'?"

"You don't even know how to write."

Jacob's words swooped down on her dream like a mallet crushing pecan shells.

"I git you to write it while I say it," Mable answered, ready to highlight her book plans until the sight of Henry Jr. humbled her. "Oh, child! Oh, child!" she sighed as his saddened eyes palpitated her heart. "We don't wanna leave dis ranch. Dis is our home, too," Mable smiled.

Eager to change the subject, Mandy began, "President Lincoln was a very important man. I believe when he died as his spirit was leaving this world, yours was entering it. I believe he helped to bring you into this world safely like a guardian angel."

"Lincoln was a special man, and you're a very special boy," Jacob chirped in.

Henry Jr. smiled, feeling good about himself, thinking it nice some man he didn't know brought him safely to his momma.

"Close your eyes and make a wish for anything you want," Mandy said sweetly.

Squeezing his eyes, he wished with all his might for a horse of his own. He'd brush it, feed it, and talk to it as he rode it through the pasture everyday. His eyes were still lidded when the door closed, jolting him, ending his dream.

"Horses are waiting to be unhitched and fed," Henry's voice echoed throughout the hall.

Jacob darted out the back door while Mable fled to the dry sink with the plates and cutlery.

Henry Jr. wanted to change his wish. He'd wish that his grandpa never came home.

Mandy looked at her father in surprise, his expression difficult to read.

Henry's eyes went from Mandy, to Mable, to Henry Jr., and finally the cake.

"It's Henry Jr.'s birthday. Would you like some cake?"

He shook his head wearily and walked away.

Mandy didn't realize that life in Virginia City had changed for him, too. Now that the gold glinted ribbon of stream ran dry, the town was drying up, as well. Businesses were closing and people were moving to Helena, or Butte, while Henry still held the deeds to a number of empty lots. Peter Warren had departed months ago, and Henry's relationship with Morgan Terrence was deeply strained.

Disrespectful remarks were becoming noticeable. In the beginning, Terrence was more interested in his rare steak than Henry's mumbled words, but his voice became more offensive and obstreperous as land values dropped.

Terrence threatened to leave town on more than one occasion, and if he did, Henry would have to pay his loans.

Henry was very angry for not selling soon enough, angrier at Morgan Terrence for not giving better business advice, and the angriest at Mandy for hanging on to the child and disobeying him. He could find very little comfort and peace. Liquor became a constant companion, helping him blot out his spiraling misfortune, helping him lash out at whoever caused him to have such a frustratingly miserable life.

Chapter 20

Henry Jr. awoke to loud noises in the deep of night. This was nothing new to him; however, the distressing sounds didn't seem to be coming from within the house. He rubbed his bleary eyes and drew back the covers, shaking the sleepiness from his bones. Peaking through his window, light was emitted from the barn, but it was the sound of a fretting horse that caused him to worry.

Before tiptoeing down the stairs, he glanced at his mother's room, but shook away the thought, moving quietly towards the wide front door. The horse's cries grew louder and harsher as Henry Jr. anxiously approached the barn. Through the open door, his grandpa could be heard howling profanities while he chastised Jefferson in his stall.

The horse whirled his fitful head, screaming, as the whip tore at his flesh.

Horrified, Henry Jr. found his voice, instinctively shouting, "Grandpa, no! You're hurting him!" Tugging roughly at his arm, he screamed, "Stop it, Grandpa!"

An angry face blazed at Henry Jr., but it was his black eyes full of fury that froze him until a hand rose with knuckles tightening around the braided handle.

Fearful, Henry Jr. ran, but the whip uncoiled in the air like a thirteen foot snake, cutting through him and pushing him down onto a bed of hay. Seething rage was unleashed with the snap of the lash, forcing him farther and farther into the tightly wound bale. It felt so hot, so excruciating, so relentless, an unstoppable momentum Henry Jr. feared would never end.

It was his mother's piercing screams that ended his punishment.

Drenched in sweat, Henry struggled for breath, seeming bewildered as his bloodied inflictor sagged lifeless to the dirt floor.

Mandy whimpered as anguish and shock paralyzed her from moving.

Still panting, Henry mounted Jefferson and vanished into the night while she wobbled to her son and slowly turned him, wiping golden grass imbedded in his small, swollen cheek.

"I'm so sorry…so very sorry," she wailed.

He whispered her name through soft lips.

Gently picking up his battered body, she rushed to the log cabin, frantic for Mable and Jacob. She kicked at the door until they answered.

"Oh, Miss Mandy!" Mable cried.

Jacob took Henry Jr. and placed him on his stomach.

"Mable, get some clean cotton and boiling water!" he cried frantically before gently grasping Mandy shaking shoulders. "You've got to get calm. Henry Jr. needs you….you've got to get calm. The shirt done save him some, but the shirt's also in his wounds. I got to get it out. You understand…you have to hold Henry Jr.'s hand. You have to keep him still!"

Mandy nodded, trembling, as tears flowed freely from fretful eyes. She clutched her son's frail hand and pressed it against her wet cheek.

"Momma's right here, my sweet child. I'll never leave you," she whimpered.

Gently curling her fingers through his matted hair, she hoped to quell his pain. Her brave boy clenched his eyes closed and squeezed her hand, but swallowed the moaning sobs that threatened the stillness of the quiet room.

The next day, Jacob placed a drowsy Henry Jr. in the wagon while Mandy packed their clothes, books, and blankets. Despite that her father hadn't returned home, she refused to stay at the ranch any longer. She gave Mable and Jacob a hurried hug and departed for her cousin's home.

Colleen was distraught at the sight of her little cousin. She knew Henry had a temper, but the sight of what he did was unfathomable.

Mandy kept her son medicated so he could sleep most of the day. While in his sluggish state, she removed the old bandages, washed his wounds, and re-applied clean cotton.

Ethan arrived home to see the weary expressions of his wife and Mandy. He was told of the previous night's attack and appeared devastated as he took Mandy's hand.

"How's Henry Jr.?"

"I've given him laudanum so he's pretty sleepy. He still moans a lot," she sighed. "Ethan, I want to head north as soon as he can travel. I'd like your help in securing a wagon, two horses, whatever supplies I will need, and some escorts. I can give you gold to take care of the costs."

"You don't have to go north. You could stay here with us," he offered.

"No, it's time for me to leave this town and find Sean. I'll go as soon as Henry Jr. is strong enough. Can you help with preparations?"

Ethan sensed her mind was made up, so he agreed, commenting that he would support her in any way possible. He even offered to take her, however she adamantly opposed him considering Colleen was due any day with her fifth child.

"Mandy, the last time I heard from Sean, he was in Fort Benton and that was a few months ago. I received a letter from him…"

"You received the letter from Sean?"

"Yes, but it was very short. He wrote that he had to high-tail it out of Helena, and was heading north to Fort Benton; and if he had to, up to Canada."

She stood and gazed out of the small kitchen window. "Then he's alive, or at least he was just months ago. Did he make mention of me?"

"No, Mandy. I didn't say anything about the letter because I ran into Frank O'Flaherty, and he boasted that Sean had been mortally wounded." Ethan continued with a remorseful face, "I apologize. I just didn't know how to tell you. You always seemed so hopeful, and I didn't want that to….change."

"My mind is firm. I will go north and if Sean is dead, I will work in Fort Benton and support Henry Jr. on my own." She didn't say that she truly believed Sean was alive, clinging to a naïve hope that she would find him.

"Do you realize that the journey will take four days, maybe longer if you have to stop and care for Henry Jr.?"

"Then you best find me two patient escorts or I'll travel on my own," she declared. "I will not stay in this town any longer!" She only needed a glimpse of her suffering son to strengthen her resolve and put to pass any doubts.

****

The next morning, Mandy went into town to procure food and cooking supplies she would need for the journey. She made hurried steps along the street, her head held discretely under a wide-brimmed hat. With eyes focused on obtaining every item from a list, her mind worried over being too far from an ailing son.

When she returned, Henry Jr. was awake and reading 'Moby Dick'. He peered up, looking sad and tired.

"I brought you chewing gum and more medicine. Are you in any pain?" she asked delicately.

"Hurt's when I move and it feels hot," he spoke gloomily. "I'll try the gum, though."

"You let me know if you want more medicine." Her fingertips brushed his head gingerly. "I love you so much I wish I could take the hurt away."

"I know. I wish I could take it away too."

His suffering eyes made her heart ache. Hesitantly, she said, "I'm going to help Colleen with supper."

After a soft kiss on his warm forehead she dragged her heavy body to the kitchen.

That evening, Ethan informed Mandy that he had a wagon, horses, and provisions: lamps, shovels, a bucket, and so on. He had a possible lead on two escorts he felt would pan out.

When Colleen left the kitchen to put the children to bed, Ethan leaned into Mandy, whispering, "I've procured you a gun, as well. You need to be able to protect yourselves. Ever used a pistol?"

"I've used a rifle. I know what to do."

Ethan was set to disagree when he recognized a familial stubborn will in her furrowed brows. "Just practice with it, please." He carefully pulled the weapon from his jacket pocket with a box of bullets. "I must tell you that I ran into Morgan Terrence today. On that ill-fated night, he was having supper with your father. Supposedly, he drank too much and was very insulting. Morgan left him sitting at the table, alone, and has since called in all of his loans."

Mandy took a moment to absorb Ethan's information.

"My father didn't need to drink to excess, to lose his temper. There's no excuse for what he did to his grandson. I'll never forgive him."

"Mandy, I have friends who were whipped as children. It's just how they're punished, sometimes."

She was horrified. "Not like that! Besides, Henry Jr. is being punished for something I did, not him! Do you know how that makes me feel?" Her face filled with immense guilt and anguish. "My mind remains unchanged. We leave as soon as you've found escorts!"

"What about Tommy. If you just give us more time….."

"Tommy's in Butte with his new wife. I don't want to disturb him, besides it would take too long." Her patience was wearing thin. "I want to leave within the next few days, so please find me some escorts!"

Finally wilting any further objections from Ethan, she walked away.

****

It took a few days for Ethan to find escorts. "Paul Hardy and his brother have made the journey before and feel confident that they can get you there safely. They can be ready to take you at sun up, tomorrow."

"The sooner, the better," she remarked, scooping up her possessions and moving to the wagon.

When darkness covered the Holden homestead, Mandy gave Henry Jr. another dose of laudanum.

"Did Grandpa ever teach you how to use a gun?"

"No, Momma. I just had the one time with the rifle," he replied, rubbing drowsy eyes.

"Well, it's pretty simple. I'll put the bullets in. All you have to know is to cock it like this, aim, and pull the trigger."

Taking the pistol, he smiled with fascination. He practiced aiming and pulling the trigger, feeling like an outlaw.

"It's not a toy," she muttered, taking it from him. "Please listen to me as I say the journey we are about to take could be dangerous. We have to be brave, protect ourselves, and pray that we can get there safely. Will you pray with me….pray that we reach Fort Benton safely?"

"Yes, Momma."

Their hands clasped together in prayer.

"Lord, tomorrow we go to Helena, then Fort Benton. Please make our travels quick, free of sickness and harm for us, Paul Hardy and his brother. Please help Henry Jr. get through his pain and suffering. And forgive me Lord for being so foolish…for not acting sooner. Please protect my only son from future harm."

Mandy gently covered Henry Jr. with a cotton sheet for he wouldn't have any heavy blankets over his tender back. "I just want you know that I wrote your father a letter and have tucked it in the Bible."

Henry Jr. was already very groggy but nodded as he pushed his head into the soft pillow. "Good for you."

She kissed his forehead and blew out the candle.

Colleen was putting two steeping cups of tea on the checkered linen tablecloth when she walked in.

"How's Henry Jr.?" Colleen asked somberly.

Shrugging her shoulders, she traced the rim of the china cup with her thumb. "The laudanum's keeping him comfortable. Help's him sleep."

"How are you, my dear cousin?"

"I feel so many things right now," she confessed. "I feel angry at Father for being so mean….mean to my mother, to me, and to Henry Jr."

Colleen studied her hands. "He wasn't just mean to the three of you."

"What are you saying?"

"Well, when I was a little girl I'd sneak out of bed to hear my parents talking late at night in the keeping room. One night my mother spoke of your father, and how he took care of the family when their own father just flat out left. Their mother didn't remarry until many years later, and by that point Henry was already a young man. One day, he came in from the barn, hands all bloodied."

"This man beat my father?" Mandy asked in disgust.

Colleen's head shook slowly. "Henry beat his stepfather, knocking him unconscious. It seems that this man didn't show enough respect for his new family, especially Henry Wilkes. So your father's temper unleashed his fist quite mercilessly."

"Why didn't anyone warn my mother?" Mandy cried.

"Maybe they felt your good-natured mother was the only one who could change Henry."

Mandy felt utterly deflated, shaking in frustration.

"Some mornings, Momma came out of her bedroom saying it was her arthritis acting up. Though I never saw marks on her face, I believe he hurt her."

She slammed her cup against the saucer, its contents splashing over the fine rim. "Now that I think about it, I never heard a kind word come out of his mouth, not one loving word, not to any of us. When he was a boy, he had a dog that kept getting pregnant. He said his father took her newborn puppies and placed them in a burlap bag, their mother foolishly following all the way to the river. My father said he never saw that 'bitch' again. That word plays over and over in my mind. I can't clear it out."

Mandy sighed. "Family's supposed to love and care for each other. He treated his pair of shoes better than he treated us. I never understood how he could be so different with his friends. They got the best of him, except for Morgan Terrence and poor Matthew Sherman. They were the only ones who ever got a taste of the real Henry Wilkes," she said with contempt. "At least there's still a chance for Henry Jr. to have a peaceful life, free from harm and ill-will."

Colleen grasped her cousin's trembling hands.

"Momma never got that chance," Mandy spoke forlornly. "If I went back to Father…if I went back to him, he'd break Henry Jr.'s gentle spirit."

Her tears flowed again at the inalterable way of life in death. "My mother deserved so much more. She was a good, faithful wife, and he had no time for her. He'd say 'Ellen Margaret you're worthless. I provide and all you do is take, take, take. What have you given me in return? Why don't you just shut up because you never have anything important to say'…."

Colleen listened intently as Mandy imitated his loud, arrogant voice. She never knew how bad it was. No one ever really knew how bad it could be. People didn't talk about their problems, especially family problems. There were so many privations like clearing the land and building homes, hunger and sickness that threatened anyone living and breathing. An abusive father was better than no father, though it left her dear cousin's family with little peace inside their home and inside themselves.

Which was why it came as no surprise to Colleen when Mandy whispered, "I still love him. However, I'll never live under his roof again. I still love him, but I'll never return," she whimpered. "He'll destroy my son!"

She shook uncertainty and fear away in her cousin's tender embrace.

Colleen silently prayed for their safety and comfort in Fort Benton while Henry Jr. silently prayed for sleep. Sinking his head deeper into the pillow, he willed the medicine to take his mind away from his mother's woeful cries, to take his mind away from feeling responsible for his mother's sadness.

****

Mandy quietly woke Henry Jr. just before dawn. "It's time to go. Let's get dressed."

"Momma, I don't want to wear a shirt. It hurts," he mumbled, scratching his sleepy head.

"I'll just cover you with this sheet, but if we stop, you put the shirt on right away. I'm going to give you another dose of medicine. It's going to be a bumpy journey."

Walking into the aroma of fried bacon, eggs and toasted bread, they ate quickly. Then Mandy hugged Colleen tightly before telling her to go back to bed.

Colleen pleaded to go outside, but Mandy refused, worrying the weeping would come. She had to show her escorts a strong, brave face.

As the sun was rising, she walked her son to the wagon. A bed with her feather tick and soft blankets had been made, and she settled him just as the Hardy brothers were arriving. The cloth covered pistol was placed beside

Henry Jr. along with a canteen of water, his gum, and a basket of food.

"When we stop, you slide that shirt on before you step outside. I love you."

He smiled weakly. "I love you, too."

Once out of the wagon, she squinted at the two men atop horses.

"Miss Wilkes, I'm Paul Hardy and this is my brother, Tim. Ah, we're hoping to get paid now," he said flatly.

Mandy eyed Tim as he spewed out a mouth of tobacco, and wiped his lips clean with the back of his hand. She turned to Paul Hardy, recognizable from the hotel many years ago, carting in liquor supplies, and offering polite gestures. But she couldn't shake the uneasiness for his younger brother, skin pock-marked and gaunt, dark eyes hollow and cold. After their parents died, Paul looked out for Tim, but it now looked like Tim watched over Paul.

"How about I give you half now and half when we arrive in Fort Benton?" She eyed Tim without flinching, knowing she would have to hold her ground.

Tim gave his brother a displeased glare, but it was ignored.

Taking a nugget from her pouch, she handed it to Paul. Ethan had given the value of her gold pieces and also negotiated the price for the escort. She paused a moment while trying to shake the uncertainty over leaving with such an unsavoury person. Every bone in her body wanted to take Henry Jr. back into Colleen's warm home, but her strong will remained steadfast.

"Well, Ms. Wilkes, are we leaving this morning or not? I want to get to Helena by nightfall tomorrow," Tim spat out, along with a ribbon of tobacco.

Mandy nervously climbed the wagon and took the reins. She then guided her precious cargo away from her cousin's home and the familiarness she had known for the past ten years.

Glancing up, she said a silent prayer. "Lord, please keep us safe from harm,"

He did on that first day of their journey.

Several stops were made to give Henry Jr. respite from the bumpy trail, and to provide fresh water for the horses. Tim also had a chance to empty his bladder that filled all too often from an unquenchable thirst.

"Momma?" Henry Jr. spoke drowsily as she lay beside him in the wagon late that night.

"Yes, Henry Jr."

"Why did we have to leave Virginia City?" He could just make out her soft silhouette as she spoke.

"It's time to find….your father."

"I'm scared, Momma."

"Oh, Henry Jr., I'm scared too. But know that I'll never leave you." She snuggled the soft quilt around her son as closely as he would allow, then held his cool hand in hers.

"I love you, my sweet boy."

"Say one of your poems, please?"

"Oh, I'm so tired…."

"It would make me feel better."

Mandy began…….

"Those dark brown locks, those eyes of blue,
Bright as thy mothers under a warm sunny hue.
Those rosy lips, cheeks of dimples that play,
And smile to steal my heart away.
Recall a time of former joy,
And touch my heart and soul, my boy."

"When will that woman ever shut up!" Tim barked.

Mandy hastily covered her sleeping son's ear.

"Tim, I'm warning you, shut your loose lips or I'll flood the ground with the rest of your booze," Paul grumbled.

Crickets and the howls of distant wolves soon replaced the voices of the two men.

Mandy slowly succumbed to exhaustion.

****

The journey would continue under a grey dawn while Henry Jr. still slept in a laudanum-induced state. Mandy gazed at the crispness of the evergreen trees against a pale sky before clucking to the horses.

A few hours into the trip, the party stopped for their first water break.

Mandy climbed into the wagon to find Henry Jr. stirring with a pained look on his face.

"Momma, I think I swallowed my gum," he spoke hoarsely.

"You'll be fine. We're carrying on a little longer."

"How much longer?" he moaned." The ride is bumpy. It hurts my back."

"We have a ways to go, son. Take a bit more medicine, and we'll stop in another hour or so. There are also biscuits in the basket and dried fruit. You get hungry, take what you want."

"What the hell's she doing in there!" Tim bellowed. "I feel like a sitting duck!"

"Shut up and stop drinking that stuff," Paul snickered under his breath. "We still have a long way to go, and I don't need to be hauling your drunken ass along with a woman and child."

Tim was apathetic, chugging from his shiny flask, reflecting the sun's brilliant rays.

Their horses slowly crept north, however Tim didn't know he was pushing the party off trail.

Mandy didn't know Tim was three sheets to the wind as another trickle of firewater ran down his gullet.

"Whoa! Whoa! You see that to your left?" Paul asked with great distraction.

Tim squinted. "I don't see nothin' but trees and rocks." He didn't confess his vision was blurry through wasted eyes. "Follow me, this way. I got to take a pis…oh pardon missus," he snorted, stumbling off of his horse. Clutching his flask, he was dousing his insatiable craving when he disappeared amongst a grove of lofty pines.

"I'm sorry about my brother," Paul said. "He promised he'd stay sober."

"He could pass out, and we might not find him for hours," she spoke prudently, scanning the densely forested area Tim vanished into. "I hear water. How close are we to the Missouri River?"

"I think it's just the leaves of the aspens quaking," he replied, looking west. "Ms. Wilkes," he stammered. "Turn your head slowly and don't make any sudden moves."

Her breath was scooped away as four Indians slowly approached. Mandy had never been this close to Indians before. Their grim faces and unflinching glares sent in icy chill through her body; her back stood as straight as a pin. Though her face remained resolutely fearless, her hands shook as she squeezed the leather reins.

Paul dropped his reins and raised hands slowly. "I believe they'll just pass through," his voice quivered. "Lift your hands carefully."

The Indians took furtive glances at the man and woman before their eyes shifted to the empty horse.

Tim came sauntering out from the trees while buttoning his pants. Squinting, he blinked his blurred vision clear, his brain stupefied by the sight of Indians holding up his party. He reached for his pistol, his wobbly hand and unsteady legs making it nearly impossible to free the weapon from its holster.

The first of his bullets fired wildly, blotting out Paul's desperate cries to stop.

The Indians were equally bewildered until a bullet whizzed too close to the head of one named 'Black Sun'. His arrow soared swift and true into Tim's chest.

The last of Tim's bullets blasted away into the midday sun.

Black Sun spun his painted pony in fury, ashen bow drawn to his ear, turkey feathers brushing his cheek as Paul's head shook, eyes pleading for his life.

When the iron tip pierced Paul's heart, his hands spread like wings and his chest sank. As his body plummeted to the ground, Mandy ran.

Henry Jr. jumped up, confused by crackling sounds and garbled voices. He frantically turned to see his mother no longer in her seat. His eyes followed the sound of footsteps alongside the wagon. He thought he heard her shouting, "Get the gun!"

Then frenzied screaming began. She couldn't reach her son and was petrified.

Henry Jr. slowly crawled his way to her hysterical voice and found her helplessly bound by an Indian's firm grip. Raising the pistol in his shaky hands, he cocked it.

His mother was all he could see, her frantic squirming and wrestling shielding the Indian.

"I can't...I can't....I can't," he whimpered, shaking his head.

He was so fixated on his mother's suffering that he was completely unaware of an Indian creeping along the far side of the wagon.

But Mandy saw him and his jutting arrow directed at her fretful child. Petrified, she bit the Indian's arm and pulled away, yelling, "Shoot the gun! Shoot the gun!"

Henry Jr. closed his eyes, squeezed the trigger, and fell back as the arrow soared, grazing his arm. Searing pain brought him to full consciousness. Grimacing, he sat up, eager to get to his mother. His shrill cry echoed throughout the desolate land when he saw her lying motionless on the ground.

"Momma!" he screamed, stumbling out of the wagon and falling to his knees in despair.

Mandy gazed up, struggling to speak, "It's not your fault.....it's not your fault."

As tears streamed down her temples and into dark hair, she touched his harrowed face. "Get the letter to your father, promise...." her voice faltered.

"Momma, please don't die...please don't die!" Henry Jr. pleaded with sheer fright.

When Mandy's shuddering stopped, he held her tightly, sobbing uncontrollably.

Black Sun took his hunting knife in hand and swiftly moved toward the boy. Grasping short hairs with his curled fingers, Henry Jr.'s head was thrust up, watery lines glistening his scarlet cheeks, throat exposed to the sharp blade.

"No more killing, today!" Eagle Horse spoke with finality. "Let the boy bury his mother!"

With asperity, Henry Jr. was cast into the stillness of his mother's chest.

The wagon shook while being pillaged of its contents. Food was stuffed into pouches; blankets were tossed out and quickly thrown over horses. Mandy's necklace was snapped from her white neck. The music sheets were freed from binding twine, and scattered, carpeting the ransacked cavern and billowing out the open ends of the canvas, taking flight from the horrific scene. Books were aimlessly tossed aside.

Henry Jr. appeared as lifeless as his mother when the Indians moved towards the river. The stoic eyes of Eagle Horse gazed at the grisly scene again with thoughts of taking the boy, but the marks stretched across his back, much like those he painted across his chest before battle, deterred him. He didn't need to bring any more sickness and death to his people. Left alone, the boy's chances of survival were slim, but that was something his tribe faced everyday.

Black Sun howled with excitement, thrilled with his first kills. Eagle Horse took in the sight of his brother with proud, solemn eyes as the blood from the scalps of the two white men ran red along the torso of his painted pony. A warrior was born, today. He would no longer be called Black Sun. When he returned to his tribe, his people would call him Canowicakte. To the white man, it would mean, Kills in the Woods.

Acknowledgements

Deepest thanks to my spouse for encouraging me to write just one of the many stories that plague my thoughts. It is with warmest gratitude to my mother, children, and cover designer/editor Theresa Leonard for encouraging me to send it out into the world. I've been inspired by talented writers Guy Vanderhaeghe and Jeannette Walls.

I wish to thank Ajax Public Library. I've trudged through the aisles gathering everything from DVDs titled 'Wild Horse Redemption' and 'Saint Patrick' narrated by Liam Neeson, to books about North American Aboriginals during mid to late 19th century.

What I found most valuable was a dusty collection of Time Life Books, titled 'The Old West' that I discovered in my mother's basement. These books, leather bound and ornately etched with western motifs, were priceless in their historical accounts using language and expressions of that era, complimentary with portraits and paintings.

In remembrance of the late Deanna Durbin for singing the Stephen Foster songs mentioned in my book, particularly Old Folks at Home. Her voice will never be forgotten. And to the poets, Shakespeare, Emerson and Elizabeth Barrett Browning, whose words will never be forgotten.

A thank you to Joy Anderson at StoneRidge Farm, and a woman named Margot at 'On the Forest Boarding' for teaching me how to ride and care for horses. Their guidance and patience have been invaluable.

About the Author

A graduate of Ryerson University, the author was also born in Toronto, Ontario, to a Sicilian father and a Canadian mother with English, Irish, and Scottish heritage. This novel is written under the name of Alek Leslie. The author's maternal Great-Grandfather was born in Assiginack, Manitoulin Island, Ontario, in 1880, and was raised by an unforgettable Ojibwe woman while his parents, immigrants from Donegal, Ireland, ran a hotel. This first published story is part of a trilogy. The journey continues with:

Montana Son – A New Name

Montana Son – A New Country